Izzy & Ann

On Their Own

By
Sherri Peterson Curtis

Izzy & Ann
On Their Own

Copyright © 2022 by Sherri Peterson Curtis

All rights reserved

Printed in the United States of America

This is a work of fiction based solely on the author's imagination. Any similarities to persons living or dead is purely coincidence.

ISBN: 979-8-986168203 (paperback)

This book is dedicated to my first and truest love, Lawrence Curtis. It was he who urged, goaded, nudged, pestered, prompted, pushed, needled, threatened, encouraged, heartened, supported, aided, reassured, and ultimately believed. Thank you my dearest friend and husband.

Your Pill

Chapter One

1965

Fifteen-year-old Ann leaned her bike against the pink stucco wall of Neighborhood Market and fished around in the pocket of her jeans. "Hey Izzy," she said to her sister, "I've got a nickel. Want to split a Popsicle?"

"I'd rather split a Coke," Izzy said.

"But a Popsicle will last longer. You only get a tiny Coke for a nickel." Ann reached for the door. "I'll get your favorite flavor."

The rusted spring on the screened door of the store made a rickety screech then shut the door with a slap.

Izzy put down the kick stand on her bike and stooped to examine her flattening tire. She found a large thorn nestled in the thin tread and used her fingernails to pull it out. Her mood was almost bad enough to press the nasty thing into her sister's tire, but not quite. Sisters, particularly twin sisters, weren't supposed to do that sort of thing. Besides, Ann was a good kid. So good in fact that there were times Izzy wanted to smack her.

Maybe it was easier to be good when you were small for your age and had rodent colored hair and a mousey voice to match. Or maybe it was harder to be good when your breasts grew in like a Playboy centerfold and your hair was a deep brooding auburn. The breasts were a serious embarrassment for Izzy, and she hid them beneath baggy shirts, but she secretly liked her hair. It hung thick and silky to the middle of her back. But late August felt too hot for long hair. She spied a rubber band on the sidewalk and used it to secure her locks into a ponytail.

Ann came out of the market trailing cool air that smelled of produce, doughnuts, and penny candy. She handed Izzy an open bottle of Coca Cola. "They were out of banana Popsicles."

Izzy glanced at the frosty drink then up at her sister. "Why didn't you get grape? You like it better anyway."

Ann shrugged, "They were out of grape, too."

"Liar." Izzy sighed and shook her head. "You drink the first half then I'll finish it."

"I'm not thirsty."

"Liar, liar."

"I'm not, I drank from the fountain in the ballpark and I feel a little sick."

Annoyed, Izzy took the cola. "Thanks," she said, but she didn't mean it.

Izzy walked her bike home because of the flat. Ann rode slowly by her side, her tattered sneakers brushing the street.

Their mother's truck was missing when they reached their driveway.

"Well, no supper," Izzy said.

"Maybe she got a job."

"Yeah! And maybe Santa's on his way to our house with a check for a million bucks right this minute."

"She might have found a job and had to work a shift right off," Ann insisted.

"I'm not saying she couldn't have. I'm saying she didn't."

"How do you know?"

"Because I just know."

Ann stopped in the middle of the gravel drive. "Why do you do that?"

Izzy dropped her bike next to the back porch. "What?"

"Act like nothing good is ever going to happen."

The girls glared at each other. Ann wilted under the hardness in her sister's eyes.

"Because," Izzy kept her voice even, "nothing ever has." The immutable truth hung between them like a wall of stone.

They ate canned tuna and crackers for dinner. It wasn't the first time their mother had not come home, and Izzy figured it wouldn't be the last.

Ann went outside to sit on the front porch steps. Izzy settled herself on the couch with a library book. Every approaching car stole her attention and after spending thirty minutes trying to focus on the same page she put the book aside and joined Ann.

"There'll be ten cars and then Mom," Izzy said. They stared down the road and counted until the eleventh car cruised slowly by before parking two houses away.

The sky darkened, but they could still make out the silhouette of the tree at the end of the driveway.

"By the time we sing 'I Wanna Hold Your Hand,' she'll be here," suggested Ann. They sang, stretching out each line.

A sliver of moon rose in the sky.

"Say the alphabet backwards," Izzy challenged.

Every pinpoint of headlights on the road nudged Izzy's reluctant heart to lift expectantly only to fall when the lights sped by. Hope was the enemy. Hope hurt.

They sat silent in the darkness. Crickets began their nightly two note lullaby. Fewer cars and finally no cars came down the road.

At midnight they went to bed.

Before Izzy's eyes were open, she felt Ann looking at her. *If I don't move, maybe she'll go away, and I can go back to sleep.* It wouldn't work. Her sister always knew when she was awake.

Izzy rubbed her eyes and yawned. Ann sat cross-legged at the foot of the bed. She was dressed and had removed the curlers from her hair. It hung in scraggly ringlets, like scrawny snakes around her face. She didn't smile.

Suddenly Izzy seemed aware of everything in the room, the pale light, the water stain on the window sill, the patched crack in the ceiling, the peeling paint on the door. She rose up on her elbows.

"What?"

"Her clothes are gone."

"What do you mean her clothes are gone?"

Ann extended empty palms. "The closet is empty, there's nothing in the dresser."

Izzy kicked off the sheet and ran to the other bedroom. Wire hangers hung askew in the closet. The only thing left in the dresser was the brown 1963 newspaper lining the drawers. Their mother was gone.

"Damn it!" She shut a drawer so hard that a mirror rattled on the wall.

Ann looked like a waif standing in the doorway. "Where could she be?"

"How the hell do I know?"

"What are we going to do?" Ann's voice trembled.

Izzy felt a surge of anger, "What do you mean what are we going to do? Again, how the hell do I know?"

"Stop asking me what I mean! I'm not speaking Egyptian. And knock off the swearing, it doesn't help."

"Not now, Ann." Izzy pushed past her.

"It has to be now."

"Well, you're the oldest, you figure it out!"

"Oh right, I'm older by twelve —" The slamming of the bathroom door cut off Ann's answer, but her sister knew the last word was "minutes."

Izzy sank onto the linoleum. The knot in her stomach spread to every muscle in her body. Mom had stayed out all night before, and once or twice she'd taken off for a weekend without telling them, but she'd never taken everything she owned with her.

Was there anyone they could call? They had a couple of aunts who married and divorced almost annually. She couldn't think what their current names were.

Nine years ago they met their grandmother. They were six years old. They'd been put to bed, end to end on a sofa in the living room. Izzy recalled the smell of floor polish and the earthy odor of house plants. The door to the kitchen was ajar and a yellow finger of light stretched across the floor of the dark living room. Mom and Grandma were having tea. Izzy heard the tinkling sound of spoons stirring in china cups and voices, quiet but not friendly.

"Oh, no you don't, Wilma Eileen," Grandma hissed, "I know what you're trying to do, and it's not going to work. I raised my kids and now you can raise yours."

"I go by Willa, now. Please Ma, I only need one year, " Mom begged.

"You'd never come back! No sirree. You show up here out of the blue, after dark with two sleeping children, Asking favors. How do I know what you're up to? Those babies are like kittens to me, I haven't even seen their eyes yet. You walk out that door and they'll be in a foster home before you get to the highway."

Izzy remembered the words even though, at six, she didn't understand. But she understood now, and calling dear old Grandma, whose name she couldn't recall--Willa kept her maiden name a bigger secret than her age--was out of the question, even if she'd known where to reach her. If she had a sheet of names and numbers it wouldn't help because they didn't have a telephone and they'd spent their last nickel on a coke.

Izzy didn't cry. Inside, where she tried to be so hard, so tough, a shuddering began that threatened to shake her to pieces. She wrapped her arms around herself. *Falling apart will only make things worse, and be a royal waste of time.*

Ann tapped on the bathroom door. "Izzy?"

"I'm coming." She glanced at her reflection in the medicine cabinet mirror. She felt so much younger than she looked. So young that she wanted to find the nearest policeman and say, "I lost my Mommy. Please help me." But past experience with the Child Welfare people reminded her that they could separate her from Ann, and right now she needed her sister, if only because her sister needed her.

They had been taking care of themselves and each other for years. Somehow, they'd have to keep doing it. She made herself stand and open the door.

Ann leaned against the wall opposite the bathroom.

Izzy took a deep breath. "We need a newspaper."

Ann nodded and headed out the door.

She was back in five minutes with a copy of The Harmony Tribune Daily.

"Where'd you get it?" Izzy asked.

"People next door must be on vacation. There were three papers on their porch. This is today's."

Izzy felt impressed, "Good work. I had no idea you could steal. That could come in handy."

Ann blushed.

They spread the paper open on the kitchen table.

"What are we looking for, Izzy?"

"A job."

"You have to be sixteen to work."

Izzy looked over at her. "How old would you guess I am?"

Ann rolled her eyes. "I know how old you are, dummy."

"No, look at me. If you didn't know me, how old could I pass for?"

Ann studied her. "Seventeen," she said, "maybe older with the right clothes and hairstyle. But Izzy you don't know how to do anything."

"Well, I better learn how to do something pretty quick."

They pored over the paper, circling ads and crossing out others. They ended with half a dozen possibilities.

"What's the date?" Ann asked.

Izzy glanced at the top of the paper, "August 21st. Why?"

"We're supposed to start school next Thursday. What will we do?" Ann asked.

"You'll start school, of course."

"What about you?"

"Ann, no one's going to believe I'm eighteen or twenty if I'm also a sophomore in high school."

"But you have to go to school!"

Izzy's eyebrow rose, "Why?"

"Isn't it the law?"

"Look, we can't think about the law and what's right and wrong for regular people. We stopped being regular people —or as regular as we ever were— sometime yesterday when our mother took off."

Ann's jaw tensed. "Then I'll get a job, too. I can pass for sixteen."

Izzy laughed. "Forget it! You barely pass for twelve." She rose from the table and folded the newspaper. "Come help me find something to wear for job hunting."

Nothing they owned was right. Their combined wardrobe was all threadbare and too casual.

"You can't look today anyway."

"Why not?"

"It's Saturday."

Izzy kicked aside the clothes. "Damn it, Willa! You could have at least left a pair of high heels!"

They went to the kitchen to rummage for breakfast and ended up eating cornflakes with canned milk.

Suddenly Ann asked, "What about the rent?"

Izzy was looking through the kitchen cabinets. "Rent? What the hell are we going to eat?"

Ann burst into tears.

"Never mind, Annie. I'll get a job on Monday. By the time the rent is due we'll be okay."

"What if you don't get a job on Monday? What then?"

Izzy's spoon and bowl clattered into the sink. "I'll get a job. End of story."

"Mom looked for two weeks and didn't find anything."

"Gee, you're a little ray of sunshine! Do you really think she was looking for work?"

"Of course—"

"She's been looking for a way to get rid of us since we were six."

"Don't say that! It's not true! She loves us . . . she's our mother."

Izzy turned away from the sink. "She gave birth to us. I don't think she knows how to love us."

"I hate you, Izzy." Ann's small frame shook. Her chair scraped the linoleum; she turned and stalked toward the bedroom.

"Yeah, well too bad you can't divorce your sister," Izzy yelled.

She wandered into the living room. It was a typical furnished rental full of things the landlord didn't want: a light blue vinyl sofa, a recliner that wouldn't completely recline or sit up, a blonde, Formica, kidney-shaped coffee table and a triple bulb floor lamp with only two working sockets. And, as an extra special treat, an old fashioned television set with doors. A row of little knobs between the larger ones for volume and channel selection gave the viewer a fighting chance at adjusting the contrast, or vertical and horizontal hold. Izzy turned it on but clicked it off when the picture came in fuzzy with snow and ghosts. At least this landlord hadn't allowed cats or smokers – Willa had had to take her Lucky Strikes out on the porch – so the only offending odors came from slightly mildewed rugs.

They needed cash right away. The girls had been gathering pop bottles, and there were a

dozen of them in an old wagon in the garage, but they only totaled twenty-five cents or so. It would take at least twenty dollars to get the right clothes for a job search. If only there was something they could sell. She looked around the house. They didn't own anything except their clothes, toiletries, bed linens and towels. The house came furnished right down to the pots and pans.

She stared at the small white spot that was all that remained of the image on the TV screen. The television! The problems with reception were likely caused by the worn out rabbit ears and could be corrected with a decent antenna. If they could get it downtown to the pawnshop without breaking, it might be worth something.

First things first. No one was going to give two kids money for a television, not without asking a lot of questions. The transformation from fifteen to eighteen would have to start now.

"Ann," she called. "Stop sulking and bring the scissors."

Chapter Two

"How short do you want it?"

Izzy tightened her grip on the towel around her neck. She frowned at her reflection. "If we cut it too short it will look all hacked up. Just below my jaw might be okay, that way I can still wear it up, sort of."

Ann gathered the thick mass into her left hand and held up the scissors. Izzy wanted to close her eyes but didn't dare. The scissors were dull and pulled and tore at her hair. Her head felt suddenly light and her sister held up twelve inches of hair.

"Put it in the trash, we've got to even it out the best we can because I still have to curl it before we can go," Izzy said, with resolve.

Normally Izzy's hair took all night to dry. They didn't own a hair dryer, so they opened the oven and turned the heat to 400 degrees. Izzy sat on the floor with her back toward the door. She propped a mirror on a kitchen chair and began plucking her eyebrows. Ann opened all the windows and the front and back doors. She brought ice cubes to cool Izzy's neck, and to numb the reddening skin above her eyes.

Eventually her hair dried in the back and Izzy's forehead felt frostbitten, but her eyebrows arched gracefully. They'd look nice once the swelling went down. She turned toward the oven and shielded her face with a towel. The thinner hair in front dried much faster.

The girls went through their clothes again, settling on a pair of pink checked pedal pushers and a pink and white knit top. They found some white sandals at the back of the closet.

The television weighed a ton! It took both of them to wrestle it onto the wagon after they unloaded the pop bottles. They tied it down with a length of clothesline.

"I'll iron your clothes," Ann offered. "You go ahead and get ready."

Izzy brushed out her curls and started teasing and spraying her hair with Aqua Net. She smoothed and combed until it looked like a burnished mushroom cap. Frowning into the mirror, she smashed the sides, grabbed the hair brush and pulled out some of the teasing. Finally it began to look less like a helmet and more like a real hairstyle.

Izzy dug out a bag of Willa castoff makeup that she and Ann shared. She spread foundation over her light freckles and patted rouge onto the 'apple' of her cheeks. Her eyes stung when she lined them with an eyebrow pencil, and they watered mercilessly when she applied mascara.

Ann laid the freshly pressed clothes out on the bed. Izzy put them on and turned to look in the mirror. The top was tight across her chest. She definitely looked older. She just didn't look good.

"Ann," she called. "You better come and see."

Ann, who had been waiting in the hall, walked in. She studied Izzy from every side.

"Well?"

"You could be eighteen."

Izzy groaned. "Is that all?"

"You'll look older when your eyebrows heal," Ann said. "And we should find you a better hairdo."

"I know. I tried, but it still looks like a hairy bowling ball."

For the first time that day, Ann laughed.

༺༻

They started down the street with the wagon. Izzy pulled and Ann steadied the television.

"I think this is stealing," Ann said.

"I'll buy another to replace it with my first check."

"How much do televisions cost?"

They eased the wagon wheels over the curb. "I don't know. I'll just have to get a good job."

"Maybe we could buy a color set," Ann suggested.

"Only if someone is giving them away! You think I'll get a job as a doctor or something?"

The Pawnshop was dark, musty and damp. But at least it was cool. The man behind the counter had one eyebrow permanently cocked in skepticism. He removed a cigarette from between his lips with long thin fingers and crushed it out in an ashtray. A smile softened his expression. His blond hair was parted on the side and combed back; a few rebellious strands had broken free of the hair cream and curled at his temples.

"Good afternoon. How may I help you ladies?"

Ladies, Izzy thought, *that has to be a good sign.* She cleared her throat. "How much can you give us for this television?"

He glanced at the wagon. "It work?"

She tried to look insulted, drew in a breath and thrust out her chest. "Of course it works."

The man looked impressed. "Well, let's have a look." He rubbed his hands together as he came around the counter. A vapor of cologne clung to him; it would have smelled nice if it hadn't made her eyes water. He pulled a jackknife from the pocket of his very tight trousers and cut through the clothesline then set the TV on the floor. It took five minutes for him to plug in the set and attach an antenna wire to it. He turned the knob and the picture came into focus.

"Not bad," he admitted and grinned. "You want to pawn or sell?"

The girls looked at each other. "What's the difference?" asked Ann.

He didn't take his eyes off of Izzy. "You pawn, I hold it here and you can buy it back later. You sell, I give you the money, and it's all over between us." He winked. "That would be a shame."

Izzy's heart beat faster. "How much to pawn?"

"I think we should sell," Ann whispered.

He ignored Ann, "To pawn, I could go as high as twenty."

Izzy pouted, "You couldn't do better?"

He laughed. "Okay, twenty-five."

"I'm sorry; did you say thirty-five? Thirty-five would be perfect. See, I need the money for rent."

"Tell you what," his gaze traveled slowly up and down Izzy, "you look like a good bet. I'll make it thirty-five if you promise to come in and visit it every week until you claim it."

"Izzy," hissed Ann.

"I'll come in every chance I get." She extended her hand. He took it in both of his and held it a second too long.

He began to fill out the paper work. "You a student at the college?"

"Not yet."

Ann was plastered to her side.

"Kid sister?" he asked.

"Yeah."

"Feel free to look around, honey," he said in Ann's direction, waving her toward the crowded shelves.

"No, thanks."

He looked annoyed but kept smiling. "She always this devoted?"

Izzy sighed and patted Ann's head. "Every minute of every day."

He showed Izzy where to sign and counted out the money. "Okay." He looked at the information on the form, "Brandy is it? May I call you Brandy?"

"Sure," she said and pocketed the cash.

"I'm Sid. I'll see you next Saturday." He shook her hand and winked again. "Maybe I could treat the kid to a movie or something."

"Maybe you could."

Ann gripped the wagon handle with one hand, and Izzy's arm in the other, and tugged them both out the door.

As soon as they were out of sight of the shop, Ann stopped. "Isabel Gardner, you are not going back there!"

Izzy shuddered. "Ann Gardner, Darn right I'm not!"

"Then why did you say you would? Why did you act like that?"

"Like what?" Izzy resumed walking.

"Like a . . . like a tramp!"

Izzy turned to her sister. Suddenly she didn't just look older, she felt older. "Because thirty-five dollars is better than twenty."

"That depends on what you have to do to get it." Ann began walking fast.

"I didn't do anything!"

"No, but you made it sound like you would."

"That's not the same as doing."

"It's the first step isn't it?"

Izzy grabbed her sister's wrist and pulled her to a stop. "I'm trying to take care of us."

Ann looked down at the pavement. "I know," she said in a small voice. "But if you can't do it without being cheap I'd rather—"

"What? Starve? Go to a foster home?" Both went silent.

"Ann, look at me."

She didn't move.

"Please Annie, just look at me."

She raised her eyes.

"Am I cheap? Am I?"

Ann's lips formed the word but no sound came out.

Izzy shook her arm. "Am I?"

"No."

"Then what's wrong?"

"I've never seen you have a chance to be cheap before, and you were awfully good at it."

Izzy hugged her sister. "It was an act, Annie. Just an act."

"And where did you get the name Brandy?" Ann asked.

Izzy chuckled. "I don't know, it just came to me. I didn't want to use Willa, I thought it might get complicated."

They went shopping at the least expensive department store they could find. Izzy picked out a dress in the Misses department. She also bought nylon stockings, a panty girdle and a pair of low heels.

Ann found an A-line skirt and a blouse for school.

"How much is left?" Ann asked as she placed their purchases in the wagon they'd left in the parking lot.

Izzy counted the bills and change. "Twelve dollars and fifty-six cents."

"We should keep it for groceries."

"Yeah, but I'm starving. Let's get hamburgers for tonight."

There was a drive-in on their way home with a couple of picnic benches beside it. They bought fifteen-cent burgers and shared an order of fries for a dime. They drank from a fountain next to the building.

Ann removed the pickle from her sandwich and offered it to Izzy, who added it to hers. "Where do you think she went?"

Izzy didn't ask who, they'd both had the same question in the back of their minds all day. She licked her fingers. "Who knows?"

"Willa always talked about Las Vegas. You think she went to Vegas?"

"Could have."

"She said there were plenty of jobs there for waitresses. Lots of tipsy gamblers. She could make a fortune."

Izzy shrugged.

They finished eating. The sun dipped below the treetops and sent angled shadows across the table.

"We'll be okay, sis," Izzy said, hoping with all her heart that it was true.

Ann smiled. "I know. We've got each other. I'm not worried."

"Liar."

"Yeah, well okay, I'm a little worried. What if they ask about you at school?"

"They won't. Why would they?"

"Because Willa told them where to send for our records."

Izzy gathered their trash and threw it in the waste bin. "You really think she even went to the school?"

Ann stiffened slightly before her shoulders drooped. "Who knows?" She lifted the wagon handle.

The heat of the day eased a bit as they walked along the shaded street. A soft breeze whispered in the leaves above them. The smell of freshly mowed lawns mingled with the delicious scent of a barbeque somewhere in the area. Neither girl commented on the sights and sounds of families settling into their homes for the evening.

The television wasn't missed that night. It was Saturday, and they tuned the kitchen radio to a top forties station.

They passed the time trying different hairstyles on Izzy until they found one more flattering. They didn't bring up their mother again, but every time an auto stopped, or they heard the sound of a car door slamming, they glanced toward the street.

Finally they went to bed. Lights from passing cars raced on the bedroom walls. Somewhere, not too far off, they could hear country music and someone calling a square dance.

Izzy felt a gradual returning tension. Her shoulders ached, her jaw clamped, and a dull pain throbbed across her forehead. She made herself look out the open window at the stars. *Think about something good,* she told herself. She thought about the new dress hanging in the closet. Until that day everything she'd worn had been secondhand. She thought about Ann starting school, about finding a job. The throbbing grew worse. She thought about what it would be like going to work. Who would hire her? Could she do anything? Her typing was fair but not fast. She didn't know shorthand. Well, she'd have to learn some things. Maybe she could waitress. After all, Willa was a waitress. Maybe she'd inherited a knack for it from her mother along with her red hair and shapely figure. She prayed she hadn't inherited her mother's sense of irresponsibility.

Willa.

Mom.

Maybe she'd wake up in the morning, and the biggest problem would be explaining to their mother where the television had gone.

The square dance ended. She heard people turning off their sprinklers. Crickets chirped. The throbbing was almost gone. She felt Ann's arm curve around her shoulder and she fell asleep.

Chapter Three

Within an hour of beginning the job hunt the new shoes wore a blister on Izzy's baby toe. The panty girdle cut into her waist and her nylons began to bag around her ankles. She longed for her bicycle, a comfortable pair of cut-off jeans and the wind on her face.

The confidence she felt when Ann gave her sophisticated French twist a final shellacking of hair spray was melting in the morning heat.

The clock on the city building struck nine times. It was too early for most of the places she'd circled in the paper. Shops didn't open until ten.

She edged into the narrow strip of shade beneath store awnings. Perspiration beaded her upper lip and dampened her neck. The French twist felt like it was listing to one side despite the fistful of pins holding it in place. A coffee shop beckoned with a banner that read, "It's COOL inside!" the word "COOL" was topped with snow and dripped with icicles. Izzy went in.

The chilled air smelled of cigarette smoke, coffee and hot fat. Frank Sinatra crooned appropriately about "High Hopes" from the jukebox.

"Sit down anywhere, honey. I'll be with you in a second," a disembodied voice called.

Izzy bypassed a few men on stools at the counter and found a booth. She picked up the menu propped between the napkin dispenser and ketchup bottle and fanned her face.

A gray-haired woman wearing a white uniform and white shoes approached the table. She could have passed for a nurse, except for the frilly green-checked apron she wore. The name tag pinned above her breast read "Ida". Izzy had observed her mother a couple of times when she waited tables. Willa had worn a kind of smirk. A sly smile that suggested she shared a secret with the customer. Ida's manner was different. Her expression looked open and welcoming. The rest of her looked slightly swollen, from her puffy eyelids, to the creases in her ankles, as if her feet had been over-inflated just the littlest bit.

"How you doing this morning?" she asked with a smile. She set a glass of water on the table and pulled out a notepad and pencil. "Coffee?"

"No, uh… thank you." Izzy pretended to read the menu.

"Take your time, sweetie. How 'bout an iced tea while you decide?"

Izzy only had a dollar with her and she didn't plan to spend it. She felt her cheeks redden.

"Listen," Ida lowered her voice, "you'd be doing me a favor. I poured it for someone by mistake, and I'll have to throw it out if you don't want it."

Izzy studied the woman's face. Ida mouthed the words, *no charge*, and winked.

"Okay." Izzy said.

While Ida went for the drink, Izzy opened the folded newspaper and began reading the ads once more.

"Looking for work?" Ida placed a small plate with a doughnut and a tall glass of amber liquid on the table and nudged the sugar container toward it.

"Yes," Izzy answered.

"What do you do?"

"I'm a waitress," Izzy said.

One of Ida's eyebrows rose.

"That's what I'm looking for, anyway." Izzy tried to look competent.

The waitress glanced around then slid onto the seat opposite Izzy. "What's your name?" Izzy told her. "Honey, you don't want to wait tables. You're young and pretty and you'd get good tips, if this were the kind of town where anyone tipped, but its crummy work: heavy lifting, on your feet the whole time. Can't you type or run a cash register or something?"

Izzy stirred her tea. "I can type a little."

Ida's hand touched Izzy's arm with hard fingers cracked on the tips. They rasped on her skin. "I know it's not my business, but you got a high school diploma?"

Izzy was prepared to lie to any number of people that day, but somehow she couldn't look into those sympathetic eyes and do it. She shook her head.

"Well, I don't know why you're not still in school, and you don't have to tell me, but I will say that your life will be a whole lot easier if you get that piece of paper."

"Thanks, but right now I need a job." Izzy picked up her purse and the newspaper and inched to the end of the bench.

"Don't rush off; I said it wasn't my business didn't I?" Ida pulled out the notepad again and retrieved the pencil she'd stuck behind her ear. "Have you done any sewing?"

Izzy blinked. "Yeah, well, some. I had two semesters of Home Economics.

Ida scribbled down a name and address. "Don't tell them that when they ask. Just say yes." She tore off the scrap of paper and pushed it toward Izzy. "They'll teach you everything you need to know. The pay is fair. I guess the work is dull, but it's more reliable than waiting tables."

Izzy frowned at the paper. "Why don't you go there, if it's so great?"

Ida chuckled. "Me? I gotta be up and moving to keep my girlish figure! I couldn't sit at a machine eight hours a day." She hefted herself off the bench and tugged at the girdle under her uniform. "If they've got shift work you might be able to go to school." She wrote on the pad again and placed the check on the table. "Don't be a stranger, Izzy," she said.

When Izzy looked at the check it only said, "Good luck!"

The factory was a large, pink, sheet-metal rectangle with a strip of grass across the front. *Sugar and Spice Clothes for Girls, High Fashion at a Low Price!* Read the sign over the entry. Two long windows flanked the front door. A beat-up picnic table was chained to the trunk of a dying elm tree doing its level best to cast a speckled shade.

Izzy patted her hair, checking for loose pins and making sure the twist was still centered on the back of her head. She pushed open the door and walked in. Cream colored linoleum gleamed with a fresh wax shine. A woman seated at a desk and talking on the phone did not look up. An electric fan on top of a file cabinet made a faint clicking sound as it turned its face left, front, right and back again. Izzy paused for a second then sat on one of the chairs against the wall. A bedraggled philodendron in search of natural light, or maybe escape, ranged along the top of an empty bookcase.

Finally the woman at the desk dropped the phone back in its cradle. She scrawled something on a piece of paper and slipped it into a wire basket. Her blonde hair had a pinkish tint and was teased into a melting cone shape on top of her head like cotton candy. She pushed a pair of white rimmed cat-eye glasses up the bridge of her nose and stared at Izzy. "Can I help ya?" she asked.

Izzy stood. "I heard you're hiring," she said.

A placard on the desk said Pauline, and beneath the name, in smaller letters, Personnel.

She pushed a clipboard toward Izzy. "When could you start?"

Izzy was already filling the blanks on the application. "Today," she said.

Pauline gave a throaty laugh. "Wow, I like your enthusiasm."

Izzy counted backwards in her head to adjust her birth year. She made up a high school in North Dakota, figuring no one would be curious enough to check. When she finished there were only three things on the application that were true: her name, her social security number, and the date.

Pauline glanced over the form as she picked up the phone. She pushed a button and waited. "I have an Isabel Gardner here with an application, available immediately." She reached for a pack of cigarettes and an ashtray while she listened. "Yes, sir, I'll send her in." She lit a cigarette and took a deep drag before waving Izzy toward the hallway behind her. "Second door on the left, name's Cudgel. Take this with you," She held out the clipboard.

Mr. Cudgel dabbed his lips with a handkerchief while he scanned the application.

"Where have you worked before?"

"Mostly hamburger places while I was in high school. You know, kid jobs."

"That would have been in…" he checked the paper, "North Dakota?"

"Yes." She made herself meet his gaze without blinking.

"You do any sewing?"

"All the time." She cleared her throat and Mr. Cudgel narrowed his eyes.

He picked up the phone and dialed. "Stan, could you step in here? Thanks."

Izzy chewed her lip and wiped her palms on her lap. She heard the door open behind her.

"Stan, this is Miss Gardner. She'd like to sew for us. Take her out on the floor and see if we can use her."

Stan was average height, slim, and not much older than Izzy was pretending to be. He held the door open and Izzy preceded him out.

They walked down a hall lined with lockers, into a room full of tables, chairs, vending machines and refrigerators, and then through wide metal doors. The mechanical whirs, hums and clicks of a hundred industrial sewing machines clattered and echoed in a large dim room. Women wearing turquoise smocks bent over machines, feeding fabric beneath staccato needles. Each machine had a lamp and it made a little pool of light at the work stations. No one looked up as they passed. To the right of each machine was a stack of shallow cardboard boxes filled with bits of cloth. On the left side, empty boxes waited to be filled.

Stan handed Izzy a smock from a cupboard and a small plastic box of tools with a lid, then led her to a machine at the very back of the room. It didn't look like any sewing machine she had ever seen. It was at least half again as big as the one she'd learned on in eighth grade. She placed her purse on a shelf, put on the smock and sat down on a metal chair.

"You ever sew in a factory?" Stan yelled over the racket.

Izzy glanced around and decided it was time to tell the truth. She shook her head.

Stan pulled up a seat. "It's different than home sewing. Machine is faster and a lot more powerful." He pointed out the lever near her knee that started and stopped the needle, and the pedal on the floor that raised and lowered the presser foot. "Move over," he shouted. She scooted her chair out of the way and he moved into place. Reaching into a box he picked up a handful of pink crescents. He pointed out the difference between and right and wrong sides of the fabric. He matched two pieces together and pushed the pedal on the floor to secure them under the presser foot. With his right hand he turned the wheel that lowered the needle into the fabric, then he put several more crescents together and set them on the machine within easy reach.

"Now watch," he said. His knee pressed the lever, and the fabric zipped under the needle. He sewed the two pieces along the outer curve and had another ready to go before Izzy had really seen exactly what he was doing. He must have seen the confusion in her face because he smiled again and said, "Just watch, it's not hard." He went slower and soon he had six crescents connected by thread like a string of little flags. He dropped them into a box marked 'collars, size two'.

"You try," he yelled, rolling his chair out of the way.

Izzy fumbled with the fabric and nearly stitched her finger on the first one. Stan placed a hand over her shaking one. "Relax, these are only for practice. It's okay to make mistakes. Just get used to the machine." He stayed beside her until she was calmer. She concentrated so hard that she was surprised when she looked up and saw him on the other side of the room, unaware that he had left her.

Bending over the collars again, she kept going. Before one box was empty another was placed beneath it. The empty box was moved to her left side. She stared so hard at the pink cloth that when she finally looked up the room had a green cast.

A shrill buzzer split through the din and every machine seemed to stop at once, every machine, except Izzy's. The sudden silence thrummed in her ears.

Stan called to her, "Break, Miss Gardner. Fifteen minutes. Come on."

The other women filed out the metal doors. Izzy stretched her neck and rolled some of the kinks out of her shoulders. Stan waited for her.

"Bring your purse, I'll show you where you can keep it."

She followed him into the room lined with vending machines and refrigerators. There were lines at the coffee machine and outside the door to the Ladies Room. Stan led her to the lockers in the hall and opened several until he found an empty one. "You'll need to get a lock if you keep anything valuable in here. Most of the girls keep cash for lunch or snacks in their smock pockets. I'll put your name down for," he checked the number on locker door, "fifty-one." He glanced at his watch before adding. "You have ten more minutes." He started to walk away, and Izzy grabbed his arm.

"Wait a second," she said. "Do you mean I got the job?"

Stan smiled. "What's your first name, Miss Gardner?"

"Isabel," she said. "Izzy."

"You've had the job for the last hour, Izzy."

Relief flooded her brain and she returned his smile, "Thank you, Mr. uh…"

"Stan. Everybody calls me Stan. You might be rethinking that 'thank you' before the week is out."

She shook her head. "No sir, I need it too much."

"Well, by way of celebration, I'll buy your first coffee."

The room was filled with chatting women. Without their matching smocks they turned into distinct individuals.

Stan found a couple of seats at a table and pulled out a chair for Izzy.

"How do you like it?" he asked gesturing at one of the vending machines.

"Cream and sugar, please." Only Willa drank coffee at home; she said it was too expensive to waste on the girls.

Stan dropped a nickel and a dime into the machine and punched some buttons. He handed a cardboard cup to Izzy and sat across from her.

Izzy blew the steam then burned her tongue on the scalding drink.

One of the women at the table pushed a cup of ice towards her.

"Shame on you, Stan! You could have warned her," she said while she tapped an unlit cigarette against the tabletop.

"Sorry. I don't drink the stuff, so I forget."

Izzy dropped a cube into her cup and held another against her tongue.

Shaking her head, the ice lady gave Izzy a sympathetic smile. "I'm Betty," she said.

"Ithy" said Izzy around the dripping cube.

Betty pulled a napkin from the container on the table and handed it to her.

"Thanth."

"What kind of name is 'Ithy'?"

"It's Izzy," Stan said. "Short for Isabel."

Betty laughed, "Your mother lose a bet or something?"

Two more women introduced themselves as Marti and Faye. Marti's hair was gun metal gray and tightly curled around her thin face. Lines radiated from her mouth and deepened each time she dragged on her cigarette. Faye was younger and not smoking. Her green eyes were too large for her small face. Thin honey-colored hair was pulled tightly back in one anemic braid that trailed down her back to her waist. She sat pleating a paper napkin into a fan. When it was done, she opened it flat and began pleating it in another direction. She had very pretty hands. The fingers were slender and every nail was a perfect oval. All three women wore jeans and short-sleeved shirts.

Izzy made a mental note to pick up a pair of Levis.

Betty lit another smoke from the stub of the first one and dropped the butt into an ashtray.

"Cudgel raiding the kinny-gartens now?" she asked Stan, jerking her head at Izzy.

Stan shrugged.

"I'm eighteen," said Izzy.

Betty gave a snort. "Maybe next year, honey." She didn't say it mean, and no one seemed to care one way or the other.

Marti finished her coffee and took a compact out of her pocket. She fussed a little with her hair, which was sprayed so stiff it didn't move a bit, then opened a tube of lipstick in an ancient shade of deep red. She applied it liberally to her thin lips and pressed them together.

Pulling a face, Betty asked, "When you gonna get a new color Marti? That one's so purple it makes your skin look like a ripe banana."

Marti put away her make-up. "I've been wearing this lipstick since my first kiss."

"Really? Was that World War one or two?"

Faye giggled, covering her mouth with her hand.

"For your information, it was Korea. When you gonna get a boyfriend?"

Betty winced. "Too late. What I need is a 'man' friend." She pushed back her chair and stood. "Let me know if you see any around here." She reached down and cupped Stan's chin in her hand. "I'd have to throw you back, punkin, you're too young. I couldn't even take you to a bar."

He brushed her hand away and smiled. "Just my rotten luck – born too late." He glanced at Izzy's still full coffee cup. "Next time I'll buy you a Coke."

A groan went around the room when Stan rose from his seat. Smokes were crushed out and coffee gulped. Everyone shrugged back into their smocks and moved toward the door.

Izzy sewed collars the rest of the morning. She had nearly finished a second box when she felt a sharp poke in her arm.

Marti stood by her chair with her hands on her hips. She curled an index finger indicating Izzy should follow her. She led her to a long table.

Shoving a box at Izzy, she said, "All these got to be done over."

Izzy stared down at the box; it looked like everything she'd sewed so far. Her cheeks burned. Picking up the box, she nodded and turned.

Marti's hand darted out and grabbed her sleeve. "Don't you wanna know why?"

Izzy gulped.

Marti pulled out a collar, "You put every damn one of these together backward!" Her voice was shrill.

"I'm sorry. I didn't know." Tears stung in her eyes. *Don't cry! Don't you dare cry!*

"Sorry don't feed the bulldog!" snapped Marti. "You put us hours behind." She held out a tool with a little hook on the end. "You know what this is, don't ya? I mean even if you can't tell right side from wrong on fabric, you do know how to unpick a seam?"

Izzy took the tool and hurried back to her machine. Bending over the box, she brushed away the one tear that managed to slide down her cheek. With shaking fingers she began undoing every stitch. She worked through her lunch without looking up. Her smock was littered with tiny bits of thread. When the afternoon break came, she went to the Ladies Room then sipped water at the fountain. Stomach growling, she returned to work.

Would they fire her? They couldn't let her stay after such a stupid mistake on her first day. Her back ached and perspiration dripped down her face and into her eyes. She had to keep this job. She had to! The little hook slipped in her damp hand and gouged her palm. Careful not to bleed on the fabric, she dabbed at the wound with scrap from the floor and awkwardly tied it around her hand.

When the last stitch slipped out, Izzy sank against the hard back of her chair and looked up at the clock. Two-thirty – she had one hour to redo what had taken three hours. She patted her bandaged hand over her forehead, pulled up to the machine and started over.

She was a little faster now but she was also three times as tired. And hungry. And scared. Her hands trembled. She stopped, took a breath and clipped the thread on a string of collars. They coiled into the empty box and she started another, then a third.

"Time to clear up, Izzy." Stan frowned at the box. He leaned over and inspected her work. "How did this happen?"

She automatically held out her hand. "I slipped with the seam ripper…"

He cut her off, "Not your hand, this." He pointed to the collars.

"I'm sorry, Stan. She showed me what I'd done and I've been unpicking. . ." a sob was rising in her throat. "I thought I could fix things by the end of the day, but it took so long."

Stan had an odd look on his face. "Izzy, what are you talking about? These are backwards!" He pointed into the box.

"What?"

He looked at the work still on the machine. "All of these are backward. Show me how you did them before."

She did.

"That's right. Who told you to redo it?"

She looked over her shoulder. Marti was cleaning her work space. She looked as tired as Izzy felt.

"I don't remember," she said. "I was upset and didn't notice."

"You said someone showed you. Who was it?"

"Someone did, but I don't remember who." Her fingers twisted in her lap, a habit she had when she lied. Carefully folding her hands, she looked Stan in the face.

"Please give me another chance. I know I can do this job."

He sighed and patted her shoulder. "Nobody gets fired the first day unless they start a fire." His mouth twitched into a lopsided smile. "No one told you to start a fire, did they?"

"Not yet," she replied.

"Finish cleaning up and go home. Tomorrow will be better."

By the time she reached the break room it was deserted. She placed her little box in the locker and pulled out her purse. Long past the point of growling, her empty stomach just plain hurt. She moaned aloud when she recalled the two mile walk to get home. It seemed like she'd been fighting back tears all day but she couldn't let them go now. She was afraid she wouldn't be able to stop. For a second she let herself wish this was a school locker and that Ann was waiting out by the bike racks. They'd ride home, change into their swimsuits and head for the canal they'd been swimming in the last two weeks. Slapping the locker shut she turned and nearly jumped out of her skin.

Stan was right behind her. "Whoa- didn't mean to startle you, kid." He held a white metal box with a red cross on it. "I have to look at your hand before you leave."

They moved to a table, and she held out her hand. A frown made a crease between Stan's eyebrows and he cut through the makeshift bandage. A couple of threads were stuck in the dried blood. He used a pair of tweezers to pull them free. "I need to clean this up so I can see it."

Izzy bit her lip and inhaled sharply when he blotted her hand with alcohol.

"Kinda deep," he muttered, "too small to need stitches." He took out a rectangular bottle of iodine, a couple of gauze squares and a roll of adhesive tape. "When was your last tetanus shot?"

"I'm not sure," she answered, praying he didn't have a hypodermic in the box. Just the thought made her light-headed. She had a deep fear of needles.

"Better follow-up with your doctor then." He applied the iodine with the tiny glass rod attached to the bottle cap. It burned like crazy and Izzy jerked her hand away.

"Hang on," he murmured, taking her hand again, "we're almost done." He placed the folded the gauze and taped it to her hand, closed the first aid kit, and scooped the little pile of cotton balls and wrappers into a nearby trash can. "You'll live," he said, "or you'll get lockjaw and die." He smiled down at her. He had friendly eyes and smooth skin that didn't appear to need shaving; though she felt sure he had to be at least twenty. They wouldn't let a kid be in charge of this place.

"You can go," he offered, "Unless you want me to kiss it better."

Izzy laughed, her voice loud in the empty room. "Thanks anyway," she said.

Stan headed for the door. "Okay." He paused and looked back. "You need a ride home?"

She was tempted but shook her head. "My boyfriend is picking me up." She lied without thinking. It was a good one though – made her sound older.

He nodded and left.

In the Ladies Room Izzy removed her nylons and panty girdle and tucked them into her purse. She could at least be comfortable walking home.

She crossed the deserted parking lot, stepping gingerly on the hot asphalt. Her shoes swung from her hand. The graham cracker she'd eaten for breakfast was long gone and she'd only had iced tea, a small donut, water, and a couple of sips of coffee all day.

Her spirits rose when she remembered the burger place only four blocks away. She still had the dollar in her purse. Ann would understand if she had a sandwich and maybe a small drink. She'd take her a Mars Bar. They were Ann's favorite.

She walked through cool grass wherever it lined the sidewalk, feeling elated and exhausted at the same time. What an amazing day.

Chapter Four

Two doors from home Izzy began pulling bobby pins out of her hair. She could hardly wait for a shower. Her skin felt sticky, the soles of her feet were black and every part of her body ached.

Opening the screen door she called for her sister. Silence.

"Ann, where are you?"

Nothing.

A scrap of paper was anchored under a salt shaker on the counter. She picked it up and read:

Izzy,
I'm babysitting. I'll be home by 7:30.
Love, Ann

It was only five o'clock. She placed the melting Mars bar in the fridge.

Normally she loved having the house to herself, usually time alone was hard to come by. But she'd been so alone all day, even in a factory full of women she'd felt isolated.

She brushed the tangles and most of the hair spray out of her hair before stuffing it under a shower cap.

The tepid water felt delicious, though it stung her punctured hand. Quickly washing off her make-up she scrubbed down to her toes then stood under the spray until it ran cold. She dried herself and donned cut-offs and a tee shirt. She found gauze and adhesive tape and bandaged her hand.

The house was stuffy and quiet. Not until she came through the door did she realize how much she had missed her sister. The Izzy who had a job in the sewing factory, and sat at a table pretending to drink coffee and listening to grown women banter, was a lie. Alone in the house it felt like she was still that lie. Brushing her hair and showering helped, but she needed Ann to break the spell and be herself again.

The remains of the stolen newspaper were folded on the drain board. She picked it up and went to the front porch. A light breeze ruffled the leaves of the sycamore that shaded the steps. Sitting down, she opened the paper. The print refused to focus under her tired gaze.

How could Ann be babysitting? They didn't know anyone in the neighborhood. She studied the houses on the street and tried to recall where she had seen small children.

She wished she had something else to read. She and Ann had found the local library within a day of moving into town and each had picked up one of their favorite books. But she had finished hers yesterday.

Frustrated, she went back into the house and switched on the radio. She found a deck of cards and dealt a hand of solitaire.

Solitaire, she thought, *is not a game a twin should even know.*

She played for an hour and was contemplating eating the Mars Bar when Ann came through the door.

"Hi," she said.

Izzy shuffled the deck. "Where have you been?"

"Babysitting. Didn't you see the note?"

"I saw it. It didn't say where you were babysitting. No address, no phone number."

"I was around the corner in that red brick house with the steep roof. I didn't know the address and we don't have a phone. Criminey! It's not even dark. What's your beef?"

Izzy flushed, embarrassed at how abandoned she'd felt. She cleared her throat. "I just didn't know where you were."

Ann made herself a glass of ice water. "So? I didn't know where you were all day. You don't see me falling apart. Get a hold of yourself for cryin' out loud!" She dropped into a chair. "This lady came to the door and said she'd seen us riding our bikes around and wondered if one of us could watch her baby while she went out. I said okay, and that was that. It was great Izzy, her name is Mrs. McKinley and she's real nice. She told me to help myself to the food so I had a sandwich and sneaked one for you, too, ham and Swiss on rye with mustard and mayo." Ann set a square, waxed-paper wrapped, packet in front of her sister. "The baby slept the whole time and Mrs. McKinley gave me seventy-five cents. I thought maybe we could go downtown to a movie."

A lump ached in Izzy's throat. She was ridiculously relieved that Ann was home. She swallowed hard. "Wow, that's great. Thanks, Ann. I'll save the sandwich for lunch tomorrow.

Her twin gave her a quick hug. "Where's that newspaper? It has movie ads in it."

Izzy looked up, "I can't go to a movie. I have to be to work at seven in the morning."

Ann shrieked. "You got a job? A real job?"

"It must be a real job. I think it is going to kill me." Izzy held up her bandaged hand.

Ann's wide eyes widened more. "What happened?"

Izzy told about her day, while she dealt the cards for a game of gin rummy. She described everyone she'd talked to and the factory. Not wanting to mar the celebratory mood, she left out the detail about Marti making her redo her work.

Ann frowned at the cards she held and discarded one. "Do you need a tetanus shot?"

Izzy shuddered, "I'd rather have tetanus. They can cure that can't they?"

"Isn't it about time you got over that fear of needles?"

"I don't have a problem with needles unless you want to put one into me."

"We've had shots before. We lived."

"Yeah, what happy times those were! Mom told us we were going to the movies or a circus to get us in the car then surprised us with vaccinations instead. We cried when it hurt and to punish us she'd say, 'okay then, we'll just go home.' Just like she really had planned to go somewhere fun."

Ann looked up. "You think she lied?"

Izzy groaned, "I think she lied every time her lips moved."

Ann frowned but made no comment.

They played cards in silence for an hour, pausing to heat a can of tomato soup diluted with water.

Ann washed the dishes.

"School starts in three days," Izzy said as she yawned. She leaned her head on her injured hand, winced and switched to her good one. "What are you going to wear?"

"My new skirt, the white blouse with the tucks and my brown loafers." She wiped out the sink and dried her hands on a dish towel.

"You need new shoes, those loafers make you walk like a duck," Izzy said.

"They do not."

"Yes, they do. Every time you wear them I expect you to quack. Where can you find cheap shoes?"

"There's a five and dime downtown."

Izzy took three dollars from the cupboard. "There's a store that advertises bargain shoes next to a coffee shop on Main Street. Try them."

Ann looked at the money. "We can't afford it. I'll wear the old loafers and save my babysitting money for new ones."

Izzy stuffed the money into her sister's pocket. "You're representing both of us now, I can't have my 'little' sister running around looking like she doesn't have a—", she stopped short, realizing what she was about to say.

Tears gathered in Ann's eyes. "'Like she doesn't have a mother who loves her?'" she finished Willa's quote. "Oh, Izzy." A small sob escaped.

Taking her sister into her arms, Izzy swallowed hard. "The hell with her! You've got a sister who loves you."

Ann sniffled against Izzy's tee shirt. "I love you, too."

"Damn! You better, I'm supporting you now."

Ann chuckled. "Stop swearing."

Izzy laughed, gave her an extra squeeze and let her go. She locked the back door.

"Get some shoes Annie. Between what I can earn and what food you can pilfer from Mrs. McKinley, we won't starve."

<hr />

The sky was still light when the girls dropped into bed, after Izzy set the alarm for five-thirty. "You don't have to do my hair in the morning. I'll just wear the make-up and curse once in a while."

Ann giggled. "That should do it."

"I don't think anyone there cares how old I am anyway." Her eyes would not stay open. "Oh, I forgot… there's a Mars Bar in the fridge for you."

"Thanks, I'll have it tomorrow."

Crickets began their song.

"Izzy?"

Silence.

"She cared enough to make us get the shots." Ann sighed. "Want me to tickle your back?"

Izzy heard but didn't answer. Locked in the soft gray space between awake and asleep she was dreaming about pink crescent moons, turquoise smocks, and old ladies in purple lipstick.

Chapter Five

Birdsong stirred the silence of the early morning streets. Lawns, flowers and trees were awash in dew. The sky was light although the sun hadn't crested the hills on the east of the valley. Izzy wondered if she could be the only person awake in the entire town. She wore the pedal pushers and pink and white top. The white sandals weren't much more comfortable for walking than the newer heels.

She passed sleeping houses, empty parks, and dark shop windows. A boy delivering newspapers rang his bicycle bell at her and waved. A milkman carrying a wire basket of empty bottles to his truck said, "Good morning. Beautiful day." Izzy agreed and kept walking.

"Hey!" called a man driving an El Camino. "Can I give you a lift?"

Izzy ignored him and walked a little faster. The car rolled along the curb.

"Come on Brandy, don't be stuck up."

Her heart gave a heavy thump as she looked over at the guy from the pawnshop.

"Sid. Remember?" He raised his sunglasses and winked. The deep blue polo shirt he wore matched his eyes.

Izzy made herself smile. "I didn't recognize you." She kept moving.

"Lemme give you a ride and I can tell you how the TV is doing."

She laughed but didn't slow down.

"Aw come on, I'll take you wherever you need to go. Had any breakfast?"

Breakfast? Her shoe caught on a crack in the sidewalk and she missed a step.

The dry cereal she had choked down —the canned milk was gone — did not stop her stomach from growling. If she accepted the ride she'd have time for breakfast.

Sid stopped the car. He leaned across the seat and opened the passenger door. "I know a great little coffee shop."

"I have to be at work by seven."

He looked at the heavy gold watch on his wrist. "It's only a minute after six, there's plenty of time."

She slid onto the seat and kept hold of the handle inside the door. Sid's right arm rested on the back of the seat. When she didn't move next to him, he shrugged and put the car in gear.

Izzy tried to relax, or at least to appear relaxed, but a movie she'd seen in grade school about never taking a ride from a stranger replayed in her mind. She and Ann had been traumatized for weeks. She leaned forward and looked at the passing pavement, calculating the possible injuries if she had to throw open the door and jump into the street.

Sid switched on the radio and whistled along with "King of the Road", his fingers tapping the beat on the steering wheel.

They drove to the coffee shop she'd visited the day before. Sid parked and walked around the car to open her door. She scrambled out before he reached it. He smiled and took her arm, guiding her into the chilled air of the cafe. He led the way to a booth in the back.

"Morning folks," said a familiar voice. Ida hovered above them with a coffeepot. Turning over the cups on the table, she filled them. "What can I . . ." She planted one reddened hand on her hip. "Well, for petesake! It's you! How'd the job search turn out?"

"I found one." Some of the stiffness in her neck relaxed. "The one you told me about."

"That's just dandy." She spotted the gauze on Izzy's palm. "What'd you do to your hand?"

"It's nothing, just a scratch."

Sid cleared his throat and Ida frowned at him.

Ignoring the look, he ordered. "We'll have some pancakes and sausages. You want eggs, too?"

Izzy shook her head and nervously spooned sugar into the coffee.

"Yes, sir." Ida moved to the next customer.

Sid offered a cigarette and Izzy shook her head again. He placed one between his thin lips and lit it. His fingers were bony, the nails a little long but clean.

"You come here much?" he asked.

Izzy poured cream and stirred her coffee. She shrugged, "No, just that one day."

She felt his eyes sweep over her. "Say Brandy, you have another outfit? I mean this one is cute, but believe me, you could do better. Why don't you come by later and we'll go shopping. My treat."

Her face grew warm. Her mother's face flashed in her mind, "No such thing as free, girls," she'd said as she picked over a heart-shaped box of chocolates, "they all want something back." She hadn't specified exactly what they wanted, but the memory made Izzy squirm and she moved a little farther away from Sid.

"No thanks. I buy my own clothes."

"Hey, just trying to be friendly."

"I know, but I . . ."

Ida appeared seemingly out of nowhere and topped off their coffee. "Food will be right along." She grinned at Sid, "You come in pretty often don't cha?"

"Now and then." He took a gulp of coffee.

"Never seen you with your daughter before, have I?"

Sid looked annoyed, "She's not my —"

"We just met the other day," Izzy interrupted.

"Church social?" Something in the way Ida said 'church social' showed she wouldn't believe that.

"Yeah," Sid sneered, "it was the Sunday picnic at Our Lady of None of Your Beeswax."

The waitress didn't flinch. "That's what I thought." She aimed a broad smile at Sid. "I'm sure you're a regular there, too."

"Look here," Sid began, but Ida walked away.

She was back in a moment with their food and a glass of milk they hadn't ordered. She set it down a little hard in front of Izzy.

It was all Izzy could do not to fall on her breakfast. Butter melted over the stack of pancakes and three sausage patties were still sizzling. She focused on pouring syrup and eating. Sid didn't eat anything, and when her plate was clean he nudged his toward her. Slathering butter and pouring more syrup she tackled her second helping.

As they left, Ida called out "Come back soon, honey." She looked directly at Izzy.

Izzy blinked then sneezed in the blinding sunlight.

"Bless you," Sid said. He handed her a monogramed handkerchief. It looked expensive but the fabric was coarse, it felt like sanding her nose.

He led her to the car and held the door for her. Where to?" Sid asked after he was seated and started the engine.

She gave him vague instructions, and had him let her off a few blocks from the factory.

"Here?" he asked. "There's no place to work here."

Izzy scrambled out of the car. "Oh, it's right around here," she said. "Thanks for the breakfast."

"See you Saturday?" he asked.

"Gotta run, can't be late." She hurried away. The El Camino's tires squealed behind her.

⚜

A dozen women were chatting in the break room when Izzy stowed her purse in the locker and put on her smock. She still didn't have a lock, so her cash, the whole dollar and sixty-five cents, went into her pocket. The paper bag with the sandwich Ann had made went into one of the refrigerators with other sack lunches.

"Izzy, over here." Faye waved from a table. "So you came back?"

"I couldn't think of anything better to do."

Faye laughed. "Sucker! Come on, I'll show you how to clock in."

Izzy aligned the marks on her time card with the notches on the clock and slid it into the slot. The punch almost as loud and sudden as a rifle shot made her jump.

"In a week you won't even notice it." Faye patted her shoulder and looked at the time card. "Your last name is Gardner? Quite a few of those in town. Any relation?"

Izzy shook her head.

"I'm a Jackson," Faye said. "You can't swing a dead cat without hitting a Jackson around here." She dropped the timecard into the rack and they joined the line moving toward the production room.

Stan held the door open. "How's the hand?"

"Sore." She held it out for him to see.

"You go to the doctor?" He prodded her palm.

"Ow! Not yet." She pulled away.

He frowned. "It's swollen. Meet me by the sink when you go on break."

Faye tugged on his sleeve. "Hey Stan, how about moving Izzy next to me today?"

"Whatever you want." He checked a stack of boxes against the papers on his clipboard.

"You'll like it better over here," Faye said, placing a thin cushion on her metal chair. "We get a little sunlight between nine and three."

Izzy followed her to a wall of shelves with labels every two feet. "Find your name and pick up what you didn't finish yesterday."

The new work space was similar to the one from the day before except it didn't face a blank wall and the lighting was better.

They got busy. Faye sewed ruffles onto skirts. She was quick and in twenty minutes had a pile stacked so high that Izzy could only see her from the neck up.

She looked into her box of work and just the sight of pink cloth made her tired. Sighing, she picked up the all too familiar collars and began unpicking.

"Where are you from Izzy?" Faye called when she paused to fill out paperwork.

"All over. Wherever Willa wanted to go."

"Who's Willa?"

Izzy swore under her breath – she hadn't meant to say that. "She was my mother."

Faye looked stricken. "Oh kid, I'm so sorry."

And just like that the problem of Willa was solved.

"It's okay, it's been a while. Just me and my kid sister now."

A man brought another box of work for Faye and removed the finished skirts.

"How old is your sister?" she asked as she changed thread.

"Fifteen," replied Izzy.

"Tough age. Is she a sophomore?"

"Yeah."

Faye scooted her chair closer. "Would you mind if I showed you something?"

She took the seam ripper from Izzy's hand and held up a collar. "If you just clip a couple of stitches a little bit apart on the same side of the material, it makes it easy to pull out the bottom thread in one piece. See how fast?"

"I wish someone had shown me that yesterday," Izzy said.

"You've been unpicking since yesterday?"

Izzy told her about Marti making her start over after she'd done them right.

"Listen," Faye leaned in and whispered, "you don't want to get on Marti's bad side. She can be mean as a snake."

"But she was wrong. What am I supposed to do?"

"Double check with me or Betty, or even Stan if we're not handy. Sometimes I wait ten minutes or so and take the work back to her. She'll usually pass it the second time."

Faye returned to her ruffles, and Izzy continued unpicking. It went much faster now that she knew how to do it, and she was stitching collars again by the time Betty reminded her that she was missing her break.

Stan waited by the sink with the first-aid kit. He'd filled an enamel bowl with very warm water and placed a clean towel next to it.

"Let's have a look." He peeled the gauze bandage away and examined the wound. It was bright red and throbbing. He frowned. "You're not going to like this," he said as he cleaned a small needle with alcohol on a cotton ball.

Izzy took a deep breath and held it. She turned her face away and shut her eyes. She felt a quick sharp pain followed by gentle pressure on her hand.

"Okay. You can look now."

Stan folded a piece of gauze and dropped it in the trash. "I got the pus out, but it's pretty infected. Must really hurt."

She shrugged. "Yeah, well . . . a little."

"Oh, tough girl." He applied more iodine and a fresh bandage. "You need to get that tetanus shot."

"I'll take care of it."

"Not that tough, huh?"

"I said I'll take care of it," she snapped, wishing she'd said that she'd seen a doctor already.

He latched the first aid kit shut. "See that you do." His smile had disappeared.

"You're not a doctor you know," she pointed out.

"If I were, you'd get that shot right now." He washed his hands. "I want to check that again before you leave today."

She watched him cross the room to the soda machine. She tried to picture him in a white coat with a stethoscope around his neck.

"Is Stan going to medical school?" she asked when she joined Faye and the others.

Betty rolled the ash off her cigarette on the edge of a partially empty cup. "In his dreams," she said and gave a snort.

Marti scowled. "You know what's wrong with you, Betty?"

Betty rolled her eyes.

"You're bitter."

"No kidding? You should write for Dear Abby."

Marti leaned forward. "Bitter as a rotten peanut. Stan's a smart guy. He could be a doctor."

"And how would you know?" Betty's cigarette hissed when she dropped it into the cup. She blew smoke at the other woman.

"It just so happens my Wendell was thinking of going to medical school."

Betty scrunched up her forehead. "Is this the same Wendell that ran out on you years ago?"

A splotchy red flush crept up Marti's neck.

"This was before. He was smart just like Stan, and a hard worker."

Faye spoke up before Betty could say anything more. "What happened, Marti? Why didn't he get to be a doctor?"

"Things came up." Marti stuffed her smokes and matches into her smock pocket.

Chairs scraped the floor; break was over.

When she and Faye were settled at their machines, Izzy asked if Betty and Marti often argued.

Faye threaded her machine. "Sometimes. They used to really get into it, but Cudgel took them into his office and told them he wasn't running a Roller Derby here, and if they couldn't behave, he'd find ladies who could."

Izzy glanced around the room. In her mind "ladies" wore dresses and got together for Bridge or a matinee on Wednesday afternoons. Their mascara wasn't so thick that it shed flakes like black dandruff on their cheeks. Ladies didn't gulp coffee or talk with cigarettes dangling in their mouths. They didn't chew big wads of gum, or scratch in public.

Willa had sneered at ladies and wasn't one herself.

Until a few days ago, a lady was what Izzy had dreamed of becoming.

She felt someone watching her and bent over her work. From the corner of her eye she saw Stan look away and walk out the door.

A square of sunlight angled onto the floor. Lint and dust motes floated lazily in the illuminated air. Izzy finished the last collar and rolled her head to relieve some of the stiffness in her neck and shoulders. It was hot. Her throat felt dry enough to make her cough dust.

"Faye," she called.

Faye looked up, strands of hair stuck on her damp forehead. "What ya need?"

"Water," answered Izzy.

"That drinking fountain in the lunchroom is the only one. Hurry, they don't like us to be away from the machines for more than a minute."

The water wasn't particularly cold but it wet her throat. She wiped her mouth with the back of her hand.

The door from the offices swung open, and Stan came in with a man in a suit.

"Hey, Isabel!"

She felt like she'd been caught stealing, "Sorry, I needed a drink. I was just going back."

"Relax, that's fine. There's someone I'd like you to meet." A hint of triumph lit his eyes as he took her arm.

The suited man stood half a head taller than Stan and looked a little older. Then Izzy saw the small black bag in his hand.

Pulling away, she asked, "What's going on?"

Stan held onto her. "This is Dr. Stewart."

Her eyes widened and there was a sense of dread in her chest.

"Doctor?" she asked.

Stan grinned openly. "A real doctor. Also my brother."

The doctor took off his coat and rolled up his sleeves. Stan led her to a chair and began removing the dressing on her hand.

Before she could protest, Dr. Stewart probed the injury. He spread some salve on her palm and wrapped it in fresh gauze.

"It will be all right," he said and smiled at Stan. "You did an excellent job."

Izzy sensed an opportunity and rose from the chair. "It feels better already." She inched away from the table. The two men exchanged looks.

"Just a minute, Miss Gardner." The doctor produced a hypodermic syringe from the bag and a small vial.

Dread exploded into full-blown panic. Stan slid her smock off her shoulder and put an arm around her waist. "Just relax, this will only take a second." His free hand pushed up her shirt sleeve.

"Wait, wait . . ." She struggled, her eyes darting around the room for someone to help. "Don't do this! Stop!"

The doctor calmly dabbed her arm with alcohol. She felt sick and numb at once. She wanted to scream, but her throat was paralyzed. Was she breathing? She saw the needle, felt the warmth of a hand on her arm and turned her face into Stan's shoulder. Overwhelming dizziness flooded her brain then everything stopped.

⧜

Acrid fumes stung her nose. Stan's arm was still around her when she opened her eyes; they were seated on the floor of the break room. Dr. Stewart checked her pulse and Stan looked worried. Her arm felt bruised.

"What happened?" she mumbled.

"You fainted," Stan accused.

"I don't faint," murmured Izzy.

The doctor shone a light in her eyes. "You sure do," he said.

She tried to get up, but the room tilted and spun.

"Izzy, I'm so sorry," Stan said.

"I– hate – needles!" she said.

"Shouldn't be working in a sewing factory then," joked the doctor. Then he added, "You had to have that shot. Haven't you ever had one before?"

"Of course I have!" She squirmed against Stan's hold. "You've got some nerve!" She pushed him away and climbed onto a chair.

"You didn't give me much choice." Stan stood and brushed the seat of his pants. "What was I supposed to do? Let you get lockjaw?"

"You could have minded your own business." The angrier she became, the less dizzy she felt.

"It is my business. You were injured at work, and it's the company's responsibility to see that you have proper medical attention."

She couldn't think of a retort. "Well, it really hurt," was all she came up with, and it sounded lame even as she said it.

Dr. Stewart bought a soft drink from the machine. "Here," he said, placing it in front of her, "this will help." He sat next to her and wrote on a small pad. "People sometimes have some fever and you can expect your arm to be a little stiff and sore for a day or so. Follow these instructions and you'll be fine." He patted her hand, "I'm sorry it hurt, but I did give you one of my best brave-girl Band-Aids." He lifted her sleeve and she saw happy Peanuts characters cavorting on a bright yellow background.

A buzzer signaled lunchtime, and women began to fill the room. They stared curiously at Stan, Izzy, and the doctor who snapped his bag shut and rolled down his shirt sleeves. He picked up his suit coat and left.

Great!" Izzy shot at Stan. "How am I supposed to sew with a stiff arm?"

"You won't have to. Take the rest of the day off. I'll drive you home."

"I'll walk, thank you very much."

"And if you faint again out in the street, what then?"

An interested group stood with their mouths hanging open, taking in the scene.

"She fainted?" someone whispered.

"What's going on?" someone else asked.

"She fainted over Stan?"

"Okay, that's enough. Show's over. Move along!" Stan's face turned bright red. "Izzy, you need anything from your locker?" he asked through gritted teeth.

"My purse." She pushed her chair back.

"Stay here," Stan ordered. "Drink your Coke. I'll get it."

He was barely out of earshot when Betty moved in. "What the hell is going on?"

Marti peeked over Betty's shoulder, her small eyes burning with questions. Izzy sipped her drink. "Nothing. Never mind."

"Oh, come on, kid. We never get this kind of excitement. What happened?" Betty took a seat and pulled out her smokes.

"You're awfully white," pointed out Marti. "A little green, too."

"I'm fine," Izzy insisted.

Stan was back with her purse. He placed a hand beneath her elbow and lifted her up. "She'll be okay. Just eat your lunch. I'll be back."

Stan's car was very clean. Old and battered but clean.

"Which way?" he asked after the engine coughed, choked and turned over.

She gave him the address.

Chapter Six

Izzy maintained what she considered a dignified silence during the ride home. She hoped Stan would ask for directions again so that she could demonstrate just how angry she was by ignoring him, but he drove straight to the house and parked in the driveway.

He kept a hand on the small of her back until they were inside.

"Is there anyone here?" he asked as he inventoried the scant furnishings of the living room.

She jerked her arm free. "You can leave now," she snapped.

A puzzled look crossed his face then he laughed.

"What's so funny?" she demanded.

"You are. If you think this is some elaborate scheme to get you alone." He wiped his eyes. "Even if you were my type—"

"I didn't think—"

A scream cut the air. Ann, wearing only towels – one as a sarong around her slim torso and the other wound turban-style on her head – stared from the kitchen.

"Oh, shoot!" Stan covered his eyes and turned away.

"What are you doing here, Izzy? Who's he?" Ann leapt out of sight.

"It's okay. I'll explain later. Didn't you hear us come in?"

"I was in the shower. Didn't you hear the water?"

"I hate to interrupt, but I have to get back to work. Do you need anything before I go?" Stan still held his hand over his eyes.

"The *only* thing I need is for you to leave." Izzy opened the front door wider.

He pulled a pen and small notebook from his pocket and wrote. "The first number is my home phone, the second is my extension at work. If you think of anything, call me. If you can't make it to work tomorrow, call me." He placed the paper on the coffee table and left.

Izzy tossed her purse next to the note and dropped onto the sofa.

"Who was that?" Ann called from the bedroom.

"He's my boss. He brought me home because I fainted."

Ann hopped across the kitchen floor, one foot caught in the slacks she was putting on, and her unfastened blouse flapping. "You fainted?" She tumbled to the living room rug, rolled onto her back and sorted out the tangled pants.

"I was jumped on and forced to have a stupid tetanus shot." Izzy pulled up her sleeve and examined the site of injury. "Do we have any aspirin?"

With her clothing properly zipped and buttoned, Ann raised up on her elbows. "You let someone give you a shot? You hate shots!"

"I didn't have a choice. It was a surprise attack. It hurts like hell. Do we or don't we have aspirin?"

Ann hurried into the bathroom and returned with a pill bottle and a glass of water.

Izzy took the medicine and slumped against the back of the couch. "Is there any soup? I left my sandwich at work."

"There's cream of mushroom. Do you want that?"

Izzy pulled a face. "Yuck! The only way I can eat that is in a casserole." She closed her eyes. "Never mind. I'm going to lie down." She didn't move. She heard her sister leave the room and return.

"Here, Izzy." Ann handed her a pillow. "Mrs. McKinley came over this morning; she wants me to babysit a few hours."

Izzy rested her head on the pillow. "Okay," she mumbled.

"I don't have to leave for an hour yet; do you want me to get something for you? I can ride my bike to the store."

"I'll be okay, Annie. I just want to rest."

She must have dozed because she woke when Ann kissed her forehead.

"You're really hot. I better not go," she said.

"I'll be fine; go ahead." Izzy forced her eyes open.

Ann sighed. "I made some Jell-O for you and there are soda crackers."

"You're a good nurse. Now go make money. I probably won't move until you get back." Her eyes shut, and she heard Ann fussing around the room, opening windows and pulling shades. Then the screen door whined open and snapped shut. She adjusted the pillow, seeking a cool spot.

Alone, and slightly more comfortable, she began a mental list of all the rotten things that had happened. In under a week she'd been abandoned, forced into a life of crime — though she would get the television back or replace it— and deceit. She could barely keep track of all the lies she'd told, her hair had been cut, her eyebrows severely and painfully plucked, she was injured at work, and then attacked with a hypodermic needle. Tears welled in her eyes; her lower lip trembled. Oh yes, and her bike had a flat tire! She turned her face into the pillow and sobbed until exhaustion took over and she slept.

Angry protestations from an empty stomach woke her to a room deep in shadow. Silence told her that Ann had not returned. Her left arm throbbed above her elbow. As she pulled off the Band-Aid, she noted with satisfaction a small spot of blood on it.

"Stupid Stan," she muttered and shuffled into the kitchen.

She found a bowl of red Jell-O in the fridge and dished some onto a saucer. The saltines were on the table and she sat down to eat. The food eased the cramps in her stomach, and she began to feel like she might survive.

Through the open window over the sink, Izzy heard the sound of bicycle tires on the gravel drive, followed by an unfamiliar laugh and Ann's giggle.

"Quiet," Ann hissed. "My sister's probably asleep."

"At eight o'clock?" whispered the other voice.

The back door opened and Ann spoke over her shoulder, "She had a really bad day at work and she doesn't feel good."

"You don't have to whisper, I'm awake." Izzy dropped the spoon onto her empty dish and wondered why Ann was wearing a swimsuit.

A tall girl with long blonde hair followed Ann into the kitchen. She wore jeans cut off above the knee and a bright yellow bikini top under an open shirt. She smiled and exposed a flash of braces on her teeth.

"This is Jill Kimball," Ann said and turned to the girl, "My sister, Izzy. Isabel really, but everybody calls her Izzy.

"You feel any better?" Ann touched Izzy's forehead. "You're still hot."

"No kidding? It's only a hundred and ten degrees in here." Izzy brushed the hand away. "You wore your swimsuit babysitting?"

Ann glanced down as if she'd forgotten. "Oh. No, we went up to the canal after."

Resentment flared in Izzy's brain. "Our canal? You went swimming?"

Ann was looking in the cupboards. "Well, yeah. It's so hot we had to do something to cool off."

Jill looked confused. "You own the canal?"

With effort, Izzy didn't roll her eyes. "Not really. We used to go there a lot."

"Every day," Ann sighed, "until a week ago."

"What happened a week ago?" It was a reasonable thing to ask.

The twins froze for a heartbeat, their eyes met.

"I got a new job," Izzy said. "No time to swim."

"Oh." Jill nodded.

"Man, there is nothing to eat here!" Ann shut the cupboard.

"Come home with me," suggested Jill. "My mom made spaghetti and she always makes way too much."

Ann looked hopeful for an instant but quickly changed her expression with a glance at Izzy. "No. I better stay here."

Izzy covered her eyes with her hands. "Go, I don't want anything. No reason you should starve."

"Thanks, Sis." Ann practically skipped out of the kitchen. "Give me a minute to change clothes, Jill."

Jill sat down across the table from Izzy. "Sorry you're sick."

Izzy shrugged. "I had a tetanus shot."

The blonde shuddered. "Ugh, I hate shots."

"Tell me about it," mumbled Izzy.

Jill took her at her word. "Well, I knew this kid in second grade, his mom made him get a polio booster and two days later he was in an iron lung."

Her blue eyes didn't blink. "The shot," she whispered dramatically, "gave him polio!"

Izzy's stomach turned over. "Really?"

Jill twisted a clump of her hair in her hand and went cross-eyed checking for split ends.

"Nah. I made that up, but I did have a cousin who passed out cold in the school gym on shot day just because he saw a needle."

"That I can believe," Izzy said.

Jill dropped the hair and turned her attention to her cuticles. "Yeah, he's kind of a sissy though. I mean he's seventeen now and doesn't even have his license. Rides his dumb bike all over then wants to talk about everywhere he's been on it."

Izzy could see how that might be dull. She changed the subject, "You live near here, Jill?"

"On the next street. Next door to Mrs. McKinley."

"Oh."

"I met Ann while she was babysitting." Cuticles and split ends adequately inspected, Jill folded her arms and waited.

The small meal Izzy had eaten roiled in her stomach.

The bedroom door opened. "Okay, I'm ready," Ann said.

"About time," Jill said.

"I'll be home before ten."

"Fine." Izzy laid her head on the table.

The bikes were barely out of the driveway when she began to gag and the Jell-O and crackers made a rude second appearance. The retching subsided after a minute. She stepped over the slippery looking puddle on the linoleum and rinsed her mouth under the faucet. Her wobbling legs weren't going to hold her up much longer. She gripped the edge of the countertop and focused on breathing. Her face felt veiled with sweat. The fever had broken. Her legs began to feel solid again. She opened a drawer where they kept cleaning rags and picked one. Avoiding looking at the mess on the floor, she wet the cloth, wrung it out, and dropped it in the general direction that needed cleaning.

Willa had been good for this sort of thing. Izzy realized there were some things she and Ann had not had to do for themselves. Her mom may not have been patient, and she would have cussed the entire time, but Willa would have sent her to lie down and cleaned the mess up herself.

But Izzy was alone.

Fighting the gag reflex in her throat, she found a bucket in the broom closet and began filling it with hot water.

The pipes rattled and knocked. What now she wondered, and shut off the water. The knocking continued. It wasn't the pipes; it came from the front door.

The living room was dark. She opened the door a couple of inches and saw the shadowed outline of a man on the porch.

"Izzy?" Stan asked.

Relief washed over her. "What are you doing here?"

He opened the screen door. "I came to check on the victim."

She stepped back and let him in. He had a grocery bag with him. He flipped the light switch.

Izzy winced, moaned, and covered her eyes.

"Man," Stan said, "you look like hell!"

"I feel like hell; so it's not a coincidence," she said.

He set the bag on the floor and gently moved her to the sofa. "Do you have any ice?"

"I don't know."

"You mind if I check?"

"Knock yourself out," she said and slid sideways onto the pillow.

She heard him moving around the kitchen, cupboard doors and the refrigerator opening and closing. "What happened here? Yuck… never mind."

"Figured it out did you?"

He carried a glass with ice to the coffee table and took a bottle of Seven-Up out of the bag. She watched it fizz as he poured, bubbles streaming up around the ice and sparkling before they popped when they met the warm air.

"Just sip this," he said, handing her the glass, then disappearing back into the kitchen with the bag.

She heard water running and chairs being moved.

"What are you doing in there?" she grumbled.

"Putting things right," he called.

She took a small sip, the carbonation burned in her throat, so she drank slowly.

Stan returned eventually with two pieces of toast on a plate. "I didn't use much butter so it shouldn't make the nausea worse." He set the plate on the coffee table and took a seat on the edge of the broken recliner.

"If you keep this down, I also brought some chicken soup. I picked up some Band-Aids, Epsom salts, and mercurochrome — it doesn't burn like iodine. Oh, and a couple of magazines because I noticed you don't have a TV."

Izzy looked sideways at him and nibbled a piece of toast. "So, am I dying or what?"

Stan grinned. "No, you'll be fine. I'm just easing my guilty conscience."

A wall of awkward silence rose between them.

Izzy swallowed, took a drink, and cleared her throat. "You do this for all your employees?" She felt some satisfaction as his face reddened.

"No." He rubbed his palms against his jeans. "Cudgel usually sends Pauline with a potted plant."

"I told you I would take care of myself," she pointed out.

"But you weren't going to."

She cocked her head, "You couldn't know that."

"You had a sort of lost look about you."

"Did I?"

"Tell me the absolute truth; would you have gone to the doctor?"

She shrugged. "I don't know." Her eyes leveled with his. "But it should have been my decision."

He sighed. "You're right. I was out of line to force you."

She licked the tip of a finger and picked up a couple of crumbs from the plate.

"Really," he continued. "I mean, I'm glad you've had the shot, but I'm sorry about the way it happened."

Izzy nodded. "Okay," her voice was barely a whisper.

Stan looked at his wristwatch. "Oh man, I didn't know it was so late." He stood.

"What time is it?"

"Nine-thirty, but I have to be at work in the morning." He studied her face. "You should stay home another day."

"I'll be there," she insisted.

"Izzy please, take another day."

"I can't afford it," she said.

Stan slapped his forehead. "I completely forgot." He reached into his pocket then handed her an envelope.

"What's this?" she asked, as she opened it.

"The company wants to be sure you are taken care of. No more infections. We don't want you to end up in the hospital. That we can't afford." He gave an awkward chuckle and was out the door before Izzy could count the money.

She peeled the bills apart. Seven twenties, a five and five ones.

For the umpteenth time that day she found it hard to breathe. Ann could get her shoes; Izzy could buy a pair of jeans. She could get the television out of hock and cross "criminal" off her list. Amazed at the number of tears that could be cried in a twenty-four hour period, she began to sob again.

But this time she was smiling.

Chapter Seven

"A hundred and fifty dollars?" Ann's eyes almost swallowed her face. She threw her arms around Izzy and squeezed.

"Ow! Annie, my arm!"

"Oh! Sorry."

Izzy rubbed the sore spot. "It's okay, you just forgot."

"But what's the money for?"

"He said it was so I would be taken care of and not wind up in the hospital. It's from the company."

"The hospital? For a shot?"

"No, for an infection," Izzy held up her bandaged hand, "but, I'm sure it'll get better on its own." She grinned, "You can get some more school clothes and new shoes."

Ann shook her head, "First thing we're going to buy is groceries."

Izzy yawned. "Whatever you want. I'm going to take a bath and go to bed."

"I'm too excited to sleep!" Ann said.

When Izzy emerged from the steamy bathroom, Ann was already in her nightgown. Curled up on the bed, she scribbled on a pad of paper.

"What are you writing?" Izzy pulled a comb through her hair.

Ann sat up. "It was a grocery list, then I added some things we need like underwear and stuff, then I remembered the television and bills that we're going to have to pay and now it's back to groceries." She held out the paper.

"Milk, eggs, bread, crackers, Jell-O, canned soup," Izzy read. "Come on, we can do a little better than that. Frosted Flakes maybe, and sliced ham for sandwiches."

Ann wrote down, corn flakes and bologna. Izzy threw a damp towel at her.

It only took a few minutes to wind her hair onto curlers with her sister's help. Ann returned the battered overnight case where they kept bobby pins and curlers to the closet shelf. She switched off the bedroom light and went into the bathroom.

Izzy gingerly adjusted the pillows and covers to protect her arm. The throbbing had nearly stopped. The bedroom windows were open, and a breeze with a surprising edge of autumn blew in.

Ann returned to the doorway. "Are you shleepy yet?" she asked around the toothbrush in her mouth.

"No."

She went back to the bathroom and ran the water, then turned out the lights.

"Is the fever back?" Ann laid down, being careful to give Izzy plenty of room.

"No. Throwing-up and taking a bath must have helped."

"When did you throw-up?"

"After I ate the Jell-O and crackers."

"Gross! You had to deal with that on top of everything else?"

"Stan cleaned it up."

They rested in silence for a minute.

"He's sort of cute." Ann yawned. After a minute, she asked "Izzy, does he like you?"

"Like me?"

"You know, I mean does he *like* you like you?"

Izzy looked at the shadowed outline of her sister. "He said I'm not his type. Anyway, he's older than me. Probably twenty-something."

"He doesn't look much older than you do. Sid is a lot older, and he definitely likes you," Ann pointed out, "but he gives me the creeps"

"Even he has his moments."

"What are you talking about?"

She told Ann about her breakfast with Sid. It seemed like it was days, not hours ago.

When she finished Ann was sitting up. "You went out with him?"

"It wasn't a date. He just bought my breakfast and gave me a ride to work."

Her sister lay down again, but didn't ask any more questions.

They talked again about the money. Izzy insisted on more school clothes for Ann, and Ann agreed to add potato chips to the grocery list. If Izzy was going to have bologna instead of ham, then she had to have chips. And sweet pickles.

Then the subject of school came up.

"I wish you were coming with me," Ann said quietly. "I've never been to school without you."

Izzy waited until she could trust her voice to answer, "I know. It's weird not planning our classes together."

There was a flash of lightening in the distance and a low rumble of thunder several seconds later.

"Maybe," Ann began, then cleared her throat, "Maybe Mom will be back soon and you can still—"

"She's not coming back," Izzy stated.

"You don't know that."

"I don't want her to come back. Ever." She hadn't meant to raise her voice.

The curtains billowed, as if the night had taken a breath and exhaled. The sweet smell of rain followed.

Izzy felt a tremor and knew Ann was crying. She reached for her hand. "We're okay, Annie. We're doing fine."

"I guess so."

The silence held much longer. Izzy was nearly asleep when Ann asked, "Don't you miss her?"

The tension seeped back in Izzy's chest. "No," she lied. "We're better off."

Ann's hand pulled free and she turned her back.

Rain pelted the leaves and grass outside.

Izzy's mind raced. Images of Willa flashed in her brain. She forced herself to think of other things: mentally she rearranged the living room furniture, she rode her bicycle through streets lined with autumn leaves, she wondered which new fall shows she would watch on the TV when it was back, what books she would find at the library.

It had been a day of one exhausting emotion after another. Her body yearned for rest, but she resisted. Once her eyes were closed the images would be back and they wouldn't be the ones she'd been focusing on. It wouldn't be Willa at her worst, sarcastic and mean. It would be that other Willa; making funny faces to get a sick child to smile, laughing at a silly story, crying at a sad movie, emptying her tip money onto the kitchen table so the girls could count it then and then sharing it with them.

It would be Mom.

Ann caught her breath in her sleep like a child who has cried to exhaustion.

Izzy left the bed and felt her way into the hall and down to the empty room at the front of the house. The door stood open. She closed it behind her and switched on the small lamp on the dressing table. The lampshade had turned the color of caramel and cast a soft yellow glow around the room.

She opened a drawer. The scent of Evening In Paris was still there, mixed with Max Factor face powder and Revlon lipstick. She swept a finger over the newspaper liner and caught several hairs. They were dyed a red rarely found in nature and glistened like copper threads under the lamplight. Carefully twining them around her fingertip she looked at her own reflection in the clouded mirror. In her shorty pajamas and without make-up, she looked just like she should. Fifteen. Her eyes were red rimmed and a little swollen. She studied her face for traces of resemblance to her mother. A tiny dimple at the side of her mouth and the way her earlobes attached to her head like the handles on a sugar bowl, were the most obvious similarities. Willa's eyes had been a strange pale blue that turned almost silver near her pupils; Izzy's looked like pools of indigo.

She closed the drawer and turned to the bed. It was still made up with the white chenille spread. Izzy sat on the edge of the mattress and picked up one of the dark pink throw pillows. She held it close to her chest, wrapping her arms across it, pulling it tight to her heart. It muffled the aching she hid. Ann couldn't find out how messed up Izzy felt inside. In one wrenching move she'd been torn from her sister, and moved from the position of twin to protector and provider.

There had been enough tears for one day, or for a week. She put the pillow back and smoothed the creases from the bedspread.

The girls had learned to pray when they were little. Willa figured out that if they went to Sunday school at a local church, she could have an extra hour or so of rest. So she sent them to the nearest congregation, and they listened to Bible stories and played with crayons and salt dough while their mother slept off a Saturday night on the town.

Izzy switched off the lamp and whispered in the dark:

"*God,*
Please watch over Ann and me. Help us know what to do." She paused, then added, "*And watch over Willa. I don't know where she is but You do. I don't care if she is hungry, and cold, and lonely, or afraid. But, please, keep her safe. Amen*"

She went back to her room. Ann mumbled in her sleep. The rain had stopped. Izzy climbed into bed and moved just close enough that her hip rested next to her sister. A kind of peace flowed between them. Her heart found its natural rhythm, and she relaxed.

Chapter Eight

"I only need one pair, Ann. What were you thinking?"

"I pictured you sitting around in your underwear waiting for your jeans to dry on the clothesline." Ann twisted in front of the mirror to see the back of her new outfit. "Do you think this is too long?"

Izzy studied the jumper and blouse her sister wore. The hem reached the top of Ann's knees. The latest magazines showed skirts three or four inches shorter. "We can take it up an inch or two. You won't want to wear it for a couple of weeks anyway. It's too hot."

"Yeah, you're right." Ann unfastened buttons. "I'll stick to summer things at first."

The bed was adrift in tissue paper and shopping bags. Knee-hi socks, underwear, a blue turtleneck sweater and a gray pleated skirt, the promised loafers in a dark oxblood and Izzy's two pair of jeans were piled in the middle.

"How much did you spend?"

Ann pulled on a tee shirt. "Thirty-eight dollars and ninety-seven cents."

"Seems like an awful lot," Izzy said.

"Oh, that was just your money. I spent my babysitting money, too." She dug through the bags until she found the one she wanted. She held it out to Izzy.

"What's this?"

"I bought something for you, from me."

Izzy opened the bag. Inside was a hooded cardigan in a deep plum color with wooden toggles down the front.

"They had other colors if you don't like it."

Izzy pulled it on carefully over her sore arm. The wool felt soft but heavy enough to keep her warm. She looked in the mirror. Her tan cheeks glowed, and her eyes shone a dark blue. "I love it, Ann." She smiled at her sister. "I really love it!" She took the cardigan off and carefully folded it.

Her sister laughed. "Great! Now we just need to get your bike fixed so you don't have to walk to work every day."

"I could sleep in 'til six!"

Izzy carried the new jeans into the kitchen and ran hot water into the old wringer washing machine next to the sink. "Can you help me with these?"

"Sure," Ann called.

Izzy sprinkled detergent into the water and used manicure scissors to snip off the tags. She dropped the pants into the machine and watched as the suds and water turned sky blue.

Her sister appeared in her summer uniform of cut-offs and tee shirt. She peered into the agitating tub. "If I end up going to my first day of high school with purple hands, it will only be because of sisterly affection."

"Your sister is grateful. I'd rather go to work naked than show up in jeans that look new!"

"For sure!"

They rinsed the jeans in the sink and ran them through the wringer until no more water squeezed out. Then they carried them to the backyard and Ann hung them on the clothesline.

"There," she said, looking at the faint blue tinge around her fingernails. "This should wear off before Monday."

"Yeah, but school starts tomorrow. Are you going to wear mittens?"

Ann laughed, "I'll add nail polish to the shopping list."

They heard footsteps on the gravel driveway.

"We're back here," Ann yelled.

Jill came around the corner of the house with a tall, blond guy in tow. "Are you ready? Hi, Izzy. I brought my brother, Paul, over to fix your tire. How you feelin'?"

"Better, thanks. Ready for what?" Izzy tugged self-consciously at her cutoff shorts and wished she'd taken the curlers out of her hair.

"We're going to rescue the television and get groceries," Ann reminded. "We'll have to take the wagon. Hi, Paul. The flat is on the red bike."

Paul nodded and went to the bike leaning against the back porch. He dropped the tools and patch kit he carried, and flipping the bike over to rest on the seat and handle bars, squatted to inspect the tire.

Ann and Jill left with the empty wagon rattling over the cracked sidewalk behind them.

"Can I get you anything, Paul?" Izzy asked.

He squinted up at her. "I need some water and dish soap." His voice was deep and she realized he was older than she first thought.

"I'll be right back," she said. In the kitchen she placed ice cubes in a glass and filled it with cold water. She got the liquid soap from the window sill over the sink and took everything out to him.

He already had the inner tube out and was looking for the puncture in it. "Do you have a pump?" he asked. Looking up, he frowned. "What's this?" he nodded at the glass.

"Water. I'll look in the garage."

The pump was half buried under some old tires. Izzy pulled it loose and carried it to the porch.

"Can I help?" she asked.

"Hold onto this." He handed her the inner tube.

Paul attached the pump and inflated the tube. Then he picked up the glass of ice water and squirted dish soap into it.

"Don't drink that!" she exclaimed.

"Really?" he said with more than a touch of irony. "Turn the inner tube slowly." He stirred the soap into the water with a finger then poured it carefully over the tube until it began to bubble. "There's the hole." He grinned. "I asked for water, not a drink." He dried the spot where the air was leaking and marked it with a little piece of chalk he pulled from his pocket.

Izzy felt her cheeks burn, "You need anything else?" she asked coolly.

"Well," he sorted the repair kit, "as long as you're up, I guess I could use a drink."

He was chuckling when she stomped past him into the house. She brought him an empty glass. "There's a hose out back."

He stood and took the glass from her hand, "If it's all the same to you, I'll use the kitchen faucet." He said it so pleasantly that Izzy felt her anger and embarrassment melt away.

He followed her inside. Filling the glass at the sink, he drank and filled it again.

"I have more ice if you want some," Izzy offered.

He shook his head. He leaned his hips against the counter and studied her for a second. "You're not much like your sister are you?"

"What do you mean?"

He shrugged. "Ann is quiet. Shy. Sweet-like. You're more. . ." he hesitated.

"Rude?" she suggested.

"I was going to say feisty." He had a killer smile: all straight white teeth and curving lips. Kind of Paul Newmanish.

"Maybe you don't know Ann as well as you think," Izzy pointed out.

"Ann's a kid, I know her as well as I need to." His gaze slid over her figure, "You, on the other hand . . ." He didn't finish.

An involuntary shiver ran down Izzy's back. Intrigued but wary, she chose not to reply.

Paul sighed, set down his glass, and went back to the porch to finish the tire.

Izzy watched from a seat at the kitchen table. When he was done, he asked if he could wash his hands.

"Of course," she said. "How much do I owe you?"

He took a minute to consider then said, "You owe me a movie on Sunday afternoon."

"A movie?"

"A movie and a hamburger afterward." He shook the water off his hands and reached for a paper towel. He didn't wait for an answer.

"I'll pick you up at 1:30. My treat. See ya'." He was out the door and striding down the drive before she could say anything.

He asked me out? She thought with amazement. *With no make-up on and my hair in curlers, he asked me out!* She couldn't say if she was more excited, mystified, or suspicious.

Izzy prepared a bowl with water and Epsom salts, following the instructions on the package. The hole in her palm looked red but not swollen or hot, and when she pressed around it there was no sign of infection. She laid it in the water to soak.

As she thumbed through a magazine, a short story caught her attention, and she began to read. It was about a girl starting college. All her clothes were corduroy or tweed, she owned a car, and shared an apartment with friendly roommates on a campus absolutely crawling with ivy and boys who also wore corduroy and tweed, plus horn-rimmed glasses. Izzy read until the water turned cold and her finger tips were pruney.

She dried her hand and applied more salve. With a fresh bandage in place, she looked for something to do and decided to straighten the bedroom. She folded the shopping bags and tissue paper and was hanging up Ann's new clothes when she heard a knock at the front door.

A woman called through the screen, "Anybody home?"

Izzy had never seen her before. She left the latch in place. "Who are you looking for?" she asked.

The woman stiffened and tugged at the door handle. "Is your mother here?"

"What do you want?" Izzy asked again.

"I want to talk to Willa Gardner," she tugged harder at the handle. "Don't think you can lock me out of my own house! Open this door!" She stomped her foot and Izzy noticed her platform heels, the kind advertised in Frederick's of Hollywood.

"This is your house?"

"Yes, this is my house," the woman mimicked. "I rented it to Willa Gardner, where is she? Let me in!"

Izzy unlocked the door and stepped back. The woman tottered in on her high heels. She wore a strapless pink sundress and a wide-brimmed white straw hat on hair the color of apricots. Slipping off a pair of sunglasses, she looked around the room then sniffed.

"Who are you?" she asked when her gaze came back to Izzy.

"I'm Isabel; Willa is my mother."

"Hunh," the woman ran a white gloved fingertip along a window sill. "I'm Mrs. Call."

Izzy glanced nervously at the spot where the television was supposed to be. "My mother isn't here right now. I can give her a message if you want."

Mrs. Call removed a glove and dug around in her straw handbag. She found a pen and a notepad and started scribbling. "Where, exactly, is Willa?"

"Work," Izzy lied.

"Give her this and tell her to call me, I'm making a few changes to the lease." She looked around the room again and frowned. "You know I rented this place clean, and I expect you to keep it that. . ." she paused, "Where the hell is the television?"

"The t-t-television?" Izzy stammered.

"The Motorola television that was right there in that corner!"

"Oh, that's right. It's at the repair shop. We couldn't get a picture on it."

Mrs. Call squinted at Izzy. "Then you busted it. It worked fine when I showed the place to your mother. Which repair place? I don't want just anybody working on it."

"I don't remember the name, but they're delivering it tomorrow."

"Uh-huh," the woman scanned the room again, "I'll be checking back." She stepped onto the porch and gave the yard a once-over. "Tell Willa it wouldn't kill her to water the grass." She tugged her glove back on and flexed her fingers. "Oh," she began, reaching to her left and flipping open the metal flap of the mailbox, "And take in your letters." She handed Izzy a stack of mail. "I don't like the place to look abandoned."

"Yes, ma'am." Izzy noted the peeling paint and the rusted window screens on the porch.

"Hunh," Mrs. Call repeated. She stalked to the pink convertible in the driveway and left.

Before Izzy could sort the mail, a familiar car stopped in front of the house.

Stan was driving, but it was Faye who climbed out of the front seat and carried a covered dish to the porch.

Izzy opened the door again, "Faye, what are you doing here?" she tried to sound happy to see her.

"I brought a casserole for the invalid." She held up the dish she had tied in a kitchen towel. "It's still hot."

A savory smell made Izzy's mouth water. "Wow," she didn't know what to say. "That's nice. You shouldn't have."

Faye followed her into the kitchen, and placed the dish on the stove. "You might really think that after you taste it. It's only chicken and rice with broccoli and cheese." She looked around the room. "Oh good, you've been soaking your hand. Stan said to remind you."

Izzy's hand flew to the curlers, and she started pulling them out. "He's not coming in, is he?"

"No, he just drove me here. He went to put gas in his car. He's coming back," she paused, "for me." Her voice came down a bit sharp on "me."

Izzy processed what had not been said. "Ooooh."

"We don't want anyone at work to know." Faye's cheeks shone pink. "Please don't say anything."

The oddest feeling, like someone had pulled a plug and all her air was leaking out, hit Izzy. She made herself take a breath and smile. "You two are, uh, going together then?" she continued pulling curlers from her hair.

Faye shrugged. "So far it's just rides home from work. He stayed for dinner a couple of times."

Izzy shook her head and raked her fingers through her curls. "That's great, Faye," she said, "Stan seems very nice."

Faye wrapped her arms around herself. "I've never met anyone like him. He's considerate and kind and smart. . ." She went on for ten full minutes before words finally failed her. She gave Izzy a sharp look, "You're not going to tell on us are you?"

"Of course not!"

"Thanks, kid." Faye squeezed Izzy's good hand. "I knew you'd be cool about it."

A car door slammed.

"Oh, he's back. I better not keep him waiting. You'll want to keep that food hot or else get it into the fridge."

"Thanks for thinking of me, Faye."

"Take care of yourself," Faye called over her shoulder from the door then she was gone.

Izzy stood rooted to the linoleum until she heard the car drive away.

What did she care who Faye was seeing? What difference did it make that Stan had a girl? Surprise, that's all it was. She was just very, very surprised. The last thing she needed right now was a crush. There'd been enough excitement in her life the last seven days.

It was just unexpected news. Maybe she was a little shocked. One thing was definite; in no way was she, not even the tiniest bit… disappointed.

She unwrapped the casserole and placed it in the oven.

Besides, she had a date for Sunday.

Chapter Nine

Ann and Jill tugged the wagon into the kitchen and slammed the door behind them before they dissolved into giggles.

Izzy looked up from the Life magazine she was reading. "What's so funny?" she asked.

Holding up her hand, Ann clutched her side as if she'd been running. "We—" she couldn't catch her breath and shook her head.

Jill wiped her brow. "We think we're being followed."

"Followed? Why?" Izzy noted the cardboard boxes and paper bags in the wagon. "Hold it! Where is the television?"

The girls collapsed onto the floor in a fresh wave of breathless laughter. Izzy folded her arms and waited.

Ann regained some composure. "The TV is at Jill's house."

"That guy, what's his name? Sid? He insisted on delivering it and kept asking where you lived, so I gave him my parents' address. I told him to leave the set by the back door if no one answered." Jill wiped her eyes.

"He had his hair slicked back and was slapping on Aqua Velva when we left." Ann snorted and that brought on a fresh bout of giggling.

"So?"

"So who knew he wouldn't wait until his shop was closed to deliver the set? We went to the store for the groceries, and when we figured the coast was clear we started back."

Jill pulled herself up to the sink and slurped from the faucet. She splashed some water over her heated face.

"We were just passing Mrs. McKinley's when Sid's car showed up. We ran up her driveway and hid until he passed."

Izzy walked to the sink and pulled the shade over the window. "Damn it!" she spat the word. "What the hell were you thinking?"

Ann was instantly serious. "We were trying to save another trip downtown."

"Save a trip? That's just great Ann! Why didn't you just bring Sid to the house?"

Jill held up her hands. "Wait Izzy, don't you get it? That's why we sent him to my place. Ann and I will get the TV after we unload the groceries."

"I don't give a crap about the stupid TV," Izzy shouted. "You just led that guy right to our front door."

"Calm down! We're not even sure he saw us."

"And even if he did, we probably lost him," Jill added.

Izzy stared at them. "Probably?"

"I'm sure he didn't follow us. I didn't see any cars after we entered the driveway," Ann said.

Izzy took an open soda from the fridge and gulped a mouthful. It was flat and sickeningly sweet.

"I'm sor—" Ann began.

"Don't! Don't tell me you're sorry, Ann." She glared at her sister. "It's not enough! You've got to use your head. You being sorry is worth squat if Sid shows up here."

Jill's face whitened, "Is he dangerous?"

"No, no. It's nothing like that. Izzy's being dramatic," Ann put in, with a warning look to her sister.

Jill didn't look convinced, "You should call the police."

"We can't," Izzy said.

"Why not? They could tell him to stay away and—"

Izzy cut her off, "We don't have a phone,"

"Call from my house then."

Izzy turned the lock on the back door, willing herself to act calm. She blew out a breath. "No," she forced a rueful smile. "Ann's right. I'm overreacting. You're right. I doubt he even saw you."

Ann touched her shoulder. "Let's put away the groceries. We'll wait 'til after dark to get the TV."

Jill sniffed, "Something smells good."

"What is it?" asked Ann.

"Chicken and rice," Izzy muttered.

Ann peeked in the oven. "Wow! Where did it come from?"

"A girl from work brought it."

Ann looked puzzled, "How'd she know where you live?"

Izzy cleared the table. "Stan brought her."

The oven door snapped shut. "He was here again?" A teasing smile played on Ann's lips.

"He just dropped her off and picked her up. They were together," Izzy placed cartons of milk and cottage cheese in the fridge. "Are together," she added.

"I thought you and Stan were. . ." Jill stopped mid-sentence.

Izzy gave Ann an exasperated look.

They filled the cupboards and set the table. Ann made a salad from lettuce and tomatoes and tossed it with a little dressing.

They tried to forget about Sid as they feasted and listened to the radio. Jill and Ann talked about school.

"I guess Izzy goes to the parent/teacher meetings and stuff," Jill said.

Ann glanced at her sister. "Yeah, that's what she usually does."

"Did you get your schedule yet? Mine came in the mail yesterday."

"Did we, I mean did I?" Ann asked.

Izzy shook her head. "I don't know, I haven't looked through the mail."

Jill shrugged, "You can pick it up in the office. I hope we have some classes together. What are you taking?"

"Probably the usual, English, History, PE, Math, I haven't decided on my electives yet. What did you choose?" Ann asked.

The chatter became background noise for Izzy's thoughts. She tried to recall if she had locked the front door behind Faye.

Jill and Ann didn't notice when she left the table and wandered to the living room.

Outside in the dusk, a few kids played Kick-the-Can. A girl anchored an empty can with one foot and covered her eyes while she counted. Half a dozen kids scattered to hide. Izzy watched them through the screen door, her hand feeling for the hook that latched it to a metal eye in the jamb. The girl who was "it" methodically gathered the first of her prisoners next to the can and sped off to find the others. Suddenly, a small redheaded boy slipped out from behind a shrub. He tip-toed to the corner of the house and waited until he was sure the coast was clear. Then, short legs churning madly, he ran up the drive and kicked the can. It clattered only a few feet but far enough for the prisoners to run and hide again. Izzy laughed. That's what she liked about Kick-the-Can — all the second chances. It only took one person to free everyone, and the game went on. It didn't have to be the biggest kid or the fastest or the smartest. There was opportunity for anyone to save the day or rather, night. Porch lights winked on, and any minute parents would begin calling their children home.

She shut the door and turned the lock.

In the kitchen, Jill washed the dishes while Ann dried. They were singing "Mrs. Brown, You've Got a Lovely Daughter," along with the radio and dancing in front of the sink.

Izzy put the leftover food away. She couldn't remember the lyrics, and her feet had forgotten how to dance.

Chapter Ten

Izzy caught herself looking at the clock again and forced her attention back to her work with an effort. Her sister should be walking into the high school right about now.

She clipped the thread on a string of collars, dropped them into the box and began another. Faye had waved Stan over to her machine and was asking him questions about something. They'd only been working for an hour and this was the third time he'd been summoned.

Faye scooted her stool to one side, and Stan leaned over to adjust the tension on the machine. Her fingers brushed against his hand.

Izzy checked the time. Eight-thirty. She was glad Ann had Jill with her. The high school was a cluster of three ancient buildings, four if you counted the one for industrial arts housed in an old storefront across the street. It would be easy to get lost. Thanks to Paul, Jill had been all over the place. She assured Izzy and Jill that she could find their classes blindfolded if she had to.

Last year's Junior High school in a different town had given Izzy a royal pain with its stuck up students and nosey teachers and that weird cabbage and vinegar smell from the chemistry room that permeated the lockers. If she hadn't had her sister with her, she would have cut class every day. Well, not every class. She liked history, and English was okay once they got past reviewing the parts of speech and punctuation and started reading something. But everything else, math, general science, health, and home economics, were a complete waste of her time. Why shouldn't she feel relieved she was through with them? She should. She did. She reminded herself of it each time she pulled her thoughts back to sewing.

Ann would be lucky if she stayed awake in class. She'd kept Izzy up half the night. No fewer than three outfits had been tried on and discarded. The first one was too shabby, the next was too tight across her bust— a fact met with a happy squeal from Ann who had feared all her curves would always be on her legs— the third outfit looked like she was trying too hard.

"Trying what too hard?" Izzy had asked, exasperated.

"You know, to make an impression." Ann frowned into the closet. "I wish I could wear the new skirt and sweater."

"Too hot," Izzy said.

"Yeah. Okay." Ann sighed. "How about the red A-line skirt and the white knit top?"

"There are going to be a jillion kids there. No one is going to pay any attention." Izzy yawned.

Ann placed a short sleeved white top over the hanger with the skirt and hung them on the closet door. She'd already laid out clean underclothes and socks. Her new shoes were polished and ready. It was after midnight when they went to bed.

Paul and the movie had been forgotten in the excitement.

When Izzy pedaled her bike out of the driveway at six a.m., Ann had already dressed.

A buzzer signaling break brought Izzy back to the factory with a jolt.

Betty and Marti picked up their coffee and were tamping cigarettes on the table. Faye dropped a coin in one of the vending machines and selected a bag of peanuts. Izzy filled a paper cup with water and joined them.

"How's it goin', kid?" Betty's cigarette waved between her lips like a conductor's baton when she spoke.

"Better, thanks," Izzy replied.

"No more fainting spells?"

"Nope."

Marti sipped her coffee noisily then said, "Your work's looking better."

"Really?" Izzy tried hard to keep the sarcasm out of her voice.

"Was the casserole okay?" Faye asked. A small brown paper bag with grease spots bleeding through sat on the table in front of her.

Izzy smiled at her. "It was great. We're making it last as long as we can. I'll have your dish for you tomorrow."

"Your kid sister start school today?" Betty brushed a bit of ash off of her blouse.

"She was ready to go when I left the house."

"First day of high school." Betty laughed. "I still remember mine. I had new saddle shoes that pinched and gave me a blister, and a day-old home permanent that smelled awful. It was wonderful."

Marti smirked. "As I recall you were a freshman about the same time I started here. Only it wasn't kids' clothes back then. Uniforms."

"For the war?" asked Faye.

The smirk dropped. "Yeah, the Civil War," Marti snarled. "How old do you think I am?"

"Give her a break. She didn't mean nothin'." Betty patted Faye's hand. "World War II was over, honey, it was nineteen-forty-eight."

"And it was work uniforms for your information." Marti was not appeased.

Stan dragged a chair to the table, squeezing in between Faye and Betty. "What uniforms?"

"The ones I used to make here," Marti answered, "for sixty cents an hour and no piece rate." She crushed her cigarette butt out in the metal ashtray.

"So, you would say things have improved around here?" Stan asked.

Marti gulped the last of her coffee. "Some things have." She glanced at Izzy, "And some things need to." Her chair scraped the floor as she stood and walked away.

"What was all that?" Stan unwrapped a stick of gum and folded it into his mouth.

"Just Marti being Marti," Betty sighed.

Faye pushed the paper bag in front of Stan and blushed.

Stan opened it and Izzy thought his face reddened. "Chocolate chip! Thanks, Faye." He took one cookie and generously passed the bag around. Betty and Izzy took one, Faye seemed too nervous to eat anything.

The buzzer sounded and everyone headed back to the production floor.

Izzy brushed crumbs from her chin and hands. "Wow Faye, you're a really good cook."

"I have to be. Nobody else at my house will do it." They took their seats.

"You live with your family?" Izzy squinted to thread her needle.

"Mom died when I was in high school. I'm the youngest, so it's just my older brother and dad." She fiddled with a knob on her machine. "Dang! This dumb thing is still not working." She craned her neck looking for Stan.

Izzy turned her attention back to sewing collar after collar. The size, color, and shape varied slightly. She was relieved when she finished with pink and started working with a floral pattern. In a few more weeks, she supposed, they would all look the same to her.

When she raised her eyes again, Stan was back in Faye's chair. "I could have sworn I had this adjusted. What happened?" he asked.

Faye twisted her fingers together. "I must have bumped it."

Stan laughed, "With what? A mallet?" He sewed on a scrap of material. After examining the stitches, he tweaked the knob again and made another line of stitches. "Okay, looks fine now." He stood and patted Faye on her head. "See if you can keep it going for a couple of hours. I can't keep running over here. People will talk!" He said it with a teasing smile, and Faye beamed. She sat down and watched him walk away, her chin resting on her hand.

The day couldn't pass fast enough for Izzy. It felt like forever until she was on her bike heading home.

Ann and Jill had changed into cut-offs and T-shirts and were drinking Cokes on the porch.

Izzy propped her bike next to the back door and grabbed a cold drink from the fridge and went out to join them.

"How was it?" she asked, still breathless from the ride.

"It was the best!" Jill said. "We have homeroom together, and we share a locker."

"I'm going to work in the cafeteria for free lunches." Ann grinned. "Oh, what time is it?"

"A little after four. Why?"

Jill jumped up. "You better get going, Ann."

A fist of disappointment punched Izzy's chest. "Going? Where?"

"McKinley's. I promised I'd sit tonight."

Izzy put down her drink. "On a school night? Don't you have homework?"

Ann picked up a book, "I can do it over there. The baby just plays by himself or sleeps. I'll be home by nine or so."

"I have to get home, too," Jill said, and the two walked away together.

Izzy picked up their empty bottles and carried them inside. The disconnected television stared mutely from the corner of the living room. She ate the last of the casserole cold and scrubbed the dish in the sink. Water gurgled down the drain when she pulled the stopper. Other than a faint mechanical hum from the clock built into the stove, it was quiet in the house. So quiet.

After the dull roar of the machines at work it should have been restful, but it wasn't. Izzy listened and felt the walls listening in return. Silence reverberated through the house. It clung to her skin and felt like a hand across her mouth. She made herself take a deep breath just to be certain that she could. She took another breath and another until she felt light-headed.

A fear compressed in her mind began to grow. All the things she'd blocked, whispered in the quiet to be heard. She paced through the rooms without seeing. Her vision turned in and grew narrow, like looking down a long tunnel with no light at the end, just darkness getting darker and darker.

Part of her brain wanted to pull her erect, shake her head and tell her to snap out of it, but the blackness was too strong. She turned abruptly and nearly scraped her nose on the screen door. Then she was outside, on her bike, the sun blinding her face, legs pumping against gravity as she climbed the street.

She rode to the canal where the pavement stopped and on to a dirt path. Dried rye grass rustled as she sped past. Startled grasshoppers popped around her. The path became a trail through poplar trees whose leathery leaves brushed her face and arms. The trail ended, and she pulled the bike to a wobbly stop.

Perspiration dripped from her forehead onto her cheeks and ran rivulets down her neck. She panted in the shade, gasping for air. Her heart pounded, her chest heaved, arms shaking but the fear was gone, the restlessness appeased. Her vision cleared. She looked over her shoulder and saw she had ridden into the foothills above the town. Insects hummed, squirrels or mice scampered in the brush, a few birds chirped. The awful silence was broken.

Izzy turned the bike around and coasted back the way she had come. In her panic she had found one clear reality. She was not okay; she was not fine. She knew exactly what was wrong and how to fix it.

The sun was slipping down on the western horizon. Shadows stretched to the east. The bike bumped over the rough path then onto pavement. Izzy rode past the canal again and over the road. There was no traffic, and she tipped her head back to drink in the wind. She passed the house where they lived and turned one corner then another.

The street was lined by neat lawns and trim hedges in front of two story brick houses trimmed with striped canvas awnings over the windows. She rode back and forth in front of each home until Ann came out of one of them. Then she parked her bike in a driveway and approached her sister.

Ann looked worried, "What's wrong?" she asked and held out her arms.

Izzy sank into her sister's embrace. "I'm lonely, Annie," her voice broke on a sob. "Please don't leave me."

Chapter Eleven

Ann led her inside the McKinley's house, down a carpeted hallway and into a pink and white bathroom. She flicked on the light above the vanity and ran water into the sink.

Izzy stared into the mirror. Her hair was wild, blown every direction like a storm cloud around her face. Dust and dirt covered her skin except where sweat and tears had cut lines.

Ann squeezed excess water out of a wash cloth and rubbed it over a bar of soap. Gently she cleaned Izzy's face, neck, and arms.

The cloth was soft, and the soap smelled of honeysuckle. Izzy closed her eyes. She heard Ann rinse out the cloth and felt it stroking her again. Ann pressed on her shoulders until Izzy was perched on the edge of the bathtub, then she picked up a brush and began removing the tangles, weeds, and a couple of leaves from Izzy's hair.

Izzy watched Ann straighten the room, replace the towels and wipe out the sink. She turned off the light and took Izzy's hand again. In the kitchen she poured a glass of icy water from a pitcher in the fridge. Izzy drank it and Ann refilled it.

They sat quietly at the table until Ann spoke. "Where did you think I'd go?"

"I don't know, I guess I didn't think you'd really go away."

Ann made a small sound like a snort. "Damn straight I wouldn't go away!"

Startled, Izzy choked on a laugh. "Annie! You swore!"

"Well I've been hanging around a bad influence."

"Jill swears?"

"No you idiot, you swear. If you didn't think I'd go away, why did you ask me not to leave?"

Izzy couldn't look at her.

"Izzy?"

She didn't answer.

"Honestly, Sis! We're in this together. I know you're the one making the sacrifices with the job and the fake identity and all, but I'm doing what I can."

Izzy swallowed. "It's not that, I just . . ." she swallowed again and looked up at the ceiling. "It feels like I'm always alone."

Ann's hand covered hers as well as a small hand can cover a larger one. They sat for several minutes without moving. "You know, you leave me, too. Every day." There was no accusation in the statement. "I hate waking up in an empty house and coming home to one. That first day you went job hunting? I thought I'd go nuts. I finally started circling the block, hoping to see you coming home."

"I'm sorry."

Ann sighed, "You don't need to be. It'll be better for me now with school. I have somewhere to be, and from now on when I'm babysitting, you come over. I don't think Mrs. McKinley will mind as long as we don't have any parties and stay out of the booze."

Izzy looked up with a little grin. "There's booze?"

Ann laughed. "Not even cooking sherry. This house is as dry as a Methodist Sunday school.

"Come on, I'll show you what they tried to teach me in math today."

They worked on Ann's homework together, pausing to look in on the baby.

When it was nearly ten o'clock, Izzy yawned and stretched. "I'd better leave, I've got to get some sleep."

Ann put the book and papers away. "Okay, they should be back any minute. I won't be long."

Izzy opened the back door and froze. An El Camino was parked across the street. A man sat behind the wheel. He struck a match, held it to a cigarette, and in the brief flame she recognized Sid. Quickly closing the door, she switched off the kitchen light.

"Hey!" Ann started, "What are you doing?"

"It's Sid!" Izzy hissed. She pulled her sister to the window above the sink. "Look! Across the street."

Ann peered out. "What's he doing here?" she whispered.

"He thinks I live around here, remember?"

Izzy crossed her arms over her chest and slid down the front of the cabinets to sit on the floor.

Ann leaned closer to the window. "It's okay, here come the McKinley's" she said.

"How's that going to help? He'll see us leave and follow us home!" Izzy scrambled to her feet and craned her neck to see.

"No, he won't. You wait on the patio while Mr. McKinley drives me home. Go out the back way, they always come in the front door."

Izzy waited until the couple was at their door before she slipped out. She peeked around a lilac bush that shielded her from the street. The El Camino was gone. Pushing her bike beside her, she found the patio and waited. In a few minutes she heard Ann's voice, then footsteps and car doors opening and closing. An engine purred and headlights came on. She heard the car back out of the driveway, and still she waited. Not until the car returned and Mr. McKinley had gone inside did she silently roll her bike to the end of the hedge next to the drive.

The street was dark except for the lights from a porch across the road. With a deep sigh, Izzy pushed her bike into motion and rode home.

Chapter Twelve

The next morning Izzy parked her bike near the picnic tables and sat down to wait. She was half an hour early for work, but it was worth it. Sid and his El Camino were nowhere to be seen.

It would be nice to rest her head on her arms and fall asleep. She felt so tired. At least she'd had a good breakfast before she left. Groceries made all the difference. She peeked into a brown bag she took from the basket on her bike. A bologna sandwich, a handful of potato chips, a few carrot sticks, and an apple made for a decent lunch.

A squirrel watched from the elm tree. Izzy sat very still and kept him in the corner of her eye. He skittered back and forth on a limb, pausing to stare with his tiny paws tucked in above his rounded tummy. He moved a little closer and sniffed the air. Very slowly, Izzy reached into her lunch sack and pinched off a bit of bread. The squirrel darted back up the tree. She tossed the bread to the end of the table and turned her back. Give him time, she thought. She tore another piece from her sandwich, and waited. When she looked again, the squirrel stood on the table busily tucking bread into his cheeks. She tossed the second piece and he scampered back to the tree.

"He likes peanut butter," a male voice said. Stan was unlocking the front door of the factory.

"How do you know?" Izzy asked.

Stan smiled and stepped over to the tree. He pulled a peanut out of his jacket pocket and held it out. The squirrel came right to him and took the treat.

"We're old friends," Stan said. "His name is Buddy." He paused before asking, "How's your hand?"

She held it up, "So much better, thank you."

"And your arm?"

Izzy smiled, "You were right, the shot didn't kill me." She stood and picked up her lunch. Her money and comb were in the pockets of her jeans so she didn't carry a purse.

Stan held the door open for her, "You're awfully early," he said when she walked in.

"You know what they say about the early bird," she said.

He moved around the room flipping on lights. "Right. The worm is all yours." He unlocked the door to the break room.

Izzy put her lunch in the refrigerator and went to her locker for her work things.

Stan sat at a table and wrote on some papers on his clipboard. She took a seat at the other end of the room. After a few minutes he looked up.

"Did my deodorant stop working or something?" he asked.

"I didn't want to crowd you," she said. Their voices sounded loud in the empty room.

Stan got up and walked to the vending machines. He dropped a couple of coins in one and bought a carton of milk, then he repeated the action to buy a second one.

"Rats!" he said, "They mixed up the milk again." He held up one plain and one chocolate flavored. "Do you drink chocolate?"

"I guess I could, if it would help you out," Izzy said with a smile.

He bought a package of small powder sugar donuts from another machine and joined her at her table. Spreading out a couple of napkins, he divided the donuts between them.

"Well," Stan said with just the slightest puff of sugar, "you survived your first week."

Izzy wiped her mouth and swallowed before answering. "Just barely."

"Next week will be much better," he paused and grinned. "It would have to be."

She returned his smile with a rueful one. "I don't even want to think how it could be worse!"

Chuckling, he finished his snack then wadded up his napkins and stuffed them into the empty carton. "For one thing, you'll get a check next Friday."

Izzy hesitated and swept some crumbs into her hand. "That reminds me, Stan, just how much am I earning?"

"It was going to be a surprise." He frowned, but there was a teasing light in his eyes. "Minimum wage, $1.25 an hour. Once you get faster you'll earn piece-rate on top of that."

"How much is piece rate?" she asked.

"It varies, depending on the piece. You'll understand once you're ready for it. First you have to meet standard numbers." He pulled a form from his clipboard and showed her the standard rates for different items. "You'll be earning more before you know it. Your base rate will go up at three months and twice a year when we give incentive raises."

Women were straggling in now, slamming lockers and buying coffee. Somewhere, someone turned on the intercom to a local radio station playing music.

Betty seated herself at their table. "I love Friday!" She smiled and lit a cigarette. "You two have weekend plans?"

"I don't know about Izzy," Stan volunteered. "I'm going to be watching my nephews tonight and tomorrow."

"The doctor skipping town?" Betty asked.

"He's taking his wife out for their anniversary. They'll be back Saturday night."

Betty turned to Izzy, "What about you, hon? Got a hot date tonight?"

"Naturally," Izzy said. She didn't say her hot date was with her sister, a bowl of popcorn, and whatever was on TV. Making things up was tiring, and keeping track of what she had and had not said proved confusing. She could have told them about Paul, but she still hadn't told Ann, and her sister should be the first.

Stan tossed his milk carton into a nearby trash bin. "Well, I have to get in there." He pushed his chair back and stood. Winking at Izzy, he added, "I'll look forward to hearing about your hot date on Monday."

Betty laughed, "I'm betting she don't kiss and tell, Stan!"

Izzy tried to look mysterious. "Maybe I don't kiss at all," she said.

Stan's eyebrows rose, and he looked like he wanted to say something, but he didn't. He picked up his clipboard and walked to the workroom.

Marti wandered in and took a seat at their table. Betty offered her a cigarette. Marti lit up and immediately began a fit of coughing. She spat into a napkin in her hand. Leaning back in her chair, she took a long drag and blew out a small cloud. "That's better."

"Think maybe it's time you changed brands?" Betty asked.

"Or quit?" added Izzy.

"Why would I quit?" she asked.

"Well, the coughing —"

Marti interrupted with a shake of her head, "As long as I can cough, I'm fine. You young kids think you're so smart. It might interest you to know that a nurse once told me that smoking helps clear my lungs."

Betty considered this statement, slowly nodding her head. Izzy, stunned by this logic, just stared.

Faye breezed through the door with barely a minute to spare. They all put on their smocks and joined the line of women making their way to the machines.

It took several minutes for Izzy to pick up her work, check over her sewing machine, and write her name and the date on her production sheet. Finally, she bent over her work. She had a box of small receiving blankets to hem. It was a simple process, and before long she was getting faster. After a stack of blankets were done, she paused to fold them.

Faye sat staring at her machine. She twisted her work in her hands but didn't move.

Izzy called her name twice before the girl blinked and turned a pale gray face towards her.

"What's wrong?" Izzy asked.

Faye only stared; she looked like she hadn't heard.

"Faye!" Izzy said, a little louder. "What's wrong?"

Without answering, Faye got to her feet and hurried out the door. Izzy moved to go after her but Stan got there first.

Turning her focus back to the blankets, Izzy could only wonder.

Break came and went with no sign of Faye or Stan. Betty and Marti seemed oblivious to the situation as they looked over a discarded Reader's Digest.

Izzy finished the blankets, and Betty carried over a box of romper fronts and showed her how to make pleats. She was picking things up easier and had half a dozen done when Faye returned.

Her color was better; she smiled shyly when she took her seat. She went to work without explanation. Izzy, preoccupied by the rompers, didn't ask any questions.

At noon she retrieved her lunch and bought a soft drink. Betty had a green salad, and Marti unwrapped her usual tuna and pickle sandwich. Faye nibbled at soda crackers and sipped a carton of milk. She declined the half sandwich that Izzy offered.

"You sick?" Izzy asked.

Faye nodded. "I must have picked up a bug somewhere."

Stan set a cola in front of Faye before taking the chair next to Izzy. "That might help."

"Thanks," muttered Faye. She was turning pale again.

"You need to go home," Marti said between bites. "I sure as hell don't need to share your bug."

"Why don't you take your lunch outside, Marti?" Stan said. It sounded like a command.

Silence fell over the table. Marti looked like she'd been slapped. Without a word she put her lunch back in the bag, picked up her coffee, and left.

Tears glistened in Faye's eyes. Betty patted her hand. "It won't hurt her to get some sun. She only *looks* like a vampire." Dabbing at her eyes, Faye gave her a grateful smile.

Stan continued eating his lunch without speaking.

Marti returned just before the buzzer sounded and moved around like a walking icicle the rest of the afternoon.

By the time the shift ended Faye looked and acted much better. She chatted while they tucked dust covers over their work and machines.

"Will you be okay?" Izzy asked. "I can't make a casserole, but I could bring over some bologna sandwiches."

"Thanks anyway, I'm so much better."

Stan caught up with them at their lockers. "I'll drive you home, Faye."

Faye nodded.

"Izzy, don't forget to wash your smock over the weekend," Stan ordered without his customary smile.

"Yes, sir," she replied coolly and hurried out to her bike.

Gliding through the afternoon heat, she wondered what had happened to Stan's easy-going nature, but not for long. The weekend stretched out in front of her. Two whole days of just being herself, except for a couple of hours on Sunday. She hadn't given much more thought to Paul, but now she recalled his teasing smile and felt a fluttering inside. She hoped it was excitement and not something she'd caught from Faye.

Chapter Thirteen

Ann was already in her swimsuit. "Hurry," she urged, pushing Izzy's suit into her hands almost before she was through the door. In no time they were riding side by side up the road to the canal. Jill was waiting for them when they got there.

All three shed their cut-offs and hung their towels on a tree limb. The water in the canal was low and slow. It was deep enough to swim in but without a strong current. They floated downstream, then swam back. Breathless, they climbed up the slippery bank to lie on the grass.

Izzy was wondering when she'd get a chance to tell Ann about her date when Jill raised on her elbows and said, "I hear you're going out with Paul."

Ann sat up abruptly, "You're what?"

Shading her eyes with her hand, Izzy sighed. "He didn't exactly ask me," she said, "he told me. He said it's payment for fixing my bike."

Jill giggled. "No, it's not," she sang. "He thinks you're cute."

"Sure he does," Izzy replied, "'Cause I'm irresistible in hair curlers. . ."

"He's seen you before, around the neighborhood," Jill said.

"That's true," Ann added. "He was so happy when we told him about your flat tire. He ran right out and bought the repair kit."

So, he planned to ask her out. It wasn't quite as casual as she'd assumed. Izzy sat up and started plucking blades of grass. "How old is Paul?"

"Nineteen," Jill said. "He's a sophomore in college."

College! What in the world could they talk about?

Ann stood and reached for her cut-offs. "Didn't you say he's studying sociology or something?"

"He changes his mind a lot. Last year it was political science."

The fluttery feeling turned into a nervous quiver. Political science? She barely knew who was president of the country. "I'm going home," Izzy said.

She was in her clothes and a block away before the others followed. She needed to talk to Ann alone. Thank heaven it wasn't a school night.

In the shower she tried to come up with a plan. Paul would probably do all the talking. She could pretend to be shy. No, he already knew that wasn't true. What had he called her? Feisty. Okay, she could play dumb. She wouldn't have to pretend for that, she thought with chagrin. She wrapped her hair in a towel and put on clean underwear. Seated on the edge of the bathtub she spread shaving cream on one leg. Her fingers shook when she picked up the safety razor. She took a steadying breath and drew the blade up her calf.

Ann rattled pans in the kitchen. Jill must have gone home because there wasn't any talking.

Izzy rinsed and lathered her other leg.

Ann appeared in the doorway "When were you going to tell me?"

"Why didn't you warn me?" Izzy returned with a glare.

"I asked you first," Ann said.

"Did you know he was going to ask me out?"

"I only knew he thought you were cute," Ann said. "Why didn't you tell me?"

Izzy pulled the razor up her shin and rinsed it under the faucet. "Well, the landlady turned up then Faye, and you and Jill came home without the TV, and I sort of forgot. I was going to talk to you about it tonight." She rinsed her leg and looked up at Ann. "What in the world am I going to talk to a college guy about?"

Ann looked puzzled, "I don't know, the same stuff you'd talk to any guy about I guess."

"What any guy? I've never been on a date."

"Hang on; I don't want to burn dinner." She disappeared.

Izzy rubbed lotion on her legs and finished dressing.

"What did you talk to Sid about at breakfast?" Ann called from the kitchen.

Izzy joined her. She rewound the towel on her head while her sister dished Beanie-Weenie onto plates.

"Nothing. I just sat and ate." She lifted a spoonful of beans and blew on it.

"What did he do?" Ann asked.

Izzy chewed and swallowed. "He watched." She sipped her milk. Then she remembered, "Oh, he offered to take me shopping for clothes."

Ann's spoon clattered to the floor. She stared with her mouth open before saying, "That's sort of . . . weird."

"I turned him down."

"No wonder you freaked when you thought he knew where you live."

Izzy got her sister another spoon. "I was really freaked-out when he turned up last night."

Ann looked thoughtful. "But if he thinks we live at Jill's house, why was he watching McKinley's?"

"Maybe he wasn't." Izzy felt some relief. She buttered a slice of bread. "I just assumed. Good. Then he still doesn't know where to find me."

Tires crunched on the driveway, a car door opened and shut, and they heard footsteps. Ann stood and looked out the window. "Do we know anyone who drives a pink convertible?" she asked.

"Damn! That's Mrs. Call. She owns the house." Izzy ducked out of sight. "I'm not here."

"Isn't she looking for Mom?" Ann asked.

"Tell her she's at work. Just get rid of her."

There was a knock at the front door. Izzy listened as Ann crossed the living room.

"Hi," her sister said.

"I need to speak to your mother," Mrs. Call snapped.

"She's at work right now," Ann said.

"What about your sister, uh, what was her name?"

"She went out."

"Hunh," said Mrs. Call. "Can I come in for a minute?"

"What for?" Ann asked.

"Here we go again." The landlady groaned and responded in an exasperated voice, "Listen, little girl, like I told what's-her-name, this is my house, and you can't keep me out!"

"How do I know this is your house?"

Izzy grinned to herself, dang but Ann was good at this.

After a brief pause, Mrs. Call snapped, "You tell Willa she's going to find herself on the street if I don't hear from her tonight! You got that?"

"You want her to phone you?" Ann asked.

"I don't care if she sends me a singing telegram! You just be sure to tell her."

There was silence until the car drove away.

"She's gone," Ann called.

Izzy's thoughts were racing. She peeked into the living room. "Ann," she whispered, "what are we going to do?"

Ann cocked her head, "You know, I think that's the first time you've ever asked me that." She paused to savor the moment. "She only wants to talk to Willa, so we'll find a telephone and have Willa," she tapped Izzy on the chest, "give her a call."

Izzy clapped a hand to her forehead. "Of course," she said. "Where is the nearest phone booth?" She pulled the towel off her head and finger-combed her damp hair.

"There's one in front of the school. Do you have a dime?"

They walked the six blocks to the high school. Warm night air dried Izzy's hair into soft curls.

"How is high school?" Izzy asked.

"So far, so good. The classes are small; there are only twelve of us in Beginning Art. That reminds me, I have a list of supplies I need for that class. The teacher told us to go to the Paint Box. It's an art supply store next to the library. It shouldn't cost more than ten dollars."

Izzy felt a shard of jealousy; she would have loved to shop for school supplies. She and Ann both adored stationery stores. They could spend hours looking at pens, pencils, rulers, notebooks, paperclips, and staplers.

Stationery was her weakness. She loved the boxes of pastel-colored onionskin paper and matching envelopes. She envisioned herself seated at an elegant writing desk, using a fountain pen to record her thoughts in flowing cursive. Then she would secure her letters with a small blob of colored wax, pressing in a brass seal to leave an imprint of her monogram. This scenario usually played through her mind until she realized she had no one to write to. She couldn't imagine she'd meet anyone who would want to exchange letters in the sewing factory.

The things she'd seen in her future were dropping away at an alarming rate. High school, parties, sitting with friends at football games, plays, concerts, dances, driving a car, prom, graduation, and college all faded and left her with the existence that stared her in the face. Her future consisted of day after day of factory work, housework, laundry, cooking, drudgery and it weighed on her soul. She squared her shoulders. *Things change, you'll get where you want, but it will be on a different road.*

The heat inside the glass phone booth hit Izzy's face like a suffocating blanket. She propped the folding door open with her foot and dropped a dime into the slot.

"Hello?" The voice on the other end of the line sounded soft and breathy.

"Mrs. Call, this is Willa Gardner. My girls said you came by the house."

"Oh," the breathiness vanished. "It's about time you called. I wanted to tell you that the rent is going up."

Izzy had no idea how much the rent was. "Up?" she asked.

"That's right. I gave you summer rates. I usually rent the place to college students during the school year. I can put four of them in there and clear a hundred dollars a month easy."

A hundred dollars? Izzy broke into a cold sweat. They'd have to move.

"But those college kids are really hard on the place. They break things, have parties, neighbors don't like it."

Izzy saw a glimpse of hope.

"So I was thinking you could stay there if you can come up with $45 a month instead of the $30 I let you have it for."

"$45?" Izzy asked.

"Due the first week of the month. That includes your gas and water."

Izzy tried to think, but numbers were adding, subtracting, multiplying and dividing in her head and making no sense.

Mrs. Call spoke more sharply, "If you can't do that, I'll need you out by the end of next week."

"No!" Izzy said, "I'll pay."

"Good. I'll expect a check next Friday." Mrs. Call snapped her chewing gum. "By the way, if anything else needs fixing, give me a ring before you send it out. You got that?"

"Sure, sorry about the television," Izzy said.

"Hunh," said Mrs. Call. "Is it working now?"

They hadn't turned it on yet, but Izzy said it was fine.

"That's good. I can't reimburse you for the repair because you didn't consult me first. But, tell you what, I'll knock five bucks off September's rent."

"Thank you." Guilt twisted Izzy's stomach; they didn't deserve a discount for pawning the television.

"Okay. I'll expect a check next Friday for $40," Mrs. Call's voice was softening again.

"A check?" Izzy asked. "Could I give you cash instead?"

"Fine, just drop it off at my place."

"And, uh, sorry I don't remember where you live."

The line was quiet.

"We talked about this before, Willa. You got some kind of problem? Like maybe you drink or something?"

"No," Izzy's brain was scrambling again. "It's been crazy getting the girls in school and working late hours."

"I hope so; I told you no smoking inside the house, and no alcohol anywhere."

"No smoking and no drinking, yeah, I remembered that. I just forgot your address."

"425 East Main Street." A click signaled the end of the call.

Izzy placed the receiver on the hook and stepped out of the booth. She wiped the sweat from her forehead with the back of her wrist. "How much money do we have?" she asked.

"A little over fifty dollars. Why? What did she say?" Ann sat cross-legged on the grass.

"The rent is going up to $45 a month and its due by next Friday." Izzy extended a hand and pulled her sister to her feet.

They retraced their path in silence. Each step struck a spark of anger deep inside Izzy. She was fifteen, technically the youngest – even if it was only by minutes. She wasn't supposed to be worried about rent and groceries! Her biggest problem right now should be nothing more than a giant zit on her nose. She could feel Ann watching her but she wouldn't look up. Her head felt heavy and she kept her gaze on the pavement. A slow, familiar throbbing began behind her eyes.

Ann didn't speak for two blocks. Finally she cleared her throat. "Come on, Izzy; it'll work out. Let's forget it for tonight. We've hardly seen each other all week." She slipped her arm through Izzy's. "Let's go home and make popcorn. *Bride of Frankenstein* is on Frightmare Theater tonight."

Izzy didn't reply. The throbbing grew stronger.

"You know how you love a romance," prodded Ann.

Izzy took a breath and let it out. The throbbing slowed. A laugh burbled up inside her. She squeezed Ann's hand. "Okay," she said. "Let's have some fun."

The television picture was just as grainy as they remembered. Supplied with icy glasses of Kool-Aid and a mounded bowl of popcorn dripping with melted margarine nestled between them on the couch, they waited for the sports segment of the newscast to end.

All of the windows and doors were open and the house was comfortably cool. The girls leaned on the pillows from their bed and propped their feet on the coffee table. The bluish glow of the TV was the only light. For the moment, everything felt perfect.

A face lit by a flashlight held under the chin appeared on the screen. They knew it was Fireman Fred from the afternoon cartoon show, but he still looked spooky in the weird light and he made his voice deep and menacing as he announced the horror movies of the night. Every Friday night there was a double feature; this week besides *Bride of Frankenstein*, they showed *The Crawling Eye*.

"Boo!" cried a voice from the porch.

Ann's glass flew out of her hand and both girls screamed.

"Wow!" said a guy, "you two are jumpy!" Paul and Jill doubled over laughing.

Izzy stomped to the door, "Very cute! What are you doing here?"

Even in the shadows she could see Paul's grin. "We thought we'd join you for Frightmare Theater." he said in a Boris Karloff voice.

Izzy glared at them.

"I told him it was too late," Jill said apologetically.

Paul thrust out his lower lip in a pout. "Aw come on, you're not really mad."

She was, but before she could tell him so, Ann spoke up. "Let him in, Izzy. He can clean up the mess he caused."

Reluctantly, Izzy lifted the hook and opened the screen door.

A contrite Paul accepted the rag and bucket of water Ann handed him, and he wiped up the spilled punch. Then he took a seat on the end of the sofa, resting his arm along the back as if he expected someone to cuddle with him. Izzy placed one hand on her hip, and with the other she pointed to the recliner. Heaving a sigh, Paul moved to the chair.

By the time they poured more drinks and portioned out the popcorn, the movie was well under way.

Izzy and Ann were used to staying up late on weekends. Willa had been fairly strict about bedtimes on school nights, but Fridays they could watch TV until the stations signed off for the night. But tonight Izzy's body began to rebel against staying awake. The early start at work, the brief swim in the canal, and the walk to and from the phone booth all combined, and she struggled to keep her head erect and her eyes open. She leaned into her pillow and curled up in the corner of the couch.

Her foot twitched. Something tickled her toes, and she kicked at it. Her eyes opened and tried to focus. Frankenstein's bride was nowhere to be seen; instead clouds were creeping down the Swiss Alps and threatening a ski lodge.

Pushing herself into an upright position, Izzy looked around the living room. Ann and Jill were gone, and Paul had moved from the chair. He sat next to her on the couch.

Izzy frowned, "Where'd everybody go?"

"To bed," Paul answered.

"Jill, too?"

"She kept falling asleep, so Ann invited her to spend the night."

"Okay." Through the fuzziness in her brain, Izzy tried to make sense of this. "What are you watching?"

Paul walked his fingers up her bare arm, "*The Crawling Eye*," he said. "I'm not sure how it's doing it, but so far several people have disappeared. The eyeball is hidden in a cloud. They haven't shown it yet, but it's pretty spooky."

She shivered.

Paul inched closer to her and slipped his arm around her shoulders. "Scared? I won't let it get you."

Izzy stiffened and he took his arm away. Turning her attention to the television, she pretended nothing had happened. Paul sat politely beside her and didn't attempt to put his arm around her again. By the time the movie ended, Izzy had pulled her legs up to her chest and covered her eyes. When she peeked through her fingers, Paul was turning off the set. He yawned loudly and stretched his arms.

"Thanks for the popcorn," he said.

"What time is it?" Izzy asked.

"Must be nearly one, can't see my watch."

Neither of them reached for a light switch.

"I better get home," Paul said. "Want me to help you lock up first?"

"Yeah, I think I do. Thanks."

He closed and latched the windows at the front of the house. "It's weird how even the dumbest movie can leave you feeling spooked," he said as he followed her into the kitchen.

"Yeah," Izzy locked the back door; Paul secured the window above the sink.

She switched on the stove light.

Paul reached out and held her fingers for a second. She didn't pull away.

"Well, thanks for letting us in," he said.

"Thanks for cleaning up the Kool-Aid." She smiled at him.

"It was the least I could do." He shrugged.

"Yes, I guess it was," she answered. They both grinned.

For a moment it seemed that something more should happen. It didn't. They walked to the front door.

"I'll see you Sunday then?" he asked.

"Okay."

He nodded and left. Izzy locked the door and leaned against it for a second.

She brushed her teeth in the bathroom and tiptoed into the bedroom to get her nightgown from the nail on the closet door. Ann had loaned Jill some pajamas and the two of them were out cold on the bed. Izzy tucked the bedspread over them.

In Willa's room, she folded down the covers and slipped in between the sheets. Leaning up, she switched off the bedside lamp. She lay on her back and studied the shadows on the ceiling. A weeping willow in the neighbors' yard created a pattern of twining limbs that seemed to be searching with their restless reaching and wriggling. It made her think of the movie. When the crawling eye had finally shown itself, it hadn't been as scary as the mysterious cloud in which it traveled. The most Izzy could say about it was that it was disgusting. She'd watched a teacher dissect a cow's eyeball in health class last year. That experience had been more disturbing than the movie creature. But in the movie the eyeball was connected to tentacles that slithered like snakes to ensnare its victims.

Think of something else, her mind ordered. *Spaghetti, long strands of delicious spaghetti waving in a breeze. No, that was stupid, why would noodles be blowing in the wind? Fringe? Like on an old fashioned buggy. What was that song? "Surry with the Fringe on Top."* So she thought about the musical *Oklahoma* until she remembered the villain and the dugout he lived in. Roots, fibrous with fine hair-like growths dangling from the dirt ceiling. Finally, Izzy turned on her stomach and put the pillow over her head.

She felt paper crinkle against her cheek. Startled, she sat up and switched on the lamp. In the yellow light she saw an envelope addressed simply "Kids" in her mother's back-slanted handwriting.

With shaking hands, she ran a finger beneath the flap and opened it. She unfolded a sheet of notebook paper and two twenty dollar bills fell out. Ignoring the money she focused on the message:

Dear Girls,
This is going to be hard for you to understand, but here goes. I been trying to find decent work and believe me I looked everywhere but I just can't do it anymore. So I didn't have any choice but to set out on my own. It brakes my heart to leave but there is lots of government programs that can see to your needs better than I ever done.

You kids is smart, smarter than me, that's for sure. You'll be better off. Don't try to find me and don't leave town. I moved you there on purpose because your grandma lives there. She's your father's mother and she don't know about you. I don't remember her first name but her last name is Gardner, duh! Maybe she'll adopt you, unless she's dead. I didn't think of that until just this minute. Bummer.

I plan on working real hard, plus maybe I'll meet a rich guy and get married again. If I do, I'll come back and get you two.

Be good girls, study hard in school so you can get real good jobs and never have to leave your children.

Keep Smiling,
Willa (you're mom, duh!)

P.S. The money is for school clothes. I don't want you to look like you don't have a mother who loves you. xxxx

Chapter Fourteen

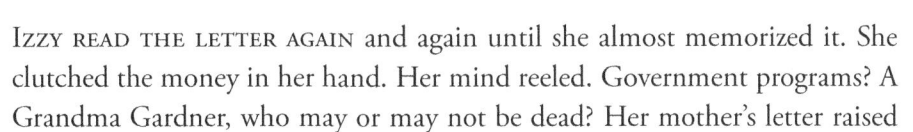

Izzy read the letter again and again until she almost memorized it. She clutched the money in her hand. Her mind reeled. Government programs? A Grandma Gardner, who may or may not be dead? Her mother's letter raised far more questions than it answered.

Any idea of sleep evaporated, the pounding in her head came back. Her first impulse was to wake Ann, but with Jill here that was impossible. She'd have to wait until Jill went home in the morning. There was one thing she could do though.

She crept into the kitchen and took two aspirin, then she found an abandoned phonebook in the broom closet. A previous tenant, who apparently could afford a telephone, had left it behind. Izzy carried it to the stove. She opened the book and flipped the pages to the Gs. Twenty-three of the listings were Gardner. She read the names, half-hoping for some kind of sign that would cause one to stand out. But they were only the names of strangers. Willa hadn't mentioned a grandfather. What if grandma was a widow and had remarried or moved away? What if they found her and she didn't want anything to do with them? She might not even believe they were her granddaughters. Whenever they had asked about their father, their mother had only said, "He could charm the garters off a corpse. And good looking? Oh man, he was handsome." Then she heaved a deep sigh and added, "But he wasn't husband material. The day I told him I was having twins, he acted all excited. Spent the last of his money on flowers and had them delivered. When I opened the card all it said was 'Good luck,' His wedding ring was in the envelope. I sold it for ten dollars. Never heard from him again."

Ann and Izzy didn't even know his name, apart from Gardner.

The clock on the stove showed three in the morning. Izzy closed the phonebook and carried it back to the bedroom. Lying on top of the covers she thumbed through the yellow pages, absently reading ads and listings while she waited for sunrise. The letter on the nightstand mocked her. She'd done a good job of relegating thoughts of her mother to the very back of her mind, but the letter pushed Willa front and center. *It was all lies. Forced to leave because she couldn't find work? Bull crap!* Izzy fought to stay angry. Anger felt strong and safe; it kept her going.

She rubbed her fists into her eyes and tried to list every rotten thing she could think of about her mother: lousy speller, crummy grammar, stupid handwriting, selfish, lazy, tramp. Izzy's throat ached like she was trying to swallow a golf ball that wouldn't budge. The ache crept up the back of her neck and into her head. Pressure gathered around her heart. Her shell of anger strained against a tidal wave of pain. Grabbing the letter, she shoved it back under the pillow where she'd found it. She buried her face in the bedding and smothered a scream, then another and another until there weren't any left, and she could only shudder. Her mouth frozen open, her lungs clenched and refused to draw breath. Her nose ran unchecked and mixed with the tears on her face. Finally, one last groan escaped, and she gasped for air. The pain behind her eyes was excruciating. She sobbed quietly until she felt empty. Then she slept without rest.

A long roll of thunder woke her. She blinked at the rain-streaked window. It was daytime, but the sky was nearly black with clouds. She sat up. Every part of her body throbbed. Her legs felt heavy when she swung them over the edge of the mattress. Her reflection in the dressing table mirror revealed eyes nearly swollen shut, lids thick and red. Recalling that it was Saturday, she crept back under the covers. Her fingers touched the envelope beneath her pillow and she was instantly wide awake.

Ann scratched softly on the door. "Izzy?" The door opened and her sister peeked in.

"I'm up," Izzy answered.

Ann stepped in and sat on the side of the bed. Her hand patted Izzy's back. "You can go back to sleep if you want."

Izzy turned over and Ann gasped when she saw her face. "What happened?" she asked.

"Where's Jill?" Izzy asked.

"She went home. She has chores on Saturdays."

Izzy pulled out the letter and handed it to Ann.

The color drained from her sister's thin cheeks as she read. When she came to the end, she started over. She shook the money out of the envelope and stared at it like she didn't know what it was. Finally she picked up the twenties and handed them to Izzy. "Well," she said with perfect calm, "there's the rent." Then she stood and walked out of the room, closing the door behind her.

Izzy jumped out of bed and followed. Ann went to the kitchen and turned on the faucet over the sink. She squirted dish soap and began washing the cups and popcorn bowls.

"Annie," Izzy reached out to touch her.

Ann jerked her arm away. "You should put a cold washcloth on your eyes." Her voice wasn't cold or angry. It was just flat.

"Okay," Izzy said. "But we need to—"

"Leave me alone, please Izzy," Ann said. She stared down at the dishwater.

Izzy poured herself a bowl of corn flakes. Her raw throat struggled to swallow.

When the dishes were done, Ann swept the floor. Then she filled a bucket with soapy water and scoured the linoleum.

Izzy took her cereal into the living room. The only sound was the swishing of the scrub brush. When the floor was done, Ann carried the bucket to the bathroom and poured the dirty water down the drain.

Izzy took aspirin, her headache was nearly gone, and let Ann be. She cleaned for the rest of the morning. Her blank expression didn't change. At noon she stopped and ate a bologna sandwich. Then she started on the windows. Izzy made the beds and dusted.

By four o'clock the house was spotless. The rain stopped and the clouds were breaking up. Izzy opened the sparkling windows, and cool, fresh air flowed in.

She heard the shower running and switched on the television. A man demonstrated a kitchen chopping tool on one channel; the other two channels had golf tournaments. She turned the set off. Her eyes didn't feel as swollen now, and the achiness was gone. She was still very tired, so she stretched out on the sofa.

After a time, Ann appeared. She had put on clean clothes and braided her hair into two short strands. She tucked some cash into her pocket.

"I'm going to the store," she said, and her voice sounded normal. "I'll be right back." She didn't ask Izzy to come with her. At least she was talking.

Izzy rested her cheek on the smooth vinyl of the couch again and dozed.

Ann brought bread, milk, and a bag of chocolate chips from the market. She mixed a batch of cookie dough. Izzy sat on a kitchen chair, watching. Everything was fine until it was time to add the chocolate chips. The bag refused to tear open. Ann pulled and tore at it and finally tried her teeth. Her face was red, and she was breathing hard from the effort. She threw the bag onto the counter top and grabbed a carving knife from a drawer. "Damn!" She plunged the knife into the bag. "Damn, damn, damn!" With every curse she stabbed the bag until it shredded and chocolate chips scattered everywhere. She dropped the knife and leaned over the counter, her shoulders quivering.

Izzy stood behind her and waited, until at last, she laid her fingers on Ann's arm. Neither girl spoke for several minutes. Ann blew her nose on a paper towel and slowly turned to look at her sister.

"I thought she'd come back," she said.

"I know you did," Izzy answered.

A deep crease appeared between Ann's eyebrows. Still looking at Izzy, she asked, "How could she just . . ." her voice trailed off.

"I don't know," Izzy said.

Ann's gaze passed her sister's face and went to the window. "We'll never see her again."

"Probably not."

Clouds gathered again. Shadows deepened in the corners of the kitchen. The thermometer on the oven clicked and a red light indicated it was hot.

Ann looked at the stove then back at the mess on the counter. A long sigh escaped her lips.

Izzy started picking bits of cellophane out of the chocolate. Most of the chips were intact, but they had flown everywhere. She brushed them into a pile and gathered some from the floor. "Good thing you cleaned," she observed. She blew away a little lint and scooped the pile of chips into the dough.

"And they will be baked," Ann pointed out.

"Perfectly safe," agreed Izzy as she set two cookie sheets on the counter.

They had warm cookies and cold milk for supper. Rain fell gently; they turned on the radio to listen to the top forty. Ann shuffled a deck of cards and dealt a hand of Gin Rummy. They played and didn't talk. All around them in the dark the air was thick with questions still unanswered and thoughts unspoken.

❦

Izzy knew she was a crummy date. Paul stopped trying to make conversation and sat staring at the street beyond the café window.

Reluctantly, Izzy took another French fry and squirted ketchup down the length of it. Most of her hamburger sat in the basket. She sipped her Coke and wiped her fingers on a napkin. She looked up and caught Paul studying her face.

"Would you rather have something else?" he asked.

"No, this is good," she said.

He stared pointedly at her uneaten food and back to her face.

"I guess I'm just not hungry," Izzy said then added, "You want my fries?"

Paul leaned toward her, "I want to know what's bothering you."

"Nothing," she said.

"Nothing," he repeated in a flat voice. "Is it me?"

"Of course not."

"I just wanted to ask because I couldn't see how it could be me," he said, straight-faced.

Izzy felt her face lift a bit.

Paul held up one hand and started counting on his fingers: "First of all, I picked you up on time; second, I said you looked nice; third, I opened the car door for you; fourth, I bought popcorn and candy at the movie; and fifth, I am exceptionally cute."

Izzy cocked her head, "Who told you that you're cute?"

Paul shrugged, "Everybody!"

"Really? Everybody?" Izzy tried to look doubtful.

"Okay, it was my mother," he hung his head for a second before adding, "and both of my grandmothers backed her up."

"Not exactly unbiased references." She grinned.

"Finally!" Paul slapped the tabletop in triumph, "I was starting to think you'd had a death in the family, or chipped a tooth." He looked at his wristwatch. "If we leave now we can get to your place in time to watch Ed Sullivan."

Izzy maintained her smile but shook her head. "I'm sorry, I can't tonight. I have too much to do before work tomorrow."

He picked up the check and slid out of the booth. She followed him to the cash register and waited while he paid the bill.

They were quiet again on the ride to the house. He killed the engine in the driveway and sat tapping his fingers on the steering wheel.

"I didn't make it up," Izzy said, "I have a ton of laundry and. . ."

He looked over at her, "I didn't think you were lying. You're too outspoken to bother with lies." He shook his head, "Nope, you are not a liar."

This was so far from the truth that Izzy's cheeks burned.

"I like you, Izzy," he said quietly, "but if you already know you don't like me, you should tell me now."

"That's not it; I like you fine but—"

"Good," he interrupted, "that's all I needed to hear." He climbed out of the car and came around to open her door. She placed her hand in the one he held out to her.

At the front door he squeezed her fingers before letting go. "I'll call," he said.

"We don't have a phone."

He leaned forward and lightly kissed her forehead. "Then I'll call in person."

She watched him drive away before going inside. Ann was babysitting so the house was quiet.

Izzy changed into her pajamas and washed her work smock in the kitchen sink. Clouds darkened outside the window once more, and by the time she was ready to hang the smock on the clothesline, large raindrops splattered on the roof. She draped the smock on the back of a chair to dry.

Ann had stacked her school books on the coffee table. Izzy spotted the copy of *Great Expectations* that was assigned reading for Ann's English class. She pulled it from the stack and thumbed through it. Settling herself in the recliner, she was soon captured by Dickens' entrancing story of the orphan Pip. These days she felt an affinity for orphans.

Chapter Fifteen

Monday dawned only marginally lighter than the night before. The rain had settled in to stay and fell steadily from the leaden sky.

Izzy clawed through the clutter of a dresser drawer until she found a folded rain cap to cover her hair. She opened it, spreading the pleats flat before tying it under her chin. Shrugging into a plastic raincoat and reasoning that Ann could stay dry enough with the only umbrella they owned, she picked up the paper bag that held her lunch, added her freshly ironed smock to it, grabbed a clean rag and went out to her bicycle.

She dried the seat with the rag, chiding herself for not parking in the garage, before climbing on and pedaling to work. The flimsy raincoat proved inadequate, and by the time Izzy parked her bike, her jeans were soaked on the front. The cold rain broke the summer heat. She shivered while she hung up the dripping coat and retrieved the things from her locker. The paper lunch bag was a soggy mess, and when she pulled out her smock, it was damp through. She took it into the Ladies Room and held it under the hand dryer. The hot air felt good and the nylon smock dried quickly. Izzy pulled it on and checked her reflection in the mirror. The rain hat had worked except for a few strands of hair that stuck to her cheeks. She reshaped the curls and used some toilet tissue to blot the smudged mascara beneath her eyes.

Faye burst through the door and dashed into one of the stalls. Izzy heard her retching and swallowed hard to keep from joining her. She heard the toilet flush and pulled a couple of paper towels from the dispenser. One of them she held under the cold running water before wringing it out. Holding the towels above the stall door she asked, "You okay?"

The door opened, and Faye, looking pale and limp, took the towels to wipe and dry her face.

"You don't look okay," Izzy said. Faye raised her eyes and Izzy saw that they were red and filled with tears. Alarmed, she asked, "Do you want me to get Betty or maybe Stan?"

Faye's shoulders began to shake. "No," she whispered. Then she added, "Oh, Izzy. I'm pregnant."

Izzy froze. "Pregnant?" she whispered.

Faye blew her nose on some toilet paper and nodded miserably. "When my dad finds out I know he'll kick me out of the house."

Izzy placed an arm around Faye. She searched for something comforting to say. "Maybe he won't. Who would do the cooking?"

Faye looked puzzled for a second then gave a mirthless chuckle. "Believe me," she said sourly, "he won't overlook this for hot meals."

The buzzer sounded from the break room. "You better go; I don't want to make you late." Faye gave her a gentle push.

Izzy hesitated, "What are you going to do? Can you go home?"

Faye shook her head. "I'll be better in a minute. Now you get in there before you're in trouble."

The break room was empty when Izzy hurried through it to the production area. Inside, Stan looked up from his clipboard and frowned at her. Ignoring him, she picked up her work and hurried to her machine. He was right behind her, and before she could settle into her chair, he said, "You're late."

"Sorry," she said as she switched on the work light and began threading the needle.

"Was it the rain? Did you have to ride your bike?"

"I said I was sorry, okay. I won't let it happen again." She wouldn't look at him.

Stan's hand touched her arm, "Your house is right on my way here. I could stop for you if you want."

Her skin began to feel hot. "No, thank you."

"Izzy," he began, but Faye ran through the door, and he hurried over to her.

Izzy watched as he picked up Faye's work boxes and gently led her to her machine. He kept a hand on her elbow and pulled out her chair for her. Squatting next to Faye, he spoke quietly. Finally, he patted Faye's hand and went back to his desk.

When morning break came, Izzy walked to the reception area to check the weather. The rain fell just as hard as it had before. She leaned her forehead on the cool glass of the door for a second and hoped that Ann got to school okay.

"That's going to leave a smudge," the receptionist said. She took the cigarette out of her mouth and laid it in the ashtray. As she exhaled smoke, she opened a desk drawer and pulled out a bottle of glass cleaner and a roll of paper towels. "Would you mind?" She held them out to Izzy who took them and wiped away the small oval mark, ignoring the dozens of fingerprints and other grime.

"There you go," Izzy said with a smile.

Pauline glared at her. "Gee, thanks," she said.

"No sweat," chirped Izzy as she passed the desk on her way back to the break room.

Betty, Marti, and Stan sat at their usual table. Faye was nowhere to be seen, but Stan kept glancing towards the ladies' room with a concerned expression. Izzy grabbed a quick drink from the fountain and returned to the production area before the buzzer.

No doubt Faye was throwing up again. Izzy wondered if she was certain she was pregnant. Had she seen a doctor? Izzy had never had a friend who was expecting. Well, she hadn't really had friends other than Ann. They'd kept to themselves.

The buzzer sounded, and Izzy bent to her work. Ten minutes later when she looked up, Faye was at her machine, her skin so pale that the sprinkling of freckles on her nose looked green. She glanced at Izzy and smiled.

"You okay?" Izzy asked.

Faye shrugged a shoulder. "I will be," she answered.

They continued working until lunch time. Izzy's sandwich and chips had been ruined by the rain. She picked through the soggy bread and ate the lettuce and the single slice of bologna. Then she took her apple and went to check on the storm again.

Pauline wasn't at her desk and sunshine dappled the grass. When Izzy stepped outside the air felt warm and humid. She climbed over the bench on the picnic table and sat down to eat. Buddy chattered up in the tree. She tipped her head back to see him. "Sorry." She held up the apple. "Only fruit and only enough for one. I'll make it up tomorrow." He turned his fluffy tail and disappeared.

A few girls that Izzy didn't know came out to share the table. They ignored her as they ate and gossiped in whispers. She caught the words "puking" and "knocked up." One of them distinctly said, "Faye? I don't believe it." This was followed by giggles and more whispers. Izzy stood and threw her apple core into the trash bin, narrowly missing one of the girls who turned to glare.

"Oops," Izzy quipped without smiling. She turned on her heel and marched back into the building.

At three-thirty there was nothing but clear blue sky showing through the window high on the wall of the production room.

Stan walked over to where Faye was clearing away her work. He picked up her boxes and said something Izzy couldn't hear. A tender smile curved Faye's lips and she nodded.

When Izzy reached her locker, she rolled up her raincoat, securing it with a rubber band and put her toolbox away.

The seat on her bike had dried in the sun. Tossing the raincoat into the basket, she climbed on for her ride home. Just as she was about to leave, she heard voices. Stan and Faye were talking next to his car. Faye's smile was gone, and Stan's forehead was creased.

"Of course I care," he was saying. "That's not the point."

Izzy couldn't catch what Faye was saying. Stan rested his hand on her shoulder, patting her back. He leaned down to look into her eyes.

Izzy felt a sudden drop in her chest, as if she missed a step coming down a flight of stairs. She pushed her bike into motion and rode into the street. It wouldn't be September until the middle of next week, but a strong feeling of autumn flowed over her. Her mind wandered during the familiar ride. Ann had babysitting jobs lined up after school for the entire week. It wasn't just the money that helped. Ann would eat dinner while she was there, and that saved expense. Between working in the lunchroom at school for her noon meal and eating at McKinley's, Ann's food cost was nearly covered.

Izzy remembered that she'd only had an apple for lunch and pedaled a little faster. She thought about having scrambled eggs and toast for supper and wondered if there was any ketchup, or eggs, or bread.

She didn't see the car until it was almost too late. The driver laid on the horn and the brakes at the same time. The bike and the car both swerved, narrowly missing each other. Izzy skidded to the curb and spilled onto the sidewalk.

A stream of swearing came from the car that had stopped in the center of the street. She looked over her shoulder and saw a man climbing out of an El Camino. "Idiot kid! Why don't you watch where . . ." His jaw dropped mid-curse. "Brandy?"

For a split second she wondered why he called her Brandy. Then Izzy did a little cussing of her own under her breath. She sat up and inspected herself for blood. "Hi, Sid."

He knelt next to her instantly. He held the sides of her head and looked at her eyes. "Damn! You okay? I didn't even see you."

"I think I'm fine. Sorry, I wasn't looking."

His hands dropped to her shoulders. "I could've killed you!" he spoke sharply.

Shrugging off his hands, Izzy tried to stand. The sidewalk flipped at an awkward angle and Sid scooped her into his arms. He carried her to the car and placed her on the seat. He then lifted her bike and put it in the back. Sitting behind the steering wheel with shaking hands, he started the engine and moved the car to the curb. He just sat for a few minutes, leaned across Izzy, and opened the glove compartment to retrieve a bottle. Unscrewing the cap he took several long swallows of amber liquid and offered the bottle to Izzy. She shook her head.

"Listen Brandy," he tightened the cap and replaced the bottle, "I think it's time we stopped playing games."

Izzy's head began a familiar throb.

"I'm driving you home. Where the hell do you live?"

Reluctantly accepting defeat in her quest to keep Sid in the dark, she gave him her address.

Chapter Sixteen

Sid refused to just drop Izzy off. He insisted she wait while he unloaded her bike then walked her to the porch. He took the items from the mail box and followed her inside.

"Uh-oh," he said and held up a small envelope.

Izzy dropped the raincoat onto the coffee table. "What is it?"

"Somebody named Willa Gardner has a shut-off notice from City Power."

"A what?" She searched for a way to get him to leave.

"You're about to have the electricity turned off." He put the envelope in her hand and wiggled a finger in front of her face. He wasn't drunk but the smell of liquor was strong.

Izzy took a step back and opened the envelope. Apparently Willa hadn't paid the bill since they moved in. If City Power didn't get $32.79 within 24 hours, the girls would be in the dark.

Sid put out his hand and asked, "How much is it?"

Izzy stuffed it in a back pocket. "Never mind," she said.

Sid looked like he was considering making a grab, but instead he said, "At least let me drive you downtown to pay it."

This was too tempting to pass up, no matter how reluctant she was to get back into his car.

"Okay. Wait here while I get my money." She found the two twenties in a jelly jar hidden on top of the water heater in her closet. "School clothes!"

she muttered to herself, even though she and Ann had planned on using the money for rent. "Stupid Willa. Good thing I'll get paid on Friday."

Sid was lounging on the sofa, but he stood when she came into the room. Someone sometime must have taught him manners. Far from being impressed, however, she found his politeness irksome.

"Let's go," she said.

Izzy was quiet during the drive to the City Power building; there was now a stabbing headache behind her eyes. She shaded them from the sun with one hand.

Sid reached over and squeezed her shoulder. His thumb plucked at her bra strap under her shirt. "Don't take it so hard, honey. It happens to everyone."

She wondered how he could tell she was getting a headache and gave him a quizzical look.

"The shut-off notice," he said, "just be glad you didn't come home to no power. That happened to me once in the middle of winter. I had to sleep at the pawnshop that night."

"That couldn't have been fun," Izzy remarked. She folded her arms.

Sid steered the El Camino into a parking lot and found a space in front of the entrance. He followed her inside, and when she hesitated, he showed her where to pay the bill.

The woman behind the counter wrote a receipt and gave her $7.21 in change. Izzy tucked the money into the front pocket of her jeans after the doors to the building closed behind them.

"Are you hungry?" Sid asked.

She wanted to lie and say she wasn't. She wanted to go home and take some aspirin, but at that moment her stomach produced a loud growl.

Sid chuckled, "I'll take that as a yes. Let's get you some dinner."

Izzy protested, "I'm not dressed to go out."

"You look fine. We'll go back to the coffee shop; they don't care what you're wearing."

She let him guide her to the car. When he was seated, he took the bottle out again for another long swallow. He held it toward her, and she said, "I don't drink."

He shrugged. "Just as well, you probably shouldn't on an empty stomach. Maybe later."

He drove them to the cafe. Once inside, Izzy looked for Ida but didn't see her. A hostess was on duty, her blonde hair piled in curls on top of her head. She wore a tight black skirt and a white ruffled blouse. The button at her bust strained to contain the abundant cleavage displayed in the deep vee of the neckline.

"Hi, Sid," the woman flashed a smile that showed gleaming teeth clear back to her molars.

"Hi baby, you got a table for two?" Sid slipped an arm around Izzy's waist.

Baby didn't give Izzy a glance. She lifted a manicured hand featuring no less than four rings and patted Sid's cheek. "Anything for you," she said and twitched her way to a booth. Izzy took a seat and Sid slid in next to her.

Izzy focused on the menu while the hostess flirted with Sid, who ate up the attention. His face flushed, and he licked his lips. At last the hostess left, and he picked up his menu. "Umm… everything looks so good." Izzy glanced up and found him nearly drooling at her. Under the table his hand found her thigh. She inched away and crossed her legs.

"How's the fried chicken?" she asked, directing his attention back to food.

"Tough and greasy," said a familiar voice. Sid groaned.

"Ida!" said Izzy, relieved and happy to see the woman again.

"How you doing, sweetie?" the waitress sniffed the air over Sid. "Let me get you folks some coffee."

Sid moved closer and put his arm around Izzy's shoulders. "Tell me, Brandy; is that old lady always here?"

Ida was back with the coffee and overheard him. "Feels to me like I live here." She gave him a thin smile.

"Feels that way to me, too," he muttered.

She ignored him. "The special tonight is country fried steak. You get soup and salad with that and a scoop of ice cream for dessert."

"What kind of soup?" Izzy asked before Sid could speak.

"Cream of chicken and it's good."

"We'll take two of the specials then," Sid put in.

"What kind of dressing on those salads?" Ida scribbled on her pad.

"What do you like, Brandy?" Sid asked.

"Thousand Island," Izzy said.

"I'll have blue cheese," Sid added.

Ida wrote the rest of the order and left.

Sid pulled coins from his pocket and leaned across Izzy to the tabletop juke box. "What would you like to hear?" he asked. His cheek rested on hers. She turned in her seat until her back was to him and studied the selections. He moved in closer behind her. She was almost sitting on his lap and had run out of room to move away. His fingers caressed her back just touching the sides of her breasts. In desperation she snapped her head back and hit him square in the nose.

"Damn!" Sid shouted and grabbed his bleeding nose.

Izzy pulled napkins from the holder and stuffed them into his hand. "Oh, Sid! I'm so sorry."

Holding the napkins to his face he glared at her. "Acthidents habben," he said thickly. "I'll be ride bad." He slid out of the booth and hurried to the men's room.

Relieved, Izzy dropped a quarter into the juke box and selected three songs.

"That was one of the slickest moves I've ever seen," complimented Ida. She set their drinks and bowls of soup on the table and winked. "I was going to pour soup in his lap."

"Thanks," Izzy said. She picked up a spoon and tasted the soup. It was rich, savory, hot, and she relished the comforting warmth of it. The pain behind her eyes dissipated.

Ida wiped up a spot of blood from the table and bench seat. "Could I ask you something?" she said.

Izzy hesitated before nodding.

"What are you doing with this guy?"

Izzy's face burned. "Nothing," she said defensively.

Keeping an eye on the men's room door, Ida continued, "You already know I'm not going to mind my own business, so I'll just say I don't think he's right for you. And why did he call you Brandy?"

"I don't want him to know my real name. He's helped me out a couple of times. I'm not dating him." Izzy crumbled a cracker into her soup.

The men's room door opened. Ida leaned down, "Make sure he knows that." She turned to Sid as he approached. "Oh my goodness," she said without sarcasm. "Would you like an ice pack?"

Sid looked suspicious. "Yeah, that would be nice."

Ida made sympathetic tch-tch sounds. "Sure thing."

"Thanks."

Izzy tucked her legs under her, taking up most of the seat. With a sigh, Sid sat down across from her.

"I'm really sorry Sid." She could tell he was skeptical.

"Uh-huh."

Izzy finished her soup and salad. Sid seemed to have lost his appetite. He ate a little soup but didn't touch the salad.

The chicken fried steaks were golden brown with a crisp coating and creamy milk gravy. Izzy could only eat half of hers. Sid ate his mashed potatoes and nothing more.

Ida brought the ice cream and the check. "Let me wrap up these leftovers for you," she said. She looked closely at Sid's face. "Think you're going to have a shiner to go with that swollen schnoz."

"Lucky me," sneered Sid.

Ida smiled pleasantly and walked away. She was back in a few minutes with the leftovers wrapped in foil packets. "Come back soon," she said.

"Are you okay to drive?" asked Izzy when they were seated in the El Camino.

"Of course," snapped Sid. The tires squealed when he jerked the car into traffic.

He stopped in front of her house.

"Thank you so much, Sid. I appreciate the ride and the dinner." She opened the car door, but before she could step out he pulled her next to him. He pressed his lips on hers. The food in her stomach churned. She felt his tongue prying and pushed on his chest. He loosened his embrace but didn't let her go. "Just a little something on account, Brandy." He nuzzled her neck, carefully protecting his nose before releasing her. His right eye was beginning to swell, but he fixed the left one on her. "One of these days I'll be expecting payment in full."

Izzy scrambled out of the car and wiped at her mouth with a shaking hand.

Sid put the car in gear and sped away.

Nausea and fear coiled in her gut. She ran into the house and locked the door behind her. Her knees trembled, and she felt desperate to shower and brush her teeth. Then she moaned aloud. She'd forgotten the leftovers in the car. They would have been so good tomorrow night. She tasted a hint of whiskey on her lips from Sid's kiss and hurried to the sink to rinse her mouth.

Chapter Seventeen

Ann walked in shortly after seven o'clock. "Now what's happened to your bike?" Her hands rested on her hips.

Izzy filled a basket with wet clothes from the washing machine. She hadn't given her bicycle a thought. "What do you mean?"

"Looks like another flat, but this time the wheel is bent."

"Oh, no!" Izzy flew outside. The front wheel had hit the curb harder than she thought and was obviously bent.

Ann followed her. "Maybe Paul can straighten it."

"Poor Paul," groaned Izzy. "He's going to think I do this stuff just to keep him coming over here."

"He'll be thrilled," Ann said. "You can take my bike tomorrow. Jill and I like walking to school."

"Thanks."

"How did it happen?" Ann asked.

"Help me hang the clothes on the line and I'll tell you all about it."

The sun had set when Izzy pinned up the last of the socks.

Ann held the empty basket and stared open-mouthed at her sister. "He kissed you?" The tone in her voice was the same one she might use to ask "He ate a live kitten?"

Izzy led the way back to the kitchen. "He thinks I owed it to him, and that's not all. He said he expects payment in full sometime."

Ann put the basket on a shelf. "What's that supposed to mean?"

"What do you think it means?" Izzy switched on the radio.

Ann switched it off. "He thinks that you'll let him . . . that you and he will . . ." She couldn't seem to find the words to say what she was thinking.

Izzy turned the radio on again. "Well, it's not going to happen."

"What if he forces you?"

Izzy told her about the head-butt she gave Sid at the café. "And that's tame compared to what I'll do if he tries anything serious."

"We should move," Ann suggested.

"Good idea. Where should we go? Oh, I know, how about those new apartments with the swimming pool and tennis courts? Or, maybe we should check in at the Holiday Inn? They say France is nice this time of year."

"You don't need to get snotty. It was just a thought."

"I wish Paul was tougher. I could ask him to scare Sid off." Izzy bit her thumbnail. She'd rather not have Paul even know about Sid.

"You'll just have to avoid him," Ann said.

Suddenly Izzy's face brightened. "Or maybe not."

"What?" Ann shrieked.

Izzy shushed her with her hands. "No, listen. What if . . .?" She hesitated. "No, I need to think this through."

"What are you thinking?" Ann asked with a frown.

Pacing between the stove and the table, Izzy paused to answer. "I think it will work but I don't want to jinx it by talking about it." She grinned at her sister. "Don't worry, Ann. It'll be all right."

Ann shook her head. "Now I know how Ethel felt when Lucy got a crazy idea."

"This isn't crazy. It might just be brilliant." Izzy touched the side of her head.

"Right" Ann replied. "That's exactly what Lucy would say."

※

Izzy rode Ann's bike the next morning. The storm on the weekend had marked the end of summer heat. The air was warm but not oppressive at dawn. It was early; she didn't want to take a chance on seeing Sid. She'd put an extra slice of bread in her lunch sack for Buddy, and she brought the copy of Great Expectations to read while she waited for the factory to open. In the bottom of the bag, she packed some items she needed later in the day.

After she parked the bike, she settled herself at the end of the picnic table. Buddy didn't appear in the tree, so she opened her book. The sun warmed her back while she read.

She couldn't tell how long she'd been sitting there when Stan's voice broke into her thoughts. "You just gonna let him starve?"

Looking up she saw Buddy at the opposite end of the table. His bright eyes stared at her while his nose twitched at the air.

Stan tossed a peanut towards the squirrel who snatched it up.

Izzy took out the slice of bread and broke off a piece.

"Don't rush him," Stan said. "Let him finish the nut before you give him something else." He stepped over the bench and sat down across from her.

"Shouldn't you be opening up?" Izzy asked.

"I came early. I'll get things going, then I'll pick up Faye."

With the mention of Faye's name, Izzy felt like the sun had gone behind a cloud. Her spine stiffened a little. "Do you know what's wrong with her?" She picked at the peeling paint on the table.

"Yeah," Stan answered. "Do you?"

Izzy cleared her throat. "She told me."

A long breath escaped Stan's lips. "Does everyone know?"

"I heard some gossip, but I don't think they know for sure."

Stan got up and stuffed his hand in his pocket. "Good." He paused and looked solemnly at Izzy. "Think we can keep it that way for a while?"

She raised her eyes to his, "I'm not telling anyone, if that's what you mean."

He nodded and walked to the doors.

At three-thirty-five, Izzy made her way to the Ladies Room. She dumped out the contents of her lunch sack. Lipstick, eye shadow, mascara and a tiny bottle of perfume clattered onto the counter. She dabbed blue eye shadow on her lids and added an extra thick coat of mascara. White lipstick obliterated her mouth. Studying her reflection, she saw that she looked hard, almost clownish, she thought, but in a frightening woman-on-the-hunt kind of way. The perfume she spritzed behind her ears and on her wrists was exotic and cloyingly sweet.

She unfastened the last buttons of her blouse and tied the shirt tails in a knot above her waist. She considered unbuttoning a button at the top but decided she shouldn't push things too far. After all, this was an experiment that could explode in her face.

When she turned the corner from Main Street she spotted the El Camino in front of the pawnshop. Parking her bike in the alley, she patted her hair a last time, crammed two sticks of peppermint gum in her mouth, and walked into the shop.

Sid was haggling with a customer. His nose looked sore, and he did have a black eye, though it wasn't swollen shut. He glanced up when the bell on the door jingled. "Be right with you," he said.

Izzy put her hands in the front pockets of her jeans and rocked back on her heels. "Sure thing, sugar," she said and cracked her gum. Sid's head snapped up, and he recognized her.

"Gimme a second," he said to the elderly man at the counter. He approached Izzy with a huge grin. Standing in front of her, he looked her up and down. Izzy stepped close to him and slid her hands around his neck.

"Ohhh!" she spoke in baby-talk. "Poor Siddy! Does it hurt much?" She kissed the tip of an index finger and touched it lightly to his nose. His face darkened to a purple that clashed with his yellow hair.

"Let me finish with this guy and you can make it better." He was almost salivating.

"I'll just look around," Izzy said and stepped over to a locked jewelry case.

Wedding bands, rings with diamonds, rubies, opals, and various birthstones gleamed under the scratched glass. Watches, broaches, bracelets and necklaces crowded the display.

A bell on the door jingled when the customer left. She heard Sid's patent leather shoes squeak as he made his way to her.

His hands stole around her bare waist from behind. "See anything you like?" he asked with a playful nip at her ear. She quelled the shudder that wanted to run down her spine.

She leaned back against him and reached up to pat his cheek. Her fingers brushed his nose. He gasped and grabbed her hand. He said a very bad word under his breath. Then he pressed his lips to her palm. "Careful baby," he whispered huskily. "Remember I'm wounded."

"What's that green one?" she asked, pointing at a ring.

He stopped nibbling her neck. "Which one?"

She tapped on the glass, "The second one over."

"That's an emerald. It's not a very good one. Least that's what I told the lady who brought it in."

"They're all so pretty," she sighed.

"Do you have a favorite?"

She stepped away from him and pouted. "I have to choose?"

Sid looked momentarily startled then chuckled. "You want all of them?"

"Maybe," she gave him a sideways look and cracked her chewing gum again.

Two men came in and Sid reluctantly left her to conduct business. She waited until he was busy then stepped behind the counter and stood next to him.

"Siddy?" she asked.

"Pardon me," Sid said to the customers. "In a minute baby, I'm helping these gentlemen."

"Give me the key?" she held out her hand.

"What key?" he frowned.

"I want to try on the jewelry." She pinched the chewing gum in her mouth and drew it out in a long thread before coiling it back in with her tongue.

One of the customers cleared his throat.

"Later," Sid whispered.

Izzy stomped her foot. "No!" she whined, "I want it now."

"Should we come back another time?" asked the customer.

Sid fumbled in his pocket and pulled out a ring of keys. "No, we're fine." He handed them to Izzy.

She squealed and kissed his cheek, leaving a streak of pasty lipstick behind.

The case opened and Izzy slipped a different colored jewel on every finger and held out her hand to admire them. She hung a string of pearls around her neck and pinned a couple of broaches to her shirt. Pulling off the rings, she dropped them into the case and tried on the diamonds. Most of them were loose on her fingers and she stacked them three deep on both hands.

The bell jingled again when the customers left, and she looked up to see Sid looking stern. He turned the lock on the door and strode across the shop to her.

Opening her eyes wide, she bit the tip of her index finger. "Ews not angwy are ew?"

He stopped in his tracks, one eyebrow dropped in a frown. She took a step towards him and peeked up through her lashes. "I'm sowee, but der so pwetty." She was beginning to make herself nauseous.

The frown lifted from Sid's face but he still looked confused. "What are you doing here?" he asked.

Izzy removed the diamonds and began placing all the rings in their slots. "Aren't you happy to see me?"

"Ecstatic," Sid said. "I'm just wondering how I got so lucky." He stepped behind and slid his hands around her midriff.

She replaced the necklaces and broaches and turned to face him. "Me, too," she said demurely. It was a good thing Sid couldn't tell the blush on her cheeks was the result of acute embarrassment.

His face sorted through expressions of surprise, suspicion, and lust. He kissed her long and slow. His mouth was hard and scrubbed back and forth against her closed lips. His hands roamed over her back.

Her breath and her lunch both caught in her throat.

Sid pulled her toward the back of the store. He opened the door to his office, and Izzy saw a lumpy looking couch against a wall. The sight of a velvet pillow matted and stained from hair cream made her scalp itch.

Sid took a seat and placed her on his lap. He nibbled at her neck, constantly moving lower while his fingers fumbled with her shirt.

Resisting the urge to run, Izzy sighed into his ear. "Which one do I get?"

"Which what?" he murmured from near her cleavage.

"Which ring?"

He paused for a split second. "You really want a ring?" He had untied the shirt tails at her waist and she felt the heat of his hand on her skin.

She nipped at his jaw. "It's customary, isn't it?"

Sid removed her hands from his hair and held them in front of her. He slid her onto the couch beside him and stared at her. "Brandy, what are you talking about?"

Izzy adjusted her shirt and patted her hair. "An engagement ring, of course."

His jaw dropped, and he choked on a laugh. "Engagement?"

She stiffened. "What else? You wanted payment in full. What else could that mean?" She gasped and covered her mouth with a hand. "Did you think that I . . . that we . . .?" She jumped up and gaped at him. "Oh Sid! You must think I'm a terrible girl!"

He looked relieved and smiled. "Brandy, I'd never think you were terrible, just a little confused maybe." He tried to pull her back to his lap but she jerked her hand away.

Izzy had a skill for crying any time she wanted, and now tears clung to her eyelashes. "I thought you wanted to marry me! I already told my father about us." She quickly retied her shirt tails.

"Whoa there. Your father?" Sid stood. "You're too young to get married," he pointed out and added, "I'm too young to get married!"

Izzy took a tissue from the desk and dabbed her eyes. "You are not! You're old and you're rich, and Daddy said you sound like a good catch, so I thought . . ."

Sid had stopped smiling. "What did you think? Wait a minute, how old do you think I am?"

She considered him for a minute, "At least forty, but I don't care about the age difference, Sid. I can take care of you, and Daddy said when we have kids, they'll keep you young." She paused and wrinkled her forehead, "You *can* still have children can't you?"

Completely flummoxed, Sid looked like he couldn't make up his mind whether to shake her or just throw her out. He swallowed a few times and moved to his desk where he opened a drawer and took out a flask. Keeping his eyes on her, he opened it and lifted it to his lips.

Izzy rushed to him and placed a hand over his mouth. "No!" she cried, "that's one thing I won't have. I will not be married to a drunk!"

Sid carefully removed her hand. "Nope," he said and deliberately took a long swig. "You sure as hell, won't!"

Izzy faked a sob, ran through the store, unlocked the door, and fled.

Chapter Eighteen

Three blocks from the pawnshop Izzy stopped at a service station and asked for the key to the restroom. She was trembling. When she looked in the mirror she saw that most of the lipstick was gone and her lips were puffy. The extra mascara had smudged onto her cheeks. She cleaned her face the best she could using powdered soap and paper towels. The eye make-up was garishly dark, but she'd have to take it off at home.

She bought a small Coke and drank it while she sat on the bike. It was nearing six, and she wondered if Sid would come after her. Not likely. The bit about him being so old was a stroke of genius. She wondered if she'd gone too far by questioning whether or not he could have children, but under the circumstances she didn't think so.

Draining the last of her soda, she dropped the empty bottle into the rack provided. Her spirits climbed with every block she put between herself and the pawnshop. She was almost giddy with relief by the time she reached the house.

When she turned into the driveway, she nearly collided with Paul. He raised a greasy hand in greeting and returned to inspecting the bent rim on her bike.

Izzy parked next to him. "Is it ruined?" she asked.

Paul looked up to answer but just stared at her face.

Izzy batted her eyelashes at him, which took some effort with an extra pound of make-up on them. "It's the latest thing," she said. "Panda eyes."

"Uh-huh," Paul responded. "Was there a costume party I didn't hear about?"

"It's such a long story and you're so . . . so young," she sighed dramatically.

"Okay then." He pulled his attention back to removing the wheel from the bike. "Ann's at McKinley's."

Izzy dropped onto a porch step. "I know."

"Dad's cooking chicken on the grill. You want to join us?"

The strain of her earlier performance had left her tired. Paul's head was bent over his work. His neck looked clean and tan, his hair a burnished gold in the sunlight. Izzy felt a pull to touch him, stroke his smooth cheek and look into friendly eyes.

Jumping up, she said, "Hold on. I'll be right back." She hurried inside to the bathroom. Willa had always used Vaseline to remove her mascara, and Izzy took a jar from the medicine cabinet and scooped out a small blob to rub over her eyes. She tissued it off and repeated the process until the black mess was gone. Without the make-up she felt different. Not like herself, exactly. Who she was or thought she would become had been derailed. Still, she felt closer to the Izzy she knew.

Reluctantly, she applied a very light coat of mascara, some blush, and lip balm. She changed into a cotton skirt and a clean blouse. Sandals would have looked nice, but she didn't have any, so she slipped her feet into a pair of flip-flops.

Paul had taken the tire and inner tube off the bike and was wiping grease from his hands when she returned to the porch. He gave her a warm smile. "Nothing against Pandas, but you look much better."

"I'd love to come to your house for dinner." She smiled back.

※

Paul and Jill's backyard was as tidy and pretty as a city park. Flower beds in a riot of colorful blooms surrounded a lush lawn. A large patio attached to the rear of the house and the side of the garage was furnished with tables, benches, gliders, and rocking chairs. A brick barbecue created a partial wall at the far end and a tall man wearing brown Huaraches, Bermuda shorts, a polo shirt, and a red and white striped apron, slathered sauce over chicken on the grill.

"Hi, Izzy," called Jill as she emerged from the sliding glass doors at the back of the house. She carried a tray piled with tablecloths and dishes.

The man at the grill turned at the sound of his daughter's voice. "Who's this, Paul?" He smiled and wiped his hands on a towel. His hair was receding a bit in front, but other than that, he looked only slightly older than his son.

"This is Izzy, Dad." Jill jumped in ahead of her brother.

"Oh, the girl with the bike." Mr. Kimball crossed the patio and extended his hand. "Good to finally know you."

"Thank you," Izzy replied shyly.

"Want to help me with the tables?" Jill asked.

"Hey, she's here as a guest," protested Paul.

"I don't mind," Izzy said.

"Why don't you get cleaned up, son? Then you can set up the badminton net," suggested Mr. Kimball.

The girls spread tablecloths and laid out the dishes.

"You have a really nice home, Jill," Izzy said.

"Don't be fooled by the yard," Jill said. "It's all done with slave labor." She pointed a finger at herself.

"What's that, Jill? You say you want to pay rent?" A small redheaded woman carrying a platter of sliced vegetables approached the tables. "Craig," she spoke over her shoulder to her husband. "You hear that? Jill's ready to get a job." She grinned at Izzy. "You must be Ann's sister. Don't believe more than half of what this girl tells you." Mrs. Kimball wasn't as tall as her daughter. Her round figure and small hands and feet made her look like a doll. Her face was sweet and still pretty.

Izzy laughed, "Can't be trusted huh?"

The woman tucked an errant strand of her daughter's hair behind an ear and patted her cheek. "She's a great kid, but sometimes she forgets she's not an only child. Paul does his share and so do Terry and Tom."

"Terry and Tom?" Izzy asked.

"The twins," Mr. Kimball said.

Izzy's jaw dropped.

"Didn't they tell you about the twins?" Mrs. Kimball asked. "They're at a ball game, but they should be here soon."

"Ann's met them. Didn't she say anything?" Jill asked.

Izzy could only shake her head. "How old are they?" she asked as she folded napkins and laid them on the plates.

"Thirteen," answered Jill. "It's hard to tell they are twins. I mean they don't look alike. Well, they wouldn't really because Terry's a girl and Tom is so much smaller."

Paul returned with his hair damp from the shower and busied himself assembling the badminton net on the lawn.

Izzy followed Jill inside to help with the food. She couldn't tell why she responded the way she had about the twins. No one here knew that she and Ann were twins. Out of nowhere a feeling of resentment rose in her. *That's stupid*, she thought. The feeling persisted, accompanied by a sense of loss. *And that's really dumb*, the voice in her head said. *You're still a twin. Nothing's changed.* Her thoughts paused then added, *except everything.*

The twins arrived just as dinner was ready. Terry shook back her blonde locks and gave Izzy a cursory glance when they were introduced. Tom, who was a head shorter than his sister and favored his mother's rounder figure, had a riot of red curls framing a freckled face. He grinned and extended his hand to Izzy with undisguised admiration in his eyes before taking his seat at the table beside Paul. Jill sat with her parents and Terry at the other table.

"I called Ann at McKinley's. She'll come over as soon as they get home," Jill said.

"Great!" Tom said through a mouthful of chicken.

Paul winked at Izzy and patted his brother's back. "Down boy," he admonished. "You're not old enough to get so excited."

Tom washed down the chicken with a gulp of lemonade before replying, "A guy can dream. I won't always be this young."

Terry sneered over her shoulder at Tom. "Won't matter how old you get, you'll still be short and fat."

An uneasy silence fell over the group. Terry raised her chin and took another bite of potato salad. Tom's head bowed, and he nudged his plate away.

Mr. Kimball softly cleared his throat. "Wow, I would have thought you'd have more appetite after your ballgame."

Terry glared at her father who nodded toward her plate and said, "You're finished, Terry. You can start cleaning the kitchen."

The plastic fork that Terry threw hit the concrete with an unsatisfactory clack. She rose, picked up her plate, and stomped into the house.

Paul spooned baked beans onto Tom's plate. "Listen sport, when I was your age I was so round it was hard to tell which end of me was up. You're in for a massive growth spurt in the next two years."

Tom gave him a hopeful sideways look.

"Paul's right," added Izzy, "and with those eyelashes and your gorgeous hair you're going to need to keep up your strength to stay ahead of the girls."

Tom smiled and picked up the piece of chicken he'd been eating. Mrs. Kimball shot Izzy a grateful look.

After dinner, Mr. Kimball and Jill went inside to help Terry with the clean-up. Tom and Paul challenged Izzy and Mrs. Kimball to a badminton game. They played until it was too dark to see the shuttlecock. No one had kept score; no one seemed to care that much about winning.

Everyone was toasting marshmallows over the dying coals in the grill when Ann turned up. Paul slipped the crisp caramelized skin off the marshmallow on the end of his roasting fork and fed it to Izzy.

Mrs. Kimball asked Ann if she was hungry. Ann said no, but was presented with a small plate of chicken and salad anyway.

Tom, who had been studying Paul and Izzy, crammed an extra marshmallow onto his fork and thrust it into the coals.

The chilly evening air made Paul's arm around Izzy's shoulders welcome. She looked at the faces in the gathering darkness. The faint glow from the embers cast the only light; occasionally a spray of golden sparks flew out of the chimney of the barbecue. They burned brightly for a split second before dying.

Izzy heard the sliding door open and saw Terry coming out to join them. She approached her twin quietly and murmured something Izzy couldn't hear. Tom put his arm around her shoulder. Kissing her brother on his cheek, she said, "I'm sorry."

Tom nodded. "Okay," he said. "But I'll get you back later."

Terry smiled and answered, "We'll see about that."

Izzy had the unsettling feeling that she had wandered from the set of *Peyton Place* into *The Donna Reed Show*. Her encounter with Sid —was it only hours ago— seemed like a bad dream. Within this circle of familial peace, she felt reassured that she truly was not the girl she had pretended to be.

But the problem remained that everything was pretend.

Chapter Nineteen

Paul drove Ann and Izzy home even though they protested that they could walk the short distance. Izzy was glad to have him with them when they entered the dark house. She half-expected to find Sid hiding behind the living room curtains. Paul stayed until they'd turned on the lights and checked under the beds. He didn't ask why she seemed nervous. He held her hand for a minute as they stood by the screen door and smiled down at her.

"I'll have your wheel and tire ready by Saturday. Do you have a way to get to work?"

"I'm riding Ann's bike. She prefers walking with Jill."

He nodded, "Those two are pretty close." His thumb stroked the back of her hand sending a flow of warmth to her heart. "Let me know if you need anything, will you?"

"Sure. Thanks for dinner."

Paul raised her chin with a finger and leaned down. His soft lips barely touched hers. She felt an insane urge to throw herself into his arms and beg him to stay.

"Good night Izzy. I'll see you soon." He pulled the door closed behind him.

Alone in the living room, Izzy dropped onto the sofa to think. She wasn't a girl who was used to being kissed. In fact the last time she'd been kissed – other than Sid, she shuddered – had been in seventh grade. It happened after a matinee dance, behind the school, in the middle of the day. The kiss itself was no more than a bumping of faces; their lips didn't even line up. She wasn't expecting it, and her reaction was to push the boy as hard as she could. He landed on his butt in a patch of weeds. She had never considered the experience as her First Kiss but she would now, if only so she wouldn't have to count the ones from Sid.

"Well?" Ann joined her on the sofa. "Did you see him?"

Izzy told her about the pawnshop. "I don't think I'll hear from him."

Ann's eyes grew huge, her mouth slightly open. She blinked a couple of times before she found her voice. "No, I . . . uh, doubt he'll want anything to do with you." She stared at her sister.

"What?" Izzy asked.

"Nothing, I'm just a little . . . I mean I didn't know what you were going to do."

Izzy's spine stiffened. "And?" she asked, defensively.

Ann blinked again before saying, "I think it was pure genius."

The tension in Izzy's body vanished. She dropped her face into her hands and moaned. "Oh, Annie it was awful. I was so scared. Afterward I could barely ride the bike. I've never been so happy to see anyone as I was to see Paul in the driveway."

"I can imagine," Ann said.

"It was so nice at his house tonight. Are they always like that?"

"What do you mean?"

"I mean, does it always feel so . . ." she searched for the word she wanted, "safe over there?"

Ann considered for a second before nodding, "Yeah, it really does."

They sat quietly then sighed in unison, which made them both smile.

"Why didn't you tell me about the twins?"

"I only met them a couple of times. I guess, with so much going on, I didn't think it was important." Ann yawned and stretched her arms.

Izzy picked at her fingernails. "It's kind of strange, but I felt jealous. Then someone said they didn't look alike, and I really resented them, like you and I are supposed to be the only twins in the world who don't look alike."

"I know what you mean, I think. It doesn't have anything to do with

Terry and Tom. It feels like we've lost something. I mean besides Mom." Ann rubbed her eyes.

Izzy stood and held out a hand to pull Ann to her feet. "Let's go to bed. It's late."

The breeze through the window had turned cold. They put another blanket on the bed and snuggled against each other. Izzy thought Ann was asleep when she suddenly spoke. "What you did at the pawnshop today could have turned out really bad."

Izzy shivered. "Don't remind me."

"You were very brave but . . ." Ann paused.

"But what?" Izzy asked.

"If you ever have to do anything like that again, you darn well better take me along!"

"Yeah, okay. Next time you can ride shotgun. I promise."

"I won't just ride shotgun. I'm bringing one with me," Ann mumbled sleepily.

The weight of the extra blanket pressed down. The warmth and scent of Ann comforted Izzy. She nuzzled her head deeper into her pillow, and in the drowsy recesses of her mind she felt peace.

※

Paychecks were distributed on Friday afternoon. Izzy opened hers in the privacy of a bathroom stall. Sixty-seven dollars and eighty-two cents. The most money she'd ever earned.

She joined Betty, Marti, and Faye in the break room. The mood was almost festive, even Marti was grinning.

"How you like getting your first check?" Betty asked.

"I like it a lot," Izzy said. "But I don't have a bank account. How do I cash it?"

"They'll cash it for you at the grocery store. Just show them your work ID," Marti said, "unless it's over five-hundred dollars." She guffawed.

"Not quite," Izzy said.

"Sweetie, you can work here for twenty years, and it'll never be that much," Betty patted her hand.

Faye drank a carton of milk and nibbled at a soda cracker. Her check lay unopened on the table.

Betty leaned forward to look Faye in the face. "You feeling punk again?" she asked.

One side of Faye's mouth lifted slightly in a smile. "A little," she said.

Stan walked up and placed an open bottle of 7-Up on the table. He sat in the chair next to Faye and poured some of the soda into a paper cup for her.

"Ahhh, Friday again." He looked around the table. "Best day of the week." He winked at Izzy, but she looked away. He turned his attention to the other women.

Izzy kept an eye on Faye. She had perked up as soon as Stan appeared. She sipped her drink, and some color returned to her face. Still, her smile looked forced, and sadness clouded her eyes.

As soon as break was over Stan approached Izzy at her sewing machine. "I need to see you in the break room." He didn't wait for her reply.

She followed him. He indicated an empty seat at a table and she took it. There was a crease between his eyebrows. He settled in the chair across from Izzy and cleared his throat. "This isn't about work," he said. "I need to ask you something."

Izzy cocked her head at him. "Like what?"

He cleared his throat again. "It has to do with Faye."

She waited.

"Her father found out about the baby," he paused. "It wasn't good. He told her to leave."

"Criminey," Izzy said, "What's she going to do?"

"Well," Stan looked in her eyes, "that's why I wanted to talk to you."

"Me?"

"Of course you can say no," he looked expectantly at her.

"Okay," she began slowly, "before I do, would you tell me what I'll be saying 'no' to?"

"Well," he said. "I was wondering if maybe Faye could move in with you and your sister?"

Izzy's heart thumped. She stared at Stan. A nerve twitched at the corner of his eye.

"Just until we figure out what to do," he added. "Could be a couple of months."

"What to do?" Izzy repeated. "A couple of months?"

"That's right," Stan seemed to appreciate how quickly she was catching on. "She'd pay half the rent and utilities and share the food cost."

Now it was Izzy's turn to clear her throat. "Until you decide what to do?" He nodded.

"If you don't mind my asking, what is there to decide?" Her throat felt tight, she had to force the words out.

Stan shifted in his chair and tapped his fingers on the table. "She hasn't decided whether or not she wants to keep the baby after it's born," he said.

Izzy stared in disbelief. "And that's okay with you?"

He frowned, "Why wouldn't it be?" he said.

Izzy stood so quickly that her chair clattered onto the floor. She started to walk away then turned back to him. "I'll talk to my sister about it. I'm sure it will be fine. When does she need to move in?" she spoke quickly, repressing the disgust she felt.

"All of her things are in my car." He hesitated. "She can stay at my mother's place for a couple of days."

"A couple of days?" She couldn't quite keep the sneer out of her voice. "Isn't that nice of you."

Stan frowned. "No, it's nice of my mother. Look, if you can't or don't want to do this just say so."

Her hand itched to pick up the napkin dispenser and smack the side of his head with it. "I need to explain to my sister, but Faye can move in tonight if she wants. She'll be welcome."

"Thanks, Izzy." He looked ridiculously relieved. "We've made plans for tonight, but is tomorrow afternoon okay?"

She stared open-mouthed. "You've made plans?"

Stan flushed, "Well, it's her birthday and my family is having a dinner for her. It's a surprise."

"I'll bet it is," Izzy said weakly. "Okay, then, tomorrow."

Stan held out his hand. She stared at it for a second before turning her back.

Her head was spinning when she reached her work station. Faye's thin shoulders were hunched over her machine. Impulsively, Izzy wrapped her arms around the girl and kissed her cheek. "Happy birthday," she whispered.

Faye looked up. "How did you know?"

Izzy started to answer but recalled the dinner was supposed to be a surprise. "You just looked a year older to me." She winked so Faye would know she was teasing and moved to her chair.

The fleeting light in Faye's face dimmed. "I feel a lot older."

Busying herself with work, Izzy avoided eye contact that would encourage further conversation.

A package of corn tortillas, a pound of ground beef, a small block of cheddar cheese, two tomatoes, and a head of lettuce didn't come close to filling the grocery cart, but with the rent to pay it was as far as Izzy dared to stretch her paycheck. She paid and tucked the change into her pocket with Mrs. Call's address.

She rode to 425 East Main Street. A pink cottage framed by flower beds of petunias and sweet alyssum made Izzy wonder for a second if somehow she'd made a wrong turn that landed her in Disneyland. She parked her bike next to the porch and carefully stepped between the little pots of flowers that lined the steps.

A tiny lady answered the door. Her white hair was curled into a riot of ringlets held back from her face with a faded ribbon; she wore a red checked dress and a white pinafore with limp ruffles; her feet were bare and the toenails painted fuchsia. The sun glinted off of a gold tooth when she smiled at Izzy. "Hello dearie." Her voice was deep and coarse and ruined the illusion created by the pinafore and ringlets.

"Is Mrs. Call at home?" Izzy asked.

The woman stared as if she hadn't heard, and asked, "Would you like some tea? I just put the kettle on."

"Uh, no, thank you. Does Mrs. Call live here?"

"My name is Puddin'," the woman replied. "Isn't that a silly name?"

Izzy took a step back and checked the house number. Puddin' cocked her head to one side and grinned. The gold tooth was her only one. "I had a doggy named Taffy." She giggled. "She died." The smile drooped, and she pulled a lace hanky from a pocket.

"I'm sorry about your dog," Izzy said. "Do you *know* a Mrs. Call?"

Puddin' made a production of blowing her nose and dabbed her powdery cheeks. "Oh, Mrs. Call isn't dead. Just the dog."

Feeling that she had finally made a connection, Izzy pushed on. "Does she live here?"

The lady frowned, "We buried her in the backyard. I guess that means she lives here. What an odd question."

"No, not Taffy. I'm sorry about Taffy and everything, but I'm looking for Mrs. Call."

Checking a tiny heart shaped watch pinned on her breast, Puddin' continued, "It's nearly five. Mrs. Call stays out late."

"But is this her house?" Izzy pressed.

"Oh yes, it's all hers. She owns everything." Her face brightened and she added, with a touch of pride, "I have my own cigarettes, though. Want one?"

"Thanks anyway, I just came by to pay the rent."

At the mention of rent the woman's eyes appeared to focus. She looked Izzy over. "Come on in. I'll get an envelope for the money."

Stepping just inside the door, Izzy couldn't help holding a hand over her nose. The place smelled like an ashtray and not a new ashtray either. This was the odor of decades of tobacco breathed into every surface. Puddin' fumbled in the drawer of a little white desk. She found a cigarette and paused to light it, striking the match on the bottom of her thickly calloused foot. "Oh, yeah," she moaned, "here it is." She held out an envelope with hearts stamped on it. It was a leftover Valentine.

Izzy took it and placed the folded twenty dollar bills inside. "Do you have a pen or pencil I could use?"

Puddin's head was tilted back, her eyes half-shut in ecstasy, as she drew another breath through her cigarette.

Izzy spotted a pencil stub on the desk and wrote, *Mrs. Call, Here is the rent for September.* She signed Willa's name.

"Mrs. uh, Puddin'? Will you see Mrs. Call gets this? It's important."

The old woman nodded, her eyes now closed tight. Izzy wondered if there might be something other than tobacco in that cigarette.

❦

Eight blocks of fresh air did little to dissipate the stench from Izzy's clothes. As soon as she reached the house, she changed into cut-offs and a T-shirt. She heard Ann call hello when she came in.

"Hi," she replied. "I paid the rent."

"Good." There was the rustle of a paper bag. "What's all this?"

"Taco's for dinner." Izzy went to the kitchen.

Ann held a package of ground beef in one hand and the tortillas in the other. "You forgot onion, and we don't have any cooking oil."

"Dang!" Izzy said, "I'll have to go back to the store."

Ann put the meat in the fridge. "Hold on, I'll run over to Jill's and see if we can borrow some."

The only thing Mexican about their tacos were the tortillas. Willa used to look disgusted when they used ketchup instead of the Tabasco sauce she preferred. "What you got there," she would say, "is a cheeseburger in a taco shell. You want pickle on that?" Izzy and Ann ignored her suggestion and looked on in awe as their mother's face went from pink to magenta the more hot sauce she ate until perspiration broke out on her forehead.

Ann returned with a jelly jar of cooking oil and half an onion. The sisters worked together chopping and frying. Izzy told about the house where Mrs. Call lived and about meeting Puddin'.

"She sounds nuts," observed Ann while she spooned fillings into her tortilla.

"No kidding," Izzy answered. "I expected a big net to drop over her any second."

They took their filled plates to the table and Izzy poured Kool-Aid into their glasses.

The tacos were good although they had to add water to the ketchup to get the last of it out of the bottle. Leaning back in their chairs, they considered the messy kitchen.

"I don't think I'll make popcorn tonight when Jill and Paul come over," Ann said.

Suddenly Izzy remembered she had to talk to Ann about Faye. "I'll do the dishes if you'll keep me company."

"You've got a deal," Ann stretched her arms and propped her feet on the edge of the table.

Once Izzy put the dishes in the sink, she turned to face her sister. "Look, there's something I have to talk to you about."

Ann's feet hit the floor; she sat up straight. "What? Is it Sid? Did he show up again?"

Izzy put up a hand, "No, it's nothing like that."

"Thank heaven!" Ann put in.

"You remember I told you about Faye from work?"

Ann nodded. "The one who brought the casserole."

"Well, she's got a big problem." Izzy began picking at her fingernails. "Her dad kicked her out."

"Why?" Ann asked.

"She, uh . . . that is . . . ," Izzy took a swallow of punch. "She's going to have a baby."

Ann stared for several seconds before asking, "Is she getting married?"

"I don't think she knows yet," Izzy said.

"How could she not know? Her boyfriend has to marry her!"

"That's what I thought, too. But I guess it's complicated. Anyway, she needs a place to stay and Stan—"

"Stan! What's he got to do with this?"

Izzy looked at her sister.

Ann's eyes grew large. "Stan?" she whispered.

Izzy shrugged. "I don't know for certain, but he asked if she could live with us for a couple of months until they figure things out."

Ann placed her hands on her hips and tossed her hair. "Seems to me Faye's father should have picked up the shotgun instead of throwing her out in the street."

"For sure," Izzy said. "But what do you think? Can she come here? Stan says she'll help with expenses—"

Ann cut her off, "Of course she can come here. Poor kid! I'll change the sheets on Willa's bed and dust the room. When is she coming?"

"Tomorrow." Izzy turned her attention to the dishes.

Ann joined her at the sink and picked up a dish towel. "I'll clear a shelf in the bathroom for her, too," she said.

"Good idea," Izzy replied.

"How pregnant is she?" Ann asked.

"I don't know. She doesn't look pregnant, yet."

"Where's her mother? What does she say?"

"Her mother died." Izzy scrubbed at a frying pan.

Ann stared out the window and chewed her lip. After a minute she spoke, "What would you do if it was you?"

Without considering, Izzy answered, "It would never be me."

"But, if it were you, what would you do?"

Izzy pulled the stopper to drain the water from the sink. "It's not me and it's not you." She looked intently at her sister. "Let's make sure it stays that way."

"Don't worry. Remember what Mom told us?"

"Keep your legs crossed and your panties on. Words to live by." Izzy nodded. "One of us ought to put that in embroidery."

Ann laughed, "Wouldn't that be cute hanging on the wall?"

❦

Paul and Jill showed up with a carton of ice cream and a jug of root beer. They drank floats while they watched Frightmare Theater. They talked more than they watched. Izzy told them about Faye coming though she did not mention the expected baby.

"So, no more sleep-overs," Jill said.

Tough! Izzy thought then felt ashamed. "I can always sleep on the couch if you want to stay over." She kept the edge of sarcasm out of her voice.

"Or Ann can stay at my house." Jill brightened.

"Sure she can," agreed Izzy and wondered if the lump so often in her throat was now becoming permanent.

Faye arrived at noon the next day. Stan carried her bag and several cardboard boxes into the house and gave her a quick squeeze before he left.

"Your room is in here, Faye." Ann led the way to the front bedroom.

The furniture was polished and the hardwood floor shone. "This is very nice. Thank you," Faye's voice was so quiet that it could have been drowned out by a falling leaf.

Izzy showed her the bathroom and the shelf assigned to her. Then the twins left her alone to unpack.

An uncomfortable formality permeated the house. Izzy felt stiff; like her skin had shrunk overnight and now her movements were jerky. She could tell Ann felt the same by the way she was talking. The courtesy was suffocating. All three girls "pleased", "thank you'd", and "pardon me'd" through the weekend. Faye only took a few bites at meals; she never put more than she ate on her plate. She scrubbed the entire bathroom every day and stayed in her room. She had a beat up radio that she played with the volume at the lowest setting.

In bed on Sunday night, Ann whispered, "It's like living with a ghost."

"I know," Izzy agreed. "I wish we could all relax."

"Well," Ann said, "she's a very tidy ghost."

Chapter Twenty

Izzy aimed the hair spray nozzle at her hair and was just about to press the button when she heard a tapping on the bathroom door.

"Izzy, I'm sorry, but I need to come in there right now," Faye said.

The girls learned over the weekend that when Faye needed the bathroom, it was because she was going to throw up. Izzy opened the door.

"Thanks," Faye blurted and rushed to the toilet.

Izzy finished her hair in her bedroom. She could hear Faye wiping down the bathroom after being sick.

Ann sat up in bed. "I am never, ever, going to have children." She gagged each time Faye was sick.

"Never say never," Izzy said. But she'd been thinking the same thing. She marveled that Faye could be so ill and immediately return to packing a lunch. Of course there was nothing in the lunch except a hardboiled egg and carrot sticks.

When Stan pulled into the driveway, Izzy and Faye were waiting. He held open the passenger door for Faye, and Izzy climbed into the backseat. The stiffness from the house carried over to the car, and no one spoke until they parked at the factory.

"Okay," Stan said, a little too cheerfully Izzy thought, "here we are."

While Stan went through the opening procedures, the girls sat in the break room.

"Izzy?" It was the first time Faye had spoken directly to her since she'd moved in.

"Yeah?"

"I've saved some money. I'll pay rent and groceries and anything else you need."

Izzy placed her hand on Faye's fingers. "We'll split the expenses, but that will really help us out."

"I can cook and clean, too," Faye added.

"Thanks. There isn't too much cooking. Ann usually eats dinner where she babysits, so it'll only be you and me most nights."

Other employees arrived and were filling the room. They bought coffee from the vending machines and lit their cigarettes to get in a last one before work began. Betty took a seat next to Faye and moved the ashtray closer. She was just about to light up when she paused and looked at Faye. "Will this bother you?" She wiggled a cigarette.

"It hasn't for the last three years," Faye said with a puzzled look.

"So, what are your plans? I mean about the baby." Betty's voice expressed sincere concern.

Faye looked embarrassed. "How did you know?"

"I saw all the signs, and I read them." Betty picked a speck of tobacco off her tongue. "I raised four kids of my own, and I've worked here for fifteen years. You're not exactly the first." She patted Faye's arm. "So will there be a wedding?"

"She's staying with me and my sister for now," Izzy interjected, hoping to turn the conversation.

Faye excused herself and hurried to the Ladies Room.

Izzy leaned toward Betty. "Does everyone know?"

The older woman shrugged. "Probably. Why's she staying at your place?"

"Her father kicked her out. Stan asked if we'd take her in."

Betty's eyebrows shot up. "What the hell? Stan? He wouldn't a been my first guess."

She crushed out her cigarette and waved to Marti across the room.

"I don't know anything for sure. He could just be trying to help. Please don't say anything," Izzy begged.

Betty studied her face for a second. "I won't say anything unless someone asks me."

"Of course they'll ask," Izzy whispered. "Just please don't mention Stan."

"What about Stan?" Marti asked as she set her coffee cup on the table.

"Might be the daddy," Betty said.

"And he might not!" Izzy added glaring at Betty.

Marti cackled. "Wow, this is interesting. One girl hopes he's not the father and the other wishes he was."

As if on cue, the intercom music came on with Dusty Springfield singing "Wishin' and Hopin'."

Betty and Marti broke into giggles. Izzy grabbed her sewing box and stalked into the production room.

At noon the break room was a buzzing hive. Furtive glances swarmed toward Faye like a cloud of gnats.

"Let's sit outside today," Izzy suggested. Faye nodded and followed her out of the room. They settled at the picnic table and opened their lunch sacks. Izzy pulled the crusts off of her peanut butter sandwich and tossed them to the end of the table in case Buddy showed up.

Faye peeled her hard-boiled egg and opened a twist of waxed paper that held a little pile of salt and pepper. She dipped the egg into the seasonings and took a bite.

Buddy scampered out of the tree, snatched a bit of crust, and ran back.

"That's so cute," Faye said. "Is he tame?"

"I don't know," Izzy said then added, "He'll eat peanuts from Stan's hand, though. So he must be."

Faye sighed, "I'd eat peanuts from Stan's hand. He's so gentle."

Izzy chewed her sandwich in silence.

"I know there's a lot of talk about me," Faye said quietly. She waited for a second before asking, "What exactly are they saying?"

Izzy took a sip of milk. She squinted up at the tree, wishing Buddy would return so she could pretend to be distracted and not answer. He did not, and Faye was waiting. "They think you're pregnant and everyone is wondering what you'll do." She hurried to add, "I didn't tell anyone, Faye. Honest I didn't."

"I know, kid. It's not the kind of thing anyone can hide for long."

Izzy felt so tense she thought her ears must be twitching.

Faye finished her egg and wiped her lips. "I'm thinking about putting the baby up for adoption," she said the words in a flat voice, without feeling or expression.

The announcement seemed to stop the world in its tracks, and for a second everything was still. Then Buddy crept slowly down the tree trunk, his beautiful fluffy tail waving behind. He reached the table and sat on his haunches while he looked over the crusts.

A tiny sob broke from Faye. She dropped her head onto her folded arms and cried quietly.

Buddy dropped the bit of bread he held and turned his bright eyes to Faye. He watched for a few seconds. Izzy could see his heart pulsing in his chest. He cocked his head to one side then the other, never taking his eyes away from the weeping girl. Izzy held her breath as the squirrel cautiously made his way over the table. He stretched out his tiny paw and placed it on Faye's shoulder. She raised her head an inch, and for a second the two of them looked at each other. Buddy then turned in a swirl of brown and gray fur and scurried back to eat another bite of crust.

"Did you see that?" whispered Faye, still looking at the squirrel.

Izzy blinked. "Stan's not the only gentle one around."

Faye blew her nose on a napkin. Izzy threw away their trash and refolded the paper sacks.

Both girls kept their focus on their work through the rest of the day. Faye ignored the glances and stares aimed at her. Izzy ground her teeth to keep herself from yelling, "What the hell do you think you're looking at?" They sewed through the afternoon break and past the quitting time buzzer. As soon as the room had emptied, they put their work away.

Stan waited for them at the lockers. He tilted his head down to look into Faye's face. "Rough day? Maybe I need to call a meeting and put a stop to the gossip."

Faye's lips twisted into a little smile. "When has that ever worked?"

Stan sighed. "Yeah, you're right."

"They'll lose interest eventually. They always do," she mumbled.

"They'll lose interest sooner if Izzy will stop giving them all dirty looks," Stan added.

Izzy stopped. "Me? What'd I do?"

"Oh nothing much, just behaved like a well-trained junkyard dog."

"I have not!" Izzy said.

"Every time you give someone that eat-dirt-and-die look, it convinces them there's a lot more to the story," Stan's raised voice echoed in the empty hallway. He and Izzy squared off, his angry face darkened. Izzy throbbed with indignation. She opened her mouth to vent her feelings, but Faye stepped between the two.

"Stop! She's only trying to protect me," she said to Stan, who didn't take his glare off Izzy. Then Faye turned to the Izzy. "But he's right. I know you're standing up for me, but it would be better if you'd ignore them."

Izzy wasn't convinced. "Bunch of nosy snoops! I'd like to slap every one of them."

"And I appreciate that," Faye put in. "Believe me, I'd be happy to hold your smock while you did it. But it's not really their fault. You can't blame a crowd for gawking at a train wreck."

The truth of the statement settled over the combatants and they each stepped back.

Stan spoke first. "I apologize, Izzy. I guess I took out my annoyance on you. I'm sorry."

She didn't want to let go of her anger. Of all the emotions tumbling through her, anger felt the safest. But Faye's eyes were pleading. "Okay," Izzy said.

Seated in the back seat of Stan's car, Izzy tried hard not to pout. She stared out the passenger side window without seeing anything. Faye talked about the doctor's appointment she had the next week and how much she liked her room.

The car slowed as they approached the house. A pink convertible sat in the driveway and Mrs. Call paced at the front door. Izzy groaned.

"Who's that?" asked Stan. He parked the car.

"It's Mrs. Call, the landlady," Izzy replied. "What does she want now?" She climbed out of the car and hurried to the porch.

The woman set her fists on her hips and tapped one foot. "Where's your mother?" she demanded.

Izzy glanced over her shoulder to see if the others had heard. They were still in the car. "At work. Why? What's wrong?"

"The rent, that's what," Mrs. Call fanned her damp face with her handbag. "I assume you'll be out by Friday."

The air left Izzy's lungs in one breath. She stared for a second before saying, "But I, I mean, *she* paid last Friday."

"Hunh!" Mrs. Call sneered.

"She did, she told me," Izzy rushed on. "She went to your house and you weren't there. Puddin' answered the door and Willa gave her cash."

"Puddin' took cash?" Mrs. Call asked skeptically. "She wouldn't. She knows she can't take money from the renters."

"But she did," Izzy protested. "Willa told me she put two twenties in an old valentine envelope and told Puddin' to be sure you got it."

Mrs. Call narrowed her eyes. "Well, somebody is lying then." She looked Izzy up and down. "But it still comes out the same. I didn't get the rent last Friday, so you, your sister, and your mother are out!"

"What's the problem?" Stan's calm voice asked. He and Faye had just reached the porch.

"Who the hell are you?" demanded Mrs. Call, sizing him up as she spoke.

Stan, who had several years' experience dealing with irate women, stood a little taller. "Never mind who I am. What do you want?"

"Rent," Izzy said. "I paid it, I mean it was paid last Friday and she says she didn't get it."

"How much is it?" asked Stan reaching for his wallet.

"It's gone up," Mrs. Call said with a gleam in her eye. "Fifty dollars a month."

"You said forty-five," Izzy argued.

The woman put on her dark glasses before replying. "That was before I knew about the sugar daddy," she smirked.

"The what?" Izzy was flummoxed.

"Forget it," Stan said and placed five ten dollar bills in Mrs. Call's hand. "We want a receipt," he added.

"Fine." Mrs. Call took a receipt book and pen from her purse and used her teeth to pull off her glove. She filled out the form and tore it out of the book for Izzy. She hesitated, "Do I give this to you, or your boyfriend?" The smirk looked like it was going to be permanent.

Stan grabbed the paper and handed it to Izzy. "Fifty dollars due the first of the month?" he asked.

Mrs. Call tugged on her glove and reached up to pat his cheek. "Unless you want to make other arrangements, honey." She lowered her sunglasses and winked.

"Good-bye, Mrs. Call," Stan said finality in his voice. The woman shrugged a shoulder and walked to her car.

The front door was unlocked, and Ann had opened all the windows before she went to babysit. Even with the airing, the house was stifling. Faye excused herself and went to her room.

"I did pay that rent!" Izzy insisted.

Stan folded his arms over his chest. "I believe you, Izzy. Mrs. Call is clearly a hustler."

"But she lied!" Izzy took the jug of ice water out of the fridge and slammed the door shut.

"She lied because she knew you couldn't prove anything," Stan explained. "That's how she operates." He got three glasses from the cupboard and took the jug.

"But," Izzy dropped into a chair and Stan handed her a drink, "I don't know when I'll be able to pay you back."

He didn't look up, just sipped his water and studied the linoleum.

Faye entered the kitchen and handed Stan a fifty-dollar bill. "Thanks," she said and took a seat at the table.

Izzy, who had never seen a fifty-dollar bill before, gazed at Faye in wonder. Before she could comment, Faye spoke, "Let's call it the first month's rent and a deposit on the room."

"Shouldn't you save it for the baby?" Izzy asked.

Faye picked up the third glass of water and took a drink before replying. "I've been saving money for more than three years." She looked down at her lap. "You're helping me out. Let me return the favor."

Stan pocketed the money. "Okay, we're all square," he said.

"We are not all square! You're the only one who's square!" Izzy answered angrily. "Mrs. Call has ninety dollars for one month's rent, Faye is out by at least twenty-five, or more like thirty since the rent was only supposed to be forty! We've been had!"

"So you've been had," Stan snapped, "now you know better! Just grow-up for cryin' out loud!" He rose and put his glass in the sink.

His words smacked Izzy in the face. Every fiber of her body wanted to scream, "Go to hell!" The injustice of it boiled in her gut. She was rigid with suppressed fury. If she opened her mouth at this point, she felt certain she would explode.

Stan glared and Faye looked worried.

The back door swung open and Ann and Jill bounced into the room. "Guess what?" Ann asked with a huge grin. Jill couldn't wait and screamed, "Ann is secretary of the sophomore class!" Squealing, the two girls grabbed each other by the shoulders and jumped up and down.

Chapter Twenty-One

"Congratulations!" Faye said.

"Way to go!" Stan added.

Something snapped in Izzy's brain. Her mind went blank.

Ann gave her a quick hug and opened the fridge. "Don't we have anything to drink?" She scanned the near empty shelves.

"Cold water," Faye offered, nudging the jug.

"Let's go to my place," Jill suggested. "There's always something there." The girls flew out the door.

Izzy's eyes and ears stopped functioning. She heard the slap of the screen door like it was a block away. Her periphery vision held a blurred picture of the kitchen, but she saw nothing in front of her. Her eyesight had retreated and turned inward, the way it did when she was thinking very hard. She felt herself push back her chair and stand. The next thing she knew, she was crouching in the stifling blackness of the clothes closet in her bedroom. Someone opened and closed cupboards in the kitchen. There was a murmur of voices, the scrape of chair legs on linoleum, and soon after a car engine turned over. The house was silent.

She wanted to sleep. Curled into the corner, she let the solid walls hold her. Her eyelids dropped, and she gave herself over to the silence.

When she awoke her hair was stuck to her face and neck, her shoulder ached, and her legs were cramped. Slowly peeling herself off the wall, she straightened her legs, and blood flowed to her feet once more. Wiping her face with her shirttail, she blinked the stinging sweat out of her eyes and felt for the door. She took a deep breath of the cooler air in the bedroom. It was late. Everything in the room looked gray in the twilight. She heard someone in the kitchen and smelled food cooking. Izzy unbuttoned her shirt and put on her bathrobe before removing her shoes and jeans. She found clean underwear in the dresser and tiptoed into the bathroom.

The tepid water of the shower sprinkling over her skin revived her. She shampooed her hair and lathered away every trace of sweat from her body. Turning the knobs, she adjusted the water temperature until the shower was as cool as a summer rain.

Her mind occupied itself burying all the things she couldn't think about anymore. She kept her surface thoughts busy with what didn't matter: television, food, clothes, and finally gossip. Thoroughly chilled, she turned off the shower and dried herself. She put on her bathrobe and wrapped her hair in a towel.

There was a tap at the door. Faye called. "Are you hungry Izzy? I made dinner."

"Starving," she said and opened the door.

The kitchen table was set for three. Izzy looked in amazement at fried chicken, mashed potatoes, milk-gravy, green beans cooked with bacon and onion, and warm biscuits. Fruit salad nestled in a lettuce leaf on each plate and a little dish of jam for the biscuits glistened next to the butter.

"Where did this come from?" she asked.

Faye took a seat and began serving. "Stan took me to the grocery. I hope you don't mind."

Izzy dropped into a chair. "No," she said, "I don't mind." She took a bite of salad. "Mmmm," she said. "I can't believe your dad would make you leave. I'd keep you around even if you'd murdered someone."

Faye looked startled and put down her fork.

Izzy saw her stricken face and exclaimed, "Oh, damn! Faye, I didn't mean that. I'm sorry."

Forcing a smile, Faye made a little shrug. "It's okay, kid. You meant it for a compliment." She cleared her throat. "But maybe the less said about my family the better."

Izzy nodded. "Sure."

They chatted about groceries and work. Faye had loaded the cupboards and fridge with essentials and extras. Izzy asked her how much it all cost.

"Well, we needed everything so I stocked up. I bought flour, sugar, canned veggies and fruit, some spices, ketchup, that kind of stuff. It wasn't terribly expensive."

Noting the extra place setting, Izzy said, "Ann will probably eat at Jill's house."

Faye blushed a little. "I didn't set it for Ann."

"Oh? Who's coming over?" Izzy took a mouthful of potatoes with gravy.

"I invited Stan," Faye began. "He said he had to run an errand but he should be here any minute."

The food in Izzy's stomach gathered into a solid mass.

"I should have asked you before I invited him." Faye shifted in her chair.

"It's okay," Izzy said. "You live here; you should be able to have someone over for dinner, especially since you paid for it and cooked it." She tried to smile, but it was a failed attempt. Offhand, she couldn't think of anyone she wanted to see less than Stan, not even Sid. No, she corrected herself; it would be a tie between the two of them.

Faye pushed her food around her plate with a fork. Izzy sensed that she was working up to something. She watched and waited.

Neatly slicing a biscuit in half, Faye spread it with butter and a spoonful of jam. Instead of eating it, she set it on the side of her plate and looked up. "Izzy," she said, "I have to ask you something."

The mass in Izzy's stomach felt like a brick. "Okay," she said cautiously. "Go ahead."

"That landlady said you and Ann and your mother would have to leave," Faye said.

"Yeah, so?" Izzy's brain tried to recreate the earlier incident in her mind.

"Didn't you tell me your mother died?"

"That's right." Izzy busied herself, cutting into a piece of chicken. She laughed awkwardly. "Mrs. Call doesn't know that. See, we were afraid she wouldn't rent to a couple of girls, so I pretended to be my mother on the phone. So far she hasn't figured it out."

Faye looked dubious but didn't pursue the topic.

Stan rapped on the screen door.

"Come in," called Izzy, pretending she didn't care she was in a bathrobe and had her hair wrapped in a towel.

"I can't," he answered, "Could you get the door for me?"

Faye jumped up to help. Stan carried a square pink bakery box in one hand and a vase of white rose buds in the other.

"What's all this?" Faye's eyes sparkled.

He held out the box. "This is dessert," he said. "And this," he indicated the flowers, "is for—"

Izzy had seen enough. She picked up her plate and utensils, "Excuse me," she said and hurried back to her room.

She finished her dinner sitting on the bedroom floor. Muffled voices, the quiet clatter of plates, forks, and spoons came through the closed door.

What is wrong with me? She wondered. *First I'm angry because he hasn't offered to marry her, and then I'm angry because he does something sweet.* She jerked the towel from her head and got out the hair curlers. Standing in front of the dresser mirror, she rolled her hair, pinned it in place, and covered it with a net.

It was after nine. She wanted to read, but her book was in the kitchen with Stan and Faye. She flipped back the covers on the bed, climbed in and turned off the lamp.

Trapped! She thought. *I'm a prisoner in my own damn house!* Somewhere on the street a radio blared. Mick Jagger sang about not getting satisfaction. *Well, join the club, Mick!* This was followed by local news and an ad for tires. Gary Lewis and the Playboys crooned, "Save Your Heart for Me." Izzy turned onto her stomach in an effort to find a spot where fewer hairpins stabbed into her scalp. Before Tom Jones could finish his musical inquiry "What's New Pussycat?" she fell asleep.

Chapter Twenty-Two

"Izzy?" Ann whispered and poked her arm. "Hey, wake up."

Forcing her eyes open, Izzy squinted at the luminous dial on the clock. It was after midnight. "What's the matter?" she mumbled.

Her sister turned on the lamp. "Look!" she said.

Izzy turned to see her. Ann sat on her side of the bed. Her light brown hair had been cut. Where it had hung in scraggly twists just touching her shoulders, it now fit her head like a cap. It couldn't have been more than a couple of inches long and framed her delicate features perfectly. Her lovely long neck looked as graceful as a swan's.

"Do you like it?" Ann asked.

Izzy hesitated. Her sister looked pretty, even stunning, but she didn't look like herself. Izzy shook her head, "What did you do?" she asked.

Ann's smile slipped. "Mrs. Kimball cut it for me. She has a beauty shop in her house. Don't you like it?"

Izzy shrugged. "It's okay," she said and turned her back. "It'll grow."

The lamp went dark. Ann moved around the room as she got into a nightgown. She lay on the bed and gave the covers a tug when she turned over.

Izzy's eyes stayed open. She felt stingy and mean. Ann looked great; she had a friend and was apparently popular enough to be a class officer. Skinny, quiet, capable, plain Ann had changed. Over the years they had argued, they got on each other's nerves, a few times they hadn't spoken to each other for a day or two, but never before had Izzy felt that she could resent her sister.

※

Sun rays sliced into the early morning kitchen. Faye fixed bacon and eggs for breakfast. Izzy did her part and made toast.

The vase of white roses sat in the middle of the table.

"Why did you run off last night?" Faye asked.

Izzy stared at her plate. She didn't answer; instead she picked up the ketchup bottle and shook some over her eggs.

"I thought you liked Stan," Faye said.

"Yeah, I thought I did, too," Izzy replied.

Faye pushed the conversation on, "What happened?"

Izzy looked directly at Faye for a second before answering, "I guess I didn't really know him." She finished her breakfast and washed her dishes.

Faye filled a pie plate with eggs, bacon, and toast, then she covered it with foil and placed it in the oven set on Warm. "I'll leave a note for Ann so she'll know her breakfast is in the oven."

"You don't need to do that," Izzy said. "Ann can fix her own food."

"It was just as easy to make enough for her, too," Faye pointed out.

"She's not a baby," snapped Izzy. "She can take care of herself."

Izzy went into the bathroom to brush her teeth. The toothpaste was almost gone. She rolled the tube and pressed it with the heel of her hand to get out the last bit. Ann would have to use baking soda today. The twinge of satisfaction this gave Izzy was not completely overshadowed by shame.

Stan honked his horn in the driveway. Izzy rinsed her mouth and dried her lips on a towel. Picking up the tube of white lipstick, she painted out her mouth and added another heavy coat of mascara to her black-lined eyes. A sense of power surged in her chest. Change was in the air and she was going to be part of it.

Faye and Stan exchanged looks when they saw Izzy. The radio played as they rode to work; Izzy stared out the window sullenly. Once inside the break room, she bought a cup of coffee and drank it black. The bitterness resonated with her mood.

Marti and Betty watched her. "When did you switch to bean brew?" Marti asked.

"Just now. You got a problem with that?" Izzy took another gulp.

"Not me." Marti put up a hand. "You want a smoke to go with it?" She extended her pack.

"Marti, leave her alone," Betty said.

"Mind your own business, Betty," Izzy said with frost on every syllable. She took a cigarette and defiantly placed it between her lips. Marti tossed a book of matches to her and sat back to watch with a crooked smile.

The first match bent in half, the second wouldn't light. The third one flared, and Izzy held it to the cigarette, but it didn't light and she had to shake out the match to keep from burning her fingers.

"You have to suck in," Marti said.

Izzy lit another match and touched it to the tobacco as she drew in her breath. Her mouth filled with smoke, and she blew it out before it reached her throat. Marti chuckled, and Betty shook her head. The buzzer sounded as Stan walked up to the table. Everyone finished their coffee, gathered up trash, and headed for the production room. Except for Izzy. She took another superficial puff on the cigarette and met Stan's glare head on. His hand darted out, snatched the cigarette from her mouth and dropped it into her unfinished coffee.

"I knew the first day you would need looking after," he said, "but I didn't think it was going to be a full-time job."

Izzy held her temper. "Is there anything wrong with my work?" she asked calmly.

"Not at all. Your work is good, almost excellent I'd say."

"Then you can stop looking after me." She threw away the coffee and put on her smock. "That should free up some time you can use somewhere else."

It turned out to be a lousy day. She sewed on bright striped fabric that gave her a horrible headache. Caffeine from the coffee she drank crept just beneath the surface of her skin so that it felt like bugs crawling over her. Curious looks from around the room were now divided between her and Faye. The only highlight was lunch. Faye had packed leftover chicken, biscuits, and the fruit salad. Izzy drank milk, and the coffee jitters wore off. She turned down a second cigarette. "I don't think I'm cut out to smoke," she said.

"You still haven't tried it. That wasn't smoking you did this morning," Marti said. "But to each her own."

"Maybe you should try chewing tobacco," Betty suggested. "Or snuff." Her tone was cool.

"Too much spitting and sneezing. I'm thinking of hard liquor," Izzy replied. "Or pot." She left the table and walked to the Ladies Room.

Izzy despised her reflection in the mirror. The mask of make-up looked hard and brittle. She imagined her face breaking into thousands of tiny glass shards, like an exploding Christmas ornament painted black and white. She scoured away the lipstick until her lips were raw and returned to her sewing.

Stan, Faye, and Izzy were the last to leave work. The afternoon was a perfect mix of end-of-summer warmth and autumn sweetness. Izzy straggled a few feet behind the others; her head was down as she watched shadows on the pavement.

"Isn't that Paul?" Faye asked.

Izzy looked up sharply. Paul's car was parked next to Stan's. Paul leaned against the hood. He grinned when he saw her. Izzy's face melted into a smile. Surprise and pleasant gratification ran through her. She hurried to him.

"What are you doing here?" she asked.

"I came to get you," he said.

Faye introduced Stan to Paul. "I'll see you at home," Faye said.

Izzy nodded.

Paul held the car door open for her, and she slid across the seat. He drove to the A&W and parked in a shady spot. "Want a root beer?" he asked. A carhop skated over and placed a plastic card on the windshield. She offered a menu, but Paul ignored it. "Two large root beers and an order of fries," he said. The girl scribbled on a notepad and rolled away.

A river bordered one side of the drive-in, and the breeze picked up the coolness of the water. Paul slid his right arm on the seat back behind Izzy. He smiled teasingly and touched her cheek. "Return of the panda?" he asked, looking at her eyes.

Izzy blushed. "Not a return, just passing through." She ducked her head. "I don't know what I was thinking this morning."

Paul's hand brushed her shoulder. "You're always pretty." The compliment felt like rain on a desert. She drank it in.

The radio played a local station. "It is 4:15, time for High School Report Cards," the deejay announced. "First up we have Janna Prescott from Harmony High right here in town."

A very enthusiastic, high-pitched voice began nervously reading. "Yesterday seniors, juniors and sophomores elected their class officers. Here are the results." She read so quickly the names ran together. Except for the last one, "Ann Gardner is secretary of the sophomore class." Izzy shut off the radio.

The carhop snapped a full tray to the window without spilling a drop. Paul handed her a dollar and told her to keep the change.

"That's great about Ann," he said as he handed a mug to Izzy.

"I guess."

He placed the basket of fries between them and opened the glove compartment to provide a tray for Izzy's drink. "Aren't you proud of her?"

Izzy squeezed ketchup the length of a hot French fry. "Sure." She nibbled the fry and sipped her root beer. She decorated another fry, this time with a zigzag pattern.

"That's cool," Paul said. "Do you write on all your food before you eat it?"

"No, only the ones that come with squeezy condiments. I'll do one for you." She selected a large fry and wrote P A U L on it in small, glistening letters.

Paul laughed and ate it. "Very good. You handle that bottle like a pro. Ever work in a bakery?"

Izzy tossed her head. "I don't do icing," she said with disdain. "Ketchup is my medium of choice."

"Ahhh, of course. Ketchup, the fifth food group."

Izzy made candy cane stripes on another fry and handed it to him. "You learn that in college?" she asked.

He was still chewing and couldn't answer. A red blob clung to his lip. She dabbed it with a napkin and held it up to show him. He caught her hand and pretended to smear the napkin on her chin. A funny chill ran up her arm. She attempted to free her hand. "Ewww," she said, "yuck!" She made a face. Paul wiped her chin with his finger. Her pulse quickened in the same instant that she stopped breathing. She knew what would happen next and raised her face. Paul's hand stroked the back of her neck. She closed her eyes. Their lips touched, and this time they lingered.

"Ahem!"

They broke apart. A middle aged man with a stack of dirty trays stood at the car door. He wore a paper hat, and a stained apron covered his clothes. His name tag said Manager.

"This isn't lover's lane, kids. We've got nice families here. They only want something to eat or drink. We don't give 'em a show."

Paul placed the mugs and basket on the tray, and the manager lifted it off the window. He removed the plastic card from the windshield. He glanced around to see if anyone was watching, then he reached into his pocket and handed Paul a dollar. "Here's a refund. Next time, wait till after dark." He winked and walked away.

"Izzy?" Paul turned on the engine and looked at her over his shoulder.

"What?" she asked.

"How long before sunset?"

She punched his arm. But just lightly.

Chapter Twenty-Three

Stan's car was in the driveway, and a telephone company van was parked in the street when they drove up. Paul stopped on the other side of the street. "What's going on?"

"No idea," Izzy said. "It can't be a repair; we don't have a phone."

A uniformed man carrying a toolbox came out of the house. Stan was with him and signed papers on a clip board before going back inside.

"Looks like you might have one now," Paul said. "Come on, let's find out. I want to get your number."

A red telephone with a very long cord hung on the wall in the kitchen. Stan was talking on it, ordering pizza. Faye hurried up to Izzy and Paul. "It's a late birthday present!" she cried. "Stan said I had to have a phone for emergencies. He paid for everything!"

"Wow!" exclaimed Paul, "That's great. No more just showing up, I can call ahead."

"Is he going to pay the bill every month?" Izzy asked churlishly.

Faye, ignoring the tone in her voice, answered happily, "It's only $8.00. I'll take care of it."

Stan hung up the receiver. "Hope everybody likes pepperoni or sausage. I got a large of each. There's plenty if you want to stay, Paul."

Izzy grabbed Stan's shirt sleeve and pulled him toward the back door. "Excuse us for a minute," she said and dragged him out to the driveway. "Hey," she whispered through clenched teeth, "what do you think you're doing?" She didn't wait for a reply. "This is not your house! You can't just install telephones and invite people to dinner and walk around like you own the place!"

Stan's eyebrows drew together in a frown. He studied her face for a few seconds. "Isabel," he said calmly, "why don't you tell me what is really wrong?"

"I just did."

"No, there's something else. Something has changed in the last week and you're upset. So, what is it?"

She pressed the heels of her palms into her eyes. "Nothing! Everything!" she shouted. "None of your business!" She turned her back to him.

He stepped around in front of her. "Okay, but why won't you let me be nice to you."

"You mean Faye, don't you? It's not me you're being nice to. You've been running around like Sir Galahad rescuing damsels in distress. Between moving people in and paying rent, rides to work and the store, bringing dessert and flowers, and now a telephone! Why don't you just solve everything and marry her?"

Stan looked like he'd been sucker punched. He leaned forward and braced his hands on his thighs while he caught his breath. When he looked up, his face was calm, mouth firm, but his eyes burned into her. "Because I don't love her," he said quietly.

Izzy could not have been more shocked if he'd claimed to be from another planet. A movement at the kitchen window caught her eye. Faye moved out of sight. Izzy's gaze turned back to Stan. His expression was sad, yet sweet. Her own eyes narrowed. "You make me sick!" she said. Pushing past him, she strode into the house.

"Everything okay?" Paul asked. He and Faye had set the table.

"Just groovy," Izzy muttered. She grabbed a loaf of bread and a jar of peanut butter from the cupboard.

"The pizza will be here any minute," Faye said.

"I don't feel like pizza." The bread tore when Izzy spread the peanut butter. She patched it the best she could and added jam.

Stan came in. He stood by the door watching her. Paul put ice in the glasses, and Faye filled them with punch. A knock sounded from the front door, and Stan answered it. He paid for the pizzas and carried them in to the kitchen.

Izzy placed her sandwich on a plate, picked up a glass of punch, and carried everything to the back porch.

The yeasty smell of fresh baked crust, sweet tomato sauce, and spicy sausage made her mouth water. She picked at her sandwich with less enthusiasm than she would have shown for picking at a scab. Setting the plate on the step below, she hunched over and rested her chin on her knees. Exhaustion consumed her. She longed to sleep; no that wasn't right; she wanted oblivion. That was the word—to fade into darkness and just not be anymore, to disappear and stop existing. Just thinking about it filled her brain with a foggy numbness.

She imagined how she looked, sitting on the step, collapsed like a child's punching toy that couldn't snap upright for another pummeling. Then she noticed a tiny train of ants that had discovered her discarded sandwich. They crept over the plate rim and gathered near the crust, picking and tasting. Finally they began the process of dismantling. Hoisting crumbs over their heads they started the long trek back to their colony. Izzy studied them until her neck was stiff and her back ached, but still she didn't move.

The screen door creaked open and someone sat beside her. She knew it was Paul without looking. She felt him watching the ants with her.

After several minutes, he asked, "Which are you, Izzy? The sandwich or the ants?"

Turning her head toward him without sitting up, she replied, "What do you mean?"

"Are you the sandwich under attack, or are you the ants taking on a huge task to survive?"

She considered the question before answering. "I don't know. Maybe I'm both," she paused, "You taking psychology this term?"

"Was it something I said?"

"Yes, Sigmund, it was." She sighed. "I'm too tired for analysis."

"You're not tired; you're discouraged." Paul took her hand in his. "We'll skip the analysis, but I do have a prescription for you."

"Thank heaven for medication!" she said.

"It's not exactly a pill—it's a bowling ball."

Surprised, Izzy sat up and chuckled. "I'll need a lot of water to swallow that!"

Paul stood and pulled her to her feet. "Very funny, I think it's working already."

Izzy shook her head. "I don't like bowling," she said.

"How could you not like bowling?" he challenged, "What other sport wears a blister on your thumb and gives you the chance to share ugly, sweaty shoes with strangers?"

She thought for a second, "Golf, maybe?"

"Come on. We'll invite Faye and Stan. It'll be fun."

"No," she spoke sharply. "Why don't we take Jill and Ann instead or maybe the twins?"

Paul was quiet.

"I'll just change my clothes; you can use the new phone to call your house." Rising onto her toes, she kissed his cheek.

Izzy put on a clean shirt and found a pair of socks without holes in them. She brushed out her hair and pinned it up again and took care of the worst of the dark smudges around her eyes. Jamming a couple of dollar bills into her pocket, she went back to the kitchen.

"Ann and Jill have homework," Paul said. "Stan had to leave, so I asked Faye to come along. Okay?"

"Where is she?" asked Izzy.

He nodded toward Faye's room. "You don't mind do you?"

Izzy smiled up at him. "Of course not. It'll be fun."

The three of them rode in the front seat of Paul's car. Neon lights from theaters, shops, and restaurants played rainbow colors over their faces. The town looked very different in the dusk. College kids back for the new school year filled the sidewalks and lined up for movie tickets. It felt like a holiday to Izzy.

Lucky Lanes had one of the best signs. White neon bowling pins trembled while a blue ball rolled toward them by means of a relay of blue circles. The ball reached the pins, and they exploded into red shards. Then the letters that made up Lucky Lanes flashed in red, white, and blue. The whole place looked like a carnival.

Inside, the lights were dim except over the lanes. A low rumbling sound, punctuated by the satisfying crack and clunk of falling pins, competed with the squeak of shoes on polished wood and sporadic cheers and moans. The place smelled of floor wax, stale smoke, beer, and French fries.

Faye and Izzy followed Paul to the rental counter and gave their shoe sizes to the employee. Paul picked up a score sheet and pencil.

"Lane one is open," the employee pointed with his middle finger. "Pick out a ball from the racks." He returned to spraying shoes with disinfectant.

They found seats and changed their shoes. "You two bowl very much?" Paul asked.

Izzy shook her head.

"I used to substitute for a league from work," Faye spoke over the noise. "I wasn't very good."

Paul stretched his legs and admired his rental shoes. "We'll just bowl for fun. We have to keep score so they can see how many games we play, but no one's going to check our numbers."

"That sounds good," Faye said. "Come on, Izzy, I'll help you pick out a ball."

Paul bowled strike after strike with an occasional spare. Faye was good, too. She didn't knock down all the pins as often as Paul, but her score was respectable. Izzy kept the gutters warm. The bowling pins seemed to relax when it was her turn. Paul's coaching was not as helpful as Faye's advice. It was difficult to pay attention when Paul's arms were around her as he demonstrated the right way to hold the ball. His British Sterling cologne was subtly fragrant and his lips almost brushed her ear as he tried to be heard over the noise. She pulled herself together, and after some practice she knocked down a few pins.

"There you go!" Paul cheered. "Keep it up; I'll get us some drinks. Cokes okay?"

"Sure," Faye said. Izzy nodded and turned her attention to the game. She approached the lane, arcing the ball back then forward. She rolled it onto the boards without an embarrassing loft and thud. It sped down the polished wood, and Izzy held her breath. The ball gained speed and crashed squarely into the pins, knocking them in every direction.

Faye jumped up from her seat. "You did it Izzy! You got a spare!" She threw her arms around Izzy.

"I can't believe it!" Izzy shouted. "Where's Paul? Oh, I wish he'd seen it!"

"I'll vouch for you if you need a witness," said a familiar voice.

Izzy turned and her heart hit the floor. Sid was standing in the next lane. He waggled a bottle of beer at her.

"What are you doing here?" Izzy asked.

"It's a free country," Sid replied. He looked Faye over. "Who's your friend?"

Izzy took a step to block his view. "She's my roommate."

Sid showed one of his smarmier smiles. "How you doin'? I'm Sid," he said and extended a hand.

Faye shook the hand briefly. "I'm Faye," she murmured.

Sid's eyes shifted back to Izzy. "I wonder if you'd excuse us for a minute Faye. I need to talk to . . ." he hesitated, his eyes boring into Izzy, "your friend here," he finished.

"I'll find Paul," Faye said and hurried away.

"I don't have anything to say to you." Izzy tried to sound confident, but her voice shook a little.

"Yeah? Well I have a question for you, Brandy." He pointed to the score sheet. "Why is everyone calling you Izzy?"

She stared and gulped. "It's a . . . a nickname."

Sid's face darkened. "Izzy is a nickname for Brandy? I doubt it." He clutched her arm. "What's going on here?"

"Nothing! Let go!" She jerked her arm and he tightened his hold. Izzy swung her free hand and struck his face with a satisfying slap. The beer bottle smashed on the floor. Sid grabbed her arms with both hands. Frantically she looked for Paul and Faye and glimpsed them talking by the snack bar.

"You think you're pretty smart," Sid snarled, his eye watering next to the print of her hand. "I'll get to the bottom of this. You and me got some unfinished business." He let go and headed for the exit.

Izzy's legs wobbled. She grabbed a chair to steady herself. The lanes near her were quiet; she felt the stares from around the room. She bent to pick up the pieces of glass. The guy from the shoe rental counter approached with a bucket and mop to clean away the puddle of beer. Paul and Faye were right behind him.

"Who was that?" Paul asked.

Faye touched Izzy's shoulder. "You okay kid?"

Izzy made herself smile. "Just a guy I used to know. No one important. I'm fine."

"What did he want?" Faye looked unconvinced.

"To make trouble," Izzy said. "Excuse me; I need to wash my hands." She dropped the broken bottle in a trash can and looked around for a Ladies Room.

"Come on," Faye said, "I'll show you where."

Inside the restroom, Izzy soaped her hands.

Faye took a comb from the back pocket of her jeans and touched up her hair. Speaking to Izzy's reflection in the mirror she said, "If I were superstitious, I'd think you must have walked under a ladder."

Izzy's forehead wrinkled. "What do you mean?"

"Bad luck. Your life seems to go from one drama to the next."

Izzy shook her hands over the sink and pulled a paper towel from the dispenser. "Says the unwed mother?" She regretted the words immediately. Faye's face blanched and turned crimson.

"Darn," Izzy said. "I didn't mean that, Faye."

"Sure you did," Faye answered flatly. "I don't blame you."

"It was a crappy thing to say," insisted Izzy. "I'm really sorry." Her throat constricted the tip of her nose began to itch and she tasted salt in the back of her throat.

Faye was already crying. She grabbed a paper towel and pressed it to the corners of her eyes. "I can't defend myself, and you know it."

Izzy felt sick, like she'd caught a rodent in a trap and then realized it was Minnie Mouse. There she was in her little red polka-dot skirt and white ruffled bloomers, tiny high heels kicking, black X's over her eyes. Cruelty wasn't really part of who Izzy was. The tears poised on her eyelids spilled over.

"Oh, Faye, I'm so sorry, please forgive me. I don't have any right to criticize you." She made herself continue. "I'm so messed up."

Faye opened her arms and enfolded Izzy in a hug. They cried together for a minute, then blew their noses on toilet paper squares. Their eyes looked bloodshot in the mirror. "Wish I had my purse," Faye said. "I carry Murine Eye Drops with me all the time these days."

"Paul's going to think we took the bus home," Izzy said, glancing at the clock on the wall. "We should get out there."

Faye nodded. "But Izzy, we do need to talk later. I want to help anyway I can."

"Me, too. I mean, I want to help you, too."

They shared a quick squeeze. Something lifted in Izzy's heart. The tension in her throat softened.

If Paul noticed they'd been gone a long time or that they'd been crying, he didn't mention it. He handed Izzy an icy cola. "Faye told me about the spare, but I'll have to see it for myself."

Setting aside the pop, she picked up her ball. "Prepare to be amazed," she said.

Concentrating on what she'd learned, she rolled the ball. Izzy didn't have much faith in miracles and she was just as amazed as everyone else when the ball slammed into the pocket and every pin dropped.

By the end of the game, Izzy's score was the same as her weight, a hundred and twelve, a big improvement since the first game when her score had been the same as her age.

Paul handed her a Band-Aid for the blister on her thumb. "You caught on quick. We'll come back soon to keep you in practice."

"Okay." Izzy grinned.

Faye finished tying her shoelaces and covered a big yawn with her hand. "Not on a work night for me. I could fall asleep right here."

They replaced their bowling balls in the racks and turned in their shoes. Paul paid the bill.

The night air smelled sweetly clean when they left the building and found the car. By the time they pulled out of the lot, Faye was asleep, her head resting on Izzy's shoulder.

Paul drove across the college campus on the way home. The school bells marked the hour. Ten o'clock. Students, their arms full of books, strolled in small clusters towards the dormitories. The classroom buildings were dark, and inside the large library with its arched windows and ivy draped facade, the lights went out room by room.

"You're awfully quiet," Paul said. "What are you thinking?"

Izzy pulled her attention back from the school. "Someday I want to be a student here," she said.

"Great! What's stopping you?"

She thought for a second before replying. "Let's see," she mused, "time, opportunity, money . . ." She ticked off each point on her fingers.

Paul took her hand in his. "Well, it's not a lack of intelligence, that's for sure. You're plenty smart."

She caught her breath. "You— you think I'm smart?"

He turned the car onto Main Street. "I don't think you're smart; I know you are. I don't date dumb girls. Talking to them is too much work."

Izzy considered this assessment. Paul, a college student nearly four years older than she was, thought she was intelligent. If she kept a diary, she would write this information on today's page in capital letters with stars and exclamation points. As it was, she looked up at Paul and said, "Thank you, I needed to hear that." He pressed his lips to her hand.

Faye stirred and opened her eyes when Paul stopped the car in the driveway. "Man, I am pooped." She reached for the door handle. "Thanks again, Paul," she said, stretching the words over a yawn.

Izzy made a move to follow her but Paul whispered in her ear, "Wait here, I'll just make sure she gets inside." He got out and walked Faye to the door. Izzy checked her face and hair in the rearview mirror. She looked tired, too.

Paul slid behind the steering wheel. Without speaking, he pulled her to him and kissed her. It was nice, but Izzy's mind was somewhere else. Back on that college campus, fat books heavy in her arms, filled with things she longed to know.

Paul hesitated and lifted his head. "Faye is nice, is she dating anyone?"

Izzy shook her head.

Then he whispered, "It's late. I have early classes tomorrow and you have work."

"That's true," she said.

He withdrew his arms and shifted to open the driver-side door. She allowed herself to be pulled from the car.

On the porch he kissed her one more time. "Can I pick you up after work tomorrow?"

"Yes, please," she answered. "Good night, thanks for teaching me to bowl."

"You're welcome," he answered. "I had a great time with you and Faye."

Izzy locked the door behind her and leaned against it. She heard his car start up and drive away. She went into the kitchen to check the time. Ann had pulled a chair next to the wall and was listening to someone on the phone, a slice of cold pizza in her hand.

"Kid, I know," she said into the receiver. "I mean, what's his beef?" She waved the pizza at Izzy. "Yeah, well we'll figure it out tomorrow. We have to start planning the Homecoming Dance, too. Can you believe it?" She listened, then snapped her fingers at Izzy, pointed to the fridge and pantomimed drinking.

Izzy poured her a glass of punch and placed it just out of reach in the living room. Ann stretched the phone cord as far as she could but only brushed the glass with her fingertips. She glared at her sister. "Okay," she said into the phone, "I've got to go. See you in the morning." She dropped the receiver onto the hook. "Why are you being such a jerk?" she asked Izzy.

Izzy tore a slice of pizza for herself. "Since when do I work for you?" she asked as she chewed. "Get your own dang drink."

"Thanks a heap," Ann said.

"You're welcome," returned Izzy. "Shouldn't you be in bed?"

Ann fumed. "Shouldn't you? Where do you get off sending me to bed? I'm the oldest, remember?"

Izzy tossed the crust from the pizza into the trash and rinsed her mouth at the sink. Wiping her chin with the back of her hand, she sized up her sister. "Oh, yeah. Guess I forgot. Stay up 'til dawn if you want."

"I will," Ann snapped. "And, by the way, the sophomore class officers are meeting here tomorrow afternoon, so maybe you could straighten the house when you get home from work."

"What? What about the babysitting job?" Izzy asked through clenched teeth.

Ann shrugged. "I have to cut back. Between class meetings and activities I have to attend, I don't have time to sit every day. Jill's going to go when I can't."

"Cut back?" Izzy said. "Uh-huh. You think we can afford that?"

"Don't let it worry you," Ann said coldly. "I won't ask you for anything." She went into the living room and turned on the television.

When did you ever have to ask? Izzy thought as she filled a cup with water, took two aspirin and went to bed. The pills stuck in her throat and dissolved into a bitter paste. She found a stick of spearmint flavored gum and chewed it to counter the bitter taste. When that didn't work, she decided to get a drink from the bathroom faucet. Before her feet hit the floor, the bedroom door swung open. It banged against the wall, leaving a dimple in the plaster. Ann flipped on the light and went to the closet, and jerked a blanket off the shelf. She snatched her pillow from the bed and left without a word. They didn't even make eye contact, yet Izzy felt like she had been slapped.

She made her way to the bathroom sink and drank. Back in bed, she pulled the covers close around herself. Voices from the TV murmured through the wall. She burrowed deeper into her pillow. Even snuggled in the blankets, she couldn't get warm.

Chapter Twenty-Four

Izzy swung a bowling ball with all her might and it rumbled down the lane. Ten pins, each with Sid's face, leered at her. Inches before it reached them, the ball burst into flames. When the smoke cleared, the ball was a pile of ashes and the pins laughed fiendishly, Izzy jerked awake.

Must have been that pizza slice, she thought drowsily. She flipped her pillow over and tugged the covers up. The events of the previous day sifted to the surface of her thoughts: the argument with Stan, the fight with Ann, the encounter with Sid. With a moan, she closed her eyes against the predawn light. She did not want to get up. Getting up was just an invitation for more trouble. But as much as she didn't want to get up, she didn't want to stay in bed. If she were in school, she would cut class. She couldn't call in sick to work because Stan would be coming by to pick her up, and he would see that she wasn't sick.

Her eyes flew open. Squinting at the alarm clock she saw that it was 5:30. Stan would be coming by in an hour. Well, that was one thing she could avoid. She leapt out of bed and scrambled into her clothes. She rushed through her hair and make-up and scribbled a note telling Faye she would see her at work. After cramming a comb, her work ID, and five dollars into her hip pocket, she mounted her bike and pedaled toward downtown.

The coffee shop wasn't open. Izzy peered through the windows. Ida was refilling salt and pepper shakers behind the counter. Izzy tapped on the glass. With a smile of recognition, the older woman came to the door and let her in.

"What're you doing out so early?" Ida ushered her to a seat at the counter.

"I'm hiding," Izzy said.

Ida frowned. "Is it that character from the pawnshop?" she asked. She set a glass of ice water in front of Izzy.

"He's only part of it," Izzy took a long drink.

"You had any breakfast?"

"Not yet."

Ida put up a finger and went to the kitchen. Izzy heard her talking to someone before she returned. "It'll be right up."

"But you're not open yet," Izzy protested.

Ida capped the salt and pepper shakers. She shrugged, "So the cook will postpone his third cup of coffee. We open in ten minutes anyway. Want orange or tomato juice? Or maybe coffee?"

Izzy chose tomato juice. Ida poured herself a coffee and a small glass of juice for Izzy. "Let's sit in the back." She led the way to a booth out of sight from the front of the café. "This way I can avoid any nasty looks from folks waiting to get in." She put sugar in her coffee and stirred. "I was at the bowling alley last night," she said casually.

Izzy choked a little on her juice. "You were? I didn't see you."

Ida sipped from her cup. "You had your hands full."

"For sure," Izzy said.

"You in over your head with this guy?"

"Yeah."

"Tell me about it," Ida invited. She pulled a couple of napkins from the dispenser and pressed them into Izzy's hand.

Izzy told everything that had happened. At least everything about Sid. She left out Willa and lying about her age to get a job.

By the time the bell rang signaling that the food was ready, Izzy was blinking back tears.

Ida patted her hand and went to pick up the order.

"Don't let that get cold," she said when she placed a plate of pancakes and ham in front of Izzy.

Izzy's empty stomach fluttered hungrily. She poured syrup and cut into the food.

Ida brought her a glass of milk and watched with her mouth drawn down at the corners and her forehead wrinkled. After a moment she spoke. "You could tell the police."

"No!" Izzy said, she took a gulp of milk. "I don't need them involved."

"Okay." Ida raised her eyebrows. She finished her coffee before continuing. "Who were those two with you last night?"

"The girl is Faye. She's a friend from work. She moved in with us. The guy is Paul. He's a college student. His little sister is friends with my sister, Ann."

"Very handsome kid," Ida said. "It looked like you two are close."

"We've been on a couple of dates. Well, last night was the second one. I think. He's in college." Izzy said. She would have said more, but Max yelled from the kitchen.

"Hey, Ida! We're open."

Ida slid out of the booth and adjusted her girdle. She held up a hand when Izzy tried to pay her. "Listen, I'm supposed to get a free breakfast every morning I work. I've been here thirty years and never have more than a cup of coffee. As far as I'm concerned, you can come in every day."

Izzy cleaned her plate and leaned against the back of the booth. With a full stomach she began to feel drowsy. She pushed the plate out of the way and rested her head on her folded arms. She'd close her eyes just for a minute. Maybe two… or five.

Someone touched Izzy's shoulder. "Hey there," Ida said. "Better wake up, sweetie."

Izzy forced her eyelids open. She sat up blinking. "Wha… where…"

Ida stood over her. "I got so busy; I forgot all about you back here. Come on, Max can watch the place while I drive you to work."

Looking around for a clock, Izzy asked, "What time is it?"

"It's ten after seven. Don't worry about your bike; I put it in the back room. You can pick it up later."

"Oh no! I'm already late!" Izzy followed Ida through the kitchen and out to the alley.

Ida opened the door on a '57 Chevy and gently pushed Izzy in. "Darn, I'm so sorry." The woman chewed at her lip and drove too fast through town. She punched the brakes when they reached the factory and Izzy nearly hit the dashboard. "Come for your bike anytime. It'll be safe at the café. Don't worry about it."

Impulsively, Izzy leaned over and kissed Ida's cheek. It felt soft and smelled of face powder.

Ida looked startled; she raised a hand and touched the spot.

"Ex—excuse me," Izzy stammered. "I don't know why I did that."

Ida's eyes looked moist, and she smiled. "Don't apologize honey. That was real nice." She cleared her throat. "You hurry along now."

Izzy closed the door and watched the car drive away. When she turned to enter the factory she saw Stan. He stood behind the glass doors and glared; he checked his watch and frowned at her.

"I'm late, I know," Izzy said before he could start. "I'll work through my breaks to make up the time. It won't happen again." She walked fast, and he kept up beside her. Neither of them said anything more. He left her at her locker and disappeared into the production area.

Izzy felt the furtive glances from the seamstresses when she made her way to her machine. She picked up her boxes and sat down to work. Faye was buried behind a wall of ruffled skirts. Izzy's box was full of romper fronts waiting for pleats. Normally she didn't mind pleats at all, but these were made up in linen which frayed like crazy and slowed her down. She focused on her task because the only thing worse than sewing on linen was unpicking and sewing on it a second time.

She worked efficiently, and by the time the break buzzer sounded there were only three left to do.

Faye stretched her arms over her head. "You coming?" she asked.

"Can't," answered Izzy. "I have to make up time."

"You weren't that late were you?"

"Twenty minutes," Izzy said.

Faye stood beside her and looked at her work box. "You're getting fast," she said. "Why don't you just finish these and come out for a few minutes?"

Izzy considered this suggestion. Her back was stiff and moving around would feel good. "Okay," she said.

Betty, Marti, Faye, and Stan sat at their usual table. Izzy hesitated. Stan rose and said something she couldn't hear, and walked away without looking at her.

Faye held up a cup of Coca-Cola. "Sit down kid, we're waiting for you."

Izzy accepted the drink. "Thanks," she muttered, "Think I'll stand though."

"Faye says you learned how to bowl last night," Betty said.

"Barely," Izzy said. Was that only last night? It seemed longer.

"Oh, come on," Faye said. "You got a spare and a strike before we left."

Marti stubbed out her cigarette. "You oughta join the league," she exhaled smoke from her nose.

"It was only one spare and one strike," Izzy said.

Betty threw back her head and laughed, "That's better than most of us! We aren't exactly setting the lanes on fire."

"Not hardly," Marti added. "We're more about the beer than the bowling." She checked her teeth in a compact mirror and picked a fleck of tobacco off an incisor.

"You're too young to drink," Betty said. Her eyes lit up. "You could drive us home afterward though!"

"I don't have a car," Izzy said quickly.

"You could drive mine," Betty offered. "Can you handle a standard transmission?"

"No," Izzy answered.

"Doesn't matter," Betty said with another laugh. "Mine's an automatic. Practically drives itself. All you gotta do is hang on to the steering wheel and aim."

Izzy gulped the rest of her drink and crushed the cup before tossing it into the trash. "I don't have time. Thanks for asking though." She practically ran back to her sewing machine.

Someone had removed her finished work and placed two more boxes on her right. Both boxes were filled with the same rompers in the same irksome fabric. Izzy swore quietly and glared around the room. Stan caught her eye, and she saw him smirk before writing on his clipboard.

"He did it on purpose! That creep!"

"Who?" Faye asked. She was changing the presser foot on her machine.

Izzy jerked her chair up to her machine with an angry scrape. "Never mind," she mumbled. With a flex of her fingers and a roll of her shoulders, she set to her task. There were four small pleats on each piece. Pinch, pinch, stitch, pinch, pinch, stitch; that was one piece finished. Concentrating on the rhythm captured her full attention. The hum and clatter of the machines became a dull cacophony in the back of her mind. Soon one box was finished, and she started on the next. She ignored the buzzer that signaled lunch and kept sewing. When the last pleat was in, she leaned away from the machine with a feeling of satisfaction. Looking around, she saw the room was empty except for Faye and herself.

Faye was sewing a stretchy panel into the front of an old pair of jeans.

"What're you doing?" Izzy asked.

"Making maternity pants," Faye replied. She lifted the hem of her shirt to show Izzy that she could no longer fasten the waistband on the jeans she wore.

"Won't you get in trouble using the machine for yourself?" Izzy pulled her paperwork closer and began filling it out.

"Naw," answered Faye, "They don't mind as long as it's on your own time. By the way, I made a tuna fish sandwich for you. It's in a paper bag with some cookies and a peach. I put it in the fridge in the break room."

Izzy looked at the clock; she still had fifteen minutes for lunch. "Thanks, Faye." She rose from her stool. "What about you? You need to eat, too."

"I'll be out in a bit. Don't wait for me."

Izzy purchased a carton of milk and took her lunch out to the picnic table. The seasons were definitely changing. Under the shade of the elm tree, the breeze was almost cold. She moved so that the sun warmed her back. She ate the sandwich all except for the crusts which she saved for Buddy if he showed up. Faye had washed and pitted the peach before putting it in a wax-paper bag. Juice dripped onto Izzy's chin when she bit into the fruit. The soft flesh melted in her mouth; the tender peel added a touch of tartness. She wiped at her chin with a napkin and licked her lips. Peaches, she decided, were her favorite fruit when they were in season. Izzy found four Oreos in the bottom of the brown bag. She tore the top off of the milk carton so she could dunk the cookies. She figured she had just enough time to visit the Ladies Room and wash up.

Her reflection in the lavatory mirror looked like she was six years old. Her chin was sticky with peach juice, and a dark chocolate cookie-ring encircled her mouth. She wiped away the juice and cookie and rinsed out her mouth. She met up with Faye walking into the production area.

"Where were you this morning?" Faye asked.

"I wanted to ride my bike so I left early," Izzy said.

"Without breakfast?"

"Oh, I had breakfast. I stopped at the coffee shop on Main Street." They had reached their machines and busied themselves organizing their work. Izzy saw with relief that the linen rompers had been replaced with yellow receiving blankets.

"I guess you'll be riding your bike home then," Faye said. She had a large spool of lace trim to attach to baby dresses.

"No, Paul is picking me up. I left the bike downtown; Ida drove me here because I was late."

"Wow that was nice of her! Didn't she get in trouble for leaving work?"

Izzy smiled, "I doubt Ida ever gets in trouble. She practically runs the place."

Faye stopped sewing and looked over at Izzy. "Do you think I could catch a ride with you and Paul today?"

"Sure, Paul won't care. What happened to Stan?"

Faye started her machine again. "He has a dentist appointment."

Izzy looked up from her work. Stan stood on the other side of the room. His arms were crossed over his clipboard, and he chewed on a pencil. Beneath a crease in his brow, he gazed at Faye.

Chapter Twenty-Five

Paul was waiting in his car when they walked out at the end of the shift. He jumped out to open the door for Izzy. "Hi, Faye," he said. Izzy explained that Faye needed a ride. "Great." He opened the rear door.

"Could you drop me downtown so I can pick up my bike?" Izzy asked.

Paul's smile faded. "Your bike? Sure, we can put it in the trunk."

Izzy hesitated for a second before replying. "I want to ride it home." She guided Faye into the front seat and climbed in the back.

After driving three blocks in silence, Paul switched on the radio.

Izzy watched the passing scenery as tree-lined streets changed to parking lots and the store fronts of Main Street.

"Where to?" Paul asked.

"It's the café next to the shoe store on your left. Just pull over please. I can walk from here."

Ever the gentleman, Paul stopped the car and came around to open her door. As soon as she was out, he caught her hand. "Is anything wrong?"

She gave him a quick smile. "Nothing at all. I just wanted to ride my bike today. I'll talk to you later. Thanks for the lift."

The traffic signal changed and Izzy hurried across the road. She heard Paul drive away behind her.

The café was empty apart from a couple of women sharing a slice of pie and drinking tea. They were dressed up for shopping and they ignored Izzy.

"Hi," Izzy spoke to a waitress behind the counter. "Is Ida around?"

The girl, she didn't look much older than Izzy was pretending to be, stopped what she was doing. "Ida went home an hour ago. You want the counter or a booth?"

"No thanks, I'm here to pick up my bike." She caught a glimpse of herself in the mirror above the counter. Her hair looked windblown, and her heavily made-up eyes were hard. She looked tired. She was tired. Why hadn't she let Paul put the bike in his car?

"Oh, yeah, Ida told me. It's in the back," she said, "you can't miss it; it's the only bike there." She guffawed at her own joke until she snorted, then showed Izzy the way through the kitchen.

Izzy rolled the bike outside. She mounted the seat and pedaled down the unpaved alley. Ivy hung from the fences by the side of the dirt path. Some of it had managed to climb up into the trees. It hung in strands and swayed in the breeze. The sky was a brilliant blue, but clouds were accumulating in the north. The air and the shady trees revived her and she pedaled harder, trying to outrun the pretense that her life had become.

She chose back streets and rode by old homes with neat yards. Little girls played hopscotch on the sidewalks and jacks or paper dolls on the porches just as she and Ann used to. Boys played ball in the middle of the road. Every block or two she came across a small grocery similar to the Neighborhood Market where she and Ann had stopped. It seemed like it had been a year since that Friday afternoon. Izzy felt a twinge. That morning had been the last time she'd seen her mother, and even then she hadn't seen much of her. Willa had been face down in the pillows on her bed, wearing only a slip, her dyed hair a frowzy mess in need of a touch-up at the roots.

She rode by the junior high. A dozen girls practiced baton twirling on the grass next to the school. They needed work; batons flew everywhere. One girl rhythmically smacked herself on the elbow. Only one of them really twirled her baton. It sparkled in the sunlight and spun like a propeller. The girl, a tall blonde, had cheerleader written plainly on her countenance from her gleaming hair to her toothy smile.

Izzy stopped to drink at the fountain next to the school. The girl who had been beating her elbow wandered over. Stepping aside to give her room, Izzy said, "You might want to soak your arm when you get home. It must hurt."

The girl looked Izzy up and down. Her eyes narrowed where the buttons on Izzy's blouse strained over her breasts. "You ever try twirling a baton?" she asked.

"Not really," Izzy answered.

The girl's lips twisted into a sneer. "Then mind your own business." She stooped to drink.

Stunned at the rudeness, Izzy was sorely tempted to shove her face into the water. Instead, she got on her bike and rode away slowly, so slowly that she heard clearly when one of the twirlers called, "Wow, there's something you don't see every day: a slut on a bicycle."

The words cut into Izzy with a pain that left her breathless. She didn't look back or increase speed. Her head was high, her face turned away from the group. No one saw how her cheeks flamed or the tears shone in her eyes. What had the girls seen in her that brought on instant contempt? Who were they, anyway? Stupid stuck-up junior high brats! She pumped the bike faster and sped across the road to an alley behind some old apartments. Her heart pounded. Most of her life she had been overlooked, dismissed, or pitied by outsiders. She had learned to ignore all that while she was still in grade school. Willa moved them so often that they didn't get to know people well enough to care what they thought or said. More importantly, she and Ann—and occasionally Willa—had each other. But now, Willa was gone, and Ann was moving toward a life the twins had dreamed of but never dared to hope for. Until a minute ago, Izzy hadn't realized how lonely and vulnerable she'd become.

She swung into the ballpark two blocks from home. Dropping her bike on the grass, she took a seat in the shade of a large Poplar. The park was abandoned, and she drew up her knees and held them close to her body. With her face hidden, she let the tears fall. Her body rocked gently. Purging sobs gurgled up from her chest and burst free. All the exhaustion, frustration, and loss of the recent weeks turned to a noxious brew that she couldn't contain. Most of all she cried in fear. She sobbed until her head ached and her body was as limp as a wrung-out rag. Still she sat. The leaves whispered over her. A breeze glided around her, tender as a blessing. Peeking through her hands at the park, she saw limbs swaying gently. The clouds had moved in and dropped, sealing the valley with a mottled gray comforter.

Izzy quickly dried her eyes on her shirt collar and picked up her bike. She splashed cold water on her face from an old tap near some picnic tables and rode toward home. The last two blocks were uphill and pedaling felt like lifting anvils with her toes.

She wanted some aspirin and a warm bath. She turned onto her street. A dozen teenagers were scattered on her front porch. Ann's class officers and committee members were still there. Ignoring them, she rode up the drive. Paul and Faye sat on the steps in front of the back door. They had glasses of Kool-Aid and shared a bowl of popcorn.

"Good," Paul said, and got to his feet. "You made it, I was starting to worry."

"I put a meatloaf in the oven," Faye said. "It should be done in half an hour."

Izzy tried to smile. "Sounds good. I'm going to lie down for a bit." She kept her face turned away when she passed them to enter the house.

Sugar ground under her shoes, punch powder was scattered on the counter. Popcorn kernals, popped and un-popped, littered the stove and floor. Empty ice cube trays were in the sink. "Just when I thought I couldn't feel worse," Izzy mumbled. She found the aspirins and shook two into her palm. Every glass and cup was either dirty or in use, so she drank directly from the water pitcher to swallow the pills.

The front door opened. Ann carried a stack of empty glasses in from the porch. She flinched when she saw Izzy's face. "I'll clean it up," she said defensively.

"You do that," Izzy muttered and turned her back. She finished the water in the pitcher.

"We're not supposed to drink from the water pitcher," Ann pointed out.

"Tough," Izzy said. Her stomach growled. She decided not to wait for meatloaf and took two slices of bread from the cupboard and found leftover tuna salad in the fridge to make a sandwich.

"Ann," a boy called through the screen door, "we need to finish up."

"Coming," Ann replied. She put the glasses in the sink and went back to her meeting.

Izzy forced herself to swallow the sandwich past the ache in her throat.

She went to her room, pulled back the bedspread and kicked off her shoes. Too tired for anything else, she rested her head on the cool pillow and pulled up the spread. Her swollen eyelids closed. The room, the kitchen, the house, Ann, and the pain disappeared, and Izzy slept.

❧

"Izzy! Wake up!" Faye's whispered voice was insistent. "Oh please, wake up."

"Whatsamatta," Izzy mumbled.

"I'm bleeding," Faye said.

"You're what?" Izzy sat up. "Where? What do you mean?" In the moonlit room she saw the ghostly pallor of Faye's face.

"Help me, Izzy. It's a lot of blood, and I'm cramping, too."

Izzy's feet hit the floor, and she was relieved to find she was still dressed. "Should I call Stan?"

Faye shook her head. "Paul."

"Paul? But Stan said—"

Faye cut her off. "I know, but I want Paul." Her voice broke.

"Sure. Okay I'll call him." She flipped the light switch on the kitchen wall and picked up the phone before she remembered she didn't know the number. Her sister was asleep in the living room. "Ann," Izzy called, "I need the Kimball's phone number."

A lump beneath the blanket on the sofa stirred.

"Annie, wake up!"

Ann looked out from the covers and blinked. "What time is it?"

Izzy glanced at the clock. "After four. I need Jill's phone number."

"You can't call her before eight a.m., they have a family rule," she moaned.

"What's the number?" Izzy stretched the phone cord and shook Ann's shoulder.

"It's on the wall by the phone." Ann grumbled. "What's the big emergency?"

Izzy dialed. "Faye is bleeding."

Ann sat up. "She cut herself?"

"Hello Mr. Kimball. This is Izzy Gardner. May I please speak to Paul?"

She rolled her eyes at Ann. "I do know what time it is. I'm sorry but it's an emergency. Thank you."

Ann seemed to catch on. She wrapped the blanket around herself and hurried from the room.

Paul sounded wide awake on the phone. "Izzy? What's the matter?"

"Faye asked me to call you. She's, uh…" Izzy paused in confusion. Paul didn't know about the pregnancy. "Sick," she said. "We need a ride to the hospital."

He didn't ask why or hesitate. "I'll be there in three minutes."

Ann was helping Faye into clean clothes. "Is he coming?" Faye asked.

"He said three minutes." Izzy found her shoes and brushed her teeth. Then Paul knocked at the door.

"Wait," Ann said. "I'll get dressed."

"You go back to bed," Izzy said. "Lock the doors behind us. I'll call and let you know what is going on." She hugged her sister. "Thanks for helping."

Ann nodded and yawned.

Faye's legs shook when she stood. Paul picked her up and carried her to the car. He gently placed her in the back seat. Izzy climbed in front with him.

"What happened?" Paul asked as he backed the car onto the street.

Izzy kept her answer vague. "She woke me up and said she was hurting."

The empty roads shimmered with dew in the headlights. Black windows in the faces of dark houses noted their passage with a blind disregard. Faye moaned softly.

"Almost there, Faye." Paul's voice sounded calm, but Izzy saw how white his knuckles looked gripping the steering wheel. He ignored stop signs, slowing only enough to see if it was clear before crossing the intersections.

Izzy looked back at Faye. She appeared asleep, but the moaning persisted. "I think she's unconscious," she said.

Paul pressed on the accelerator and sped through the last three blocks. The car jerked to a stop in front of the Emergency Entrance sign. "Get some help," he ordered Izzy with a nod toward the glass doors. But help was on the way before she could get out of the car. Two men in white dragged a gurney toward them.

Paul opened the back car door and quickly stepped out of their way. Once Faye was on the stretcher, he walked beside it holding her hand. "Do you think it might be appendicitis?" he asked Izzy over his shoulder.

She trotted to keep up. "I don't know."

The strident odor of rubbing alcohol, laundry starch, and antiseptic assailed them inside the hospital.

"Over here please," said a nurse behind a counter. "Are you a relative?"

"I'm her roommate."

"Fill this out, please," the nurse instructed and pushed a clipboard in Izzy's direction.

Her tired eyes refused to focus on the blanks. There was so much she didn't know. Faye's birthday? She thought back to a day at work; the day before Faye moved in and wrote down the date. The address and phone number were the same as her own, no problem there. Next of kin? She left it blank and moved on. She tried to make reasonable guesses about age, height and weight, but when she placed the clipboard on the counter, the nurse frowned at the empty spaces.

"When can we see her?" Paul asked.

"Someone from the ER will let you know what's going on. Take a seat in the waiting area, please."

The wall clock showed the time as four-forty. Paul slumped in an easy chair between a dark window and a potted fern. His chin rested on his chest. His eyes were closed. Izzy took a seat across from him and picked up a bedraggled magazine. It was a copy of *Seventeen* from August of 1964. An article about the Beatles was missing, including the photos from *A Hard Day's Night*. Izzy didn't mind until she discovered the short story she was reading had concluded on one of the missing pages. She looked at the clock again. Five-fifteen. The sky faded from black to gray in the window. She hunched her back and stretched her neck and shoulders. Paul breathed deeply, not quite snoring.

At five-thirty a new nurse took over at the counter.

Paul awoke and blinked. "What's happening?" he asked.

"Don't know," Izzy said.

"How's Faye?"

Izzy shrugged. "Haven't heard."

Rubber-soled shoes squeaked against the linoleum floor and a man in a white coat came into the waiting area. Izzy and Paul were the only ones there, and he approached them.

"I'm Dr. Lewiston," he said, and pushed magazines out of his way to sit on the coffee table. He looked at Paul. "Are you the father?" he asked.

Paul frowned. "No. Wait . . . what father?"

The doctor paused and looked again at the chart in his hand. "You would be the roommate?" he spoke to Izzy.

She nodded.

"Where is Mr. Jackson?"

Paul answered, "Her father kicked her out of the house. I don't think Faye would want to contact him."

"Is she okay, Doctor Lewiston?" Izzy asked.

"Mrs. Jackson will be fine. But I'm going to order bed rest for the next three or four weeks. It could be for the remainder of her pregnancy."

"I thought Faye's mother was dead…" Paul began then his mouth dropped open. He recovered and asked, "What pregnancy?"

"Oh Paul, please be quiet," Izzy said. "It's Miss Jackson, doctor. Faye isn't married.

Doctor Lewiston shook his head. "Well your friend is around 24 weeks pregnant, seems the fetus is small. Is there anyone who can care for her at home?"

"I work, and my sister is in school. She'll probably be alone between eight and four." Izzy bit a fingernail.

The doctor scribbled a note on the chart. "I can arrange for home care. Someone to come to the house to take a temperature and check blood pressure and pulse. They can fix a meal, help with baths. Does she have health insurance?"

Izzy nodded. "We get it from work."

"That's good. They'll pay something for the home care. I'm going to keep her here at least twenty-four hours for observation. They're getting her settled in the Obstetrics Ward. You can go up and see her if you'd like, but don't stay too long. She's lost blood and needs rest." The doctor stood. He handed a prescription to Izzy. "Who's her obstetrician?" he asked.

"I don't know."

Dr. Lewiston shook his head again. "Well, her own doctor may have her on prenatal vitamins already, but just in case, she can use that if she needs to." He turned and walked away.

Izzy looked at Paul. He hadn't moved since the pregnancy had been announced. She gave him a soft poke in his arm. "What are you thinking?" she asked, pretty sure she knew.

Only Paul's eyes turned to her. "Is Stan the father?"

She hadn't expected that. "I don't know. People at work think he might be."

"She didn't tell you?"

"No."

"Do Ann and Jill know about this?"

"Ann does. I don't know if she told Jill. I don't think so."

Paul slowly shook his head. "She's so sweet. It's hard to believe. He rose from his seat. "Well, let's go see her."

Izzy got up and they went in search of the obstetrics ward.

Chapter Twenty-Six

Early light passing through venetian blinds next to Faye's bed made a pattern of narrow bars over her. Her pale face matched her pillow, and her braid wound a thin stream of honey on the covers. Izzy saw Faye's eyes move under her closed lids before she raised them to look at Paul.

He stroked the sheet near her shoulder. "How do you feel?" His whisper sounded loud in the silent room.

Faye turned her face to the window and didn't answer. A tear slipped down her cheek.

Izzy leaned over her and brushed the tear away. She kissed her forehead and touched her hair. "It will be okay," she said feebly.

"I'm supposed to stay in bed," Faye said. "I don't know what to do, I have to work." Her large eyes blinked back more tears.

"Ann and I will take care of you, Faye. Don't worry," Izzy said, and in her heart she wondered how.

A nurse came in and pulled the curtains around Faye's bed, blocking her from the other three beds in the room. "She needs to rest." She pulled back one of the curtains far enough for Izzy and Paul to exit.

"Just sleep now," Izzy said. "I'll be back after work to see you."

"Visiting hours are between two and four afternoons," the nurse informed, "and six to eight in the evening. No more than three people at a time."

Izzy kissed Faye's cheek and Paul squeezed her hand and smiled.

The hospital was waking up. Day-shift nurses arrived. Laundry, linen, and food trolleys clattered through the hallways. The elevator was nearly full when

Izzy and Paul got on. Sleepy eyed night workers yawned and fumbled in coat pockets and purses for car keys. The doors slid open near the lobby.

Paul squinted at the bright light now streaming through the windows. He looked over at Izzy. "You hungry?" he asked.

"Famished."

"Hospital Coffee shop is open," he said. "Let's get something before we leave."

She followed him to a stool in the cramped café. As soon as she sat down, she dropped her head onto her folded arms.

"What'll ya have?" asked the cook.

"Hot chocolate, bacon, eggs, toast," she heard Paul say. "For both of us."

Izzy forced her eyes open. A red and white sign above the grill invited her to "Have a Coke and a Smile." She'd settle for either one, she thought. A clock next to the sign told her she had to be at work in an hour.

Two plates, two mugs and utensils appeared on the counter. Paul and Izzy ate in silence, unless you counted the chatter all around them, the sizzle and hiss from the grill, and the jangling of the cash register. Paul paid for the food and they left.

Izzy shivered in the chill morning air.

Paul finally spoke when he opened the car door for her. "Why didn't you tell me?"

She hesitated before answering. "I didn't think you needed to know."

He seemed to consider her reply. "Yeah, you're probably right." He walked around to the other side of the car and climbed in.

Ann looked up when Izzy entered the kitchen. "How is she?"

"She's lost some blood. The doctor kept her at the hospital. She has to stay in bed for a while, maybe the rest of the pregnancy."

"Seriously? The rest of the pregnancy?" Ann dried her hands on a dish towel. "How long is that?"

Izzy fought a yawn before answering. "I guess it's about three months."

"THREE MONTHS?" Ann shouted. "How can anyone stay in bed for three months?"

"I guess we'll find out. She could lose the baby if she doesn't."

Ann stared out the window, her brow furrowed. "Izzy," she hesitated for a second, "do you think that might be for the best?" Ann's voice was very quiet.

A deep coldness grew in Izzy's chest. "Ann, how can you even ask that?"

"I know it sounds awful. But how is Faye going to take care of a baby? Whoever the father is, he doesn't care. Will she put it up for adoption? Move back home with her family? What?"

Now Izzy looked out the window, vaguely hoping there might be an answer out there in the warmth and light. The exhaustion she felt took on another dimension as it pushed at the back of her neck and tugged at her heart and lungs like a weight pulling her into a ball. "I don't know Annie. I don't know what she'll do." She spoke slowly and with an effort.

The clock hummed into the quiet. *I need to sleep, that's what this feeling is. That's why I'm collapsing. I'm curling like a cat in front of a fire. When I wake up, I'll know the answer. What to do.* The room was slipping away. Izzy sensed her sister's arm around her. She saw her unmade bed through a haze and felt her blouse and jeans being removed. She barely noted the softness of the sheets and the welcome weight of a blanket. On the precipice of unconsciousness she felt Ann's kiss on her cheek.

Eyes still closed, Izzy groped for the alarm clock. Her fingers touched paper and she squinted to see an envelope with her name on it. Rising up on an elbow, she removed a single sheet of notebook paper and read:

Izzy,
Stan came by this morning and I told him Faye was in the hospital and that you had been with her most of the night. He wants you to call him at work as soon as you wake up.

There's a football game after school and a dance, so I'll be late tonight. Give Faye a hug for me. I'll be thinking of you and of her.

Love you,
Ann

It was 11:45 according to the alarm clock. If she hurried, she could be at work by 1:00 and only miss part of a day.

She washed her face and under her arms, changed her underwear and put on clean clothes. In thirty minutes she was pedaling her bike toward the factory.

Walking into work in the middle of the day felt odd. Izzy punched in. Lunch break was in progress, so she made her way into the production room without drawing attention.

She saw Stan seated at his desk and averted her eyes. She felt him watching as she picked up her work and went to her machine. He was by her side before she could change the thread.

"What happened?" he asked.

"Ann told you, I was at the hospital with Faye."

"Why?"

Izzy rubbed her temples with her fingertips. "She started . . ." she paused, "She had a problem with the baby."

"What sort of problem?"

The weight she'd felt earlier rose furiously in her chest. Her jaw clamped tight. How did she get in the middle of this? Her life was complicated enough!

"I asked you—"

"I heard you Stan," she snapped. Her eyes flashed at him. "I'm not her mother or her

sister. I'm not even a cousin. Talk to Faye. She's on the Obstetrics floor at the hospital."

Stan's face flushed. He looked away. "Why didn't you call me?"

His voice sounded sad, and after a deep sigh, Izzy answered mildly, "Faye asked for Paul. I don't know why. Maybe because he lives closer."

"You look awful. Do you want me to take you home?"

"No. I just want to do my job and be left alone." She finished threading the machine, expertly licking the end of the thread before slipping it through the needle's eye.

After the lunch break the hum of Izzy's machine joined all the rest of the factory and she found her place in the rhythm. Piece after piece slid under the pulsating needle. Izzy focused on her stitching, pausing only to fill out papers, clip stray threads, or adjust her chair. Twice she caught herself glancing over at Faye's chair, and each time she was startled to see it empty. She returned to her task, not allowing her mind to wander.

News of Faye's hospitalization buzzed around the production room. Izzy felt it swarming toward her and concentrated intently on her work. Marti tapped her on the shoulder. She was holding a piece of Izzy's work. "These seams are a little close to the edge," she began. Izzy set her jaw and narrowed her eyes; there was nothing wrong with the seam. She looked up. Marti saw her expression and took a step back. "I mean they're fine; I just wanted to let you know not to get too close." Izzy nodded curtly and went back to work. She heard Marti's shoes squeaking away. She knew Marti wanted details about Faye. It gave her a sour bite of satisfaction to know she had disappointed the nosey woman.

The shift ended. Izzy went through the closing routine automatically and left. Stan caught her at the bike rack.

"I'm going to the hospital. Do you want a ride?"

"No, I'll go later." She avoided his eyes. She didn't tell him that visiting hours would end in twenty minutes, or what floor the Obstetrics Ward was on. He knew where the hospital was; he could find out for himself. The sourness inside her had grown more pronounced.

<hr />

The air inside the house smelled like dirty socks and curdled milk. Izzy opened the kitchen window and the front and back doors. The remains of Ann's breakfast – a nearly empty bowl of milk with a limp corn flake floating in it – sat on the drain board. Izzy rinsed out the dish and left it in the sink. She found a pitcher of cherry punch in the fridge and poured herself a drink. She had more than an hour to kill before going to the hospital. She decided to start the laundry. Faye's blood-stained sheet was soaking in the bathtub. Pushing up her sleeves, Izzy unplugged the drain and began wringing. Back in the kitchen, she filled the washing machine with hot water, added bleach and detergent, and dropped the sheet in to soak. She stripped the remaining sheets from the beds in the house and pushed them under the steaming water before starting the agitator. Chlorine scented steam rose and turned the kitchen into a sauna. Izzy poured herself another glass of punch and watched the suds pulse and roll in the washer. Five minutes before the agitation was to stop, she dragged the rinse tubs up to the sink and began filling them with clean water. When she finished rinsing and wringing, she carried the sheets to the line in the backyard and hung them to dry. She picked up the empty basket and started toward the house.

Her stomach growled and her thoughts were on food, so she didn't see Mrs. Kimball on the back porch before she nearly ran over her.

"Careful dear," Mrs. Kimball said. She held a tray covered with a tea towel.

"Oh!" Izzy exclaimed, "You scared me." She opened the kitchen door.

"I was just about to knock." Mrs. Kimball stepped inside and placed the tray on the kitchen table. She turned and looked at the washing machine and tubs. "You poor thing! To think you work all day and have to come home to laundry and dishes! I brought you a plate of dinner. Hope you haven't already eaten."

Izzy's mouth watered, "No, I haven't."

Mrs. Kimball whisked away the dishtowel with a magician's flair.

Izzy went weak-kneed at the sight of chicken, potato salad, and corn on the cob, homemade biscuits, and a wedge of chocolate cake. Food! Real food, cooked by a mother! Izzy dropped into a chair and picked up a fork. She felt Mrs. Kimball's hand stroke her hair.

"Dig in, honey. Don't mind me."

The invitation proved unnecessary as Izzy had already taken a bite of chicken. She savored every mouthful while Mrs. Kimball straightened the kitchen, poured a glass of milk, and set it near the chocolate cake. Pulling out a chair, she took a seat.

Izzy licked a fingertip and used it to pick up the last crumbs of cake from the plate. She swallowed the final gulp of milk and wiped her mouth on the napkin provided. It was so nice to have a mother around. Even if it wasn't her own mother. Maybe especially because it wasn't.

"Goodness, you were hungry!" Mrs. Kimball said.

Izzy smiled, not caring if there were corn kernels or bits of cake stuck in her teeth. "It was so good," she said.

Mrs. Kimball's cheeks turned pink. "Thank you."

Izzy saw that it was five-thirty. She needed to leave soon to visit Faye. She pushed her chair back from the table.

"Just a minute Izzy," Mrs. Kimball began, "I need to talk to you." Her tone was serious, and Izzy, sensing bad news, wondered if she'd just eaten her last meal.

Mrs. Kimball cleared her throat. Her rosy face darkened a shade. "Paul told me about Faye."

Izzy felt heat rising in her own cheeks, and at the same time a cold shiver slipped down her spine.

Mrs. Kimball cleared her throat a second time. "Please don't misunderstand me. I'm not one to judge anyone…"

"Of course not," murmured Izzy. *Then why aren't you looking at me?*

"We all love Ann and you of course…"

If your face gets any redder it's going to explode.

"I believe your heart is in the right place, I mean helping Faye out and all. But I wonder if you've considered how this setup might not be good for your sister."

"I…" Izzy frowned, "What do you mean?"

Mrs. Kimball forced herself to meet Izzy's gaze. "It's one thing for you to reach out to a girl in trouble, but it's different for Ann. She's so young."

"She's…" Izzy completed the statement in her mind, *twelve minutes older than I am!*

"Jill says that Ann is doing very well in school. I mean, she's on the student council and everyone likes her. Mr. Kimball and I are concerned that if people find out about her situation at home they might…" She paused.

Tick . . . Tick . . . Tick . . .

"Oooh," Izzy said, "I see."

Mrs. Kimball took Izzy's hands in hers. "I'm not entirely sure you do dear. You've done a wonderful job raising Ann on your own. Who knows what could have happened to her if it weren't for you." Mrs. Kimball's half-smile looked grim.

Izzy gently pulled her hands free and laid them in her lap. "Yes, who knows?"

"We're worried that if the authorities find out that Ann is living in a house with an unwed mother and only a sister as guardian, they might try to remove her."

"They can't!" Izzy cried, leaping to her feet.

Mrs. Kimball was beside her, curling an arm around her shoulders. "Izzy, it will be all right. We have a solution. We'd like Ann to come and live with us."

Izzy stared.

"There's plenty of room for Jill to share with her, and mixed in with the brood we've already got. She'll hardly be noticed."

She'd be noticed here.

Mrs. Kimball continued, "You'd have one less mouth to feed, and she'd only be around the corner. You could still see each other."

The silence in the kitchen was palpable, even the clock seemed to stop. Deep in her chest, Izzy's heart kept beating. She was aware of her breathing, but everything else felt numb. She tried to clear her throat and choked on a sob, which she awkwardly covered with a cough.

"Have you talked to Ann?" she asked.

"No. We wanted to see how you felt about it first."

Izzy nodded. "Thank you." She squared her shoulders. "I'll talk to her about it when she comes home tonight."

Mrs. Kimball hugged her. "You're a remarkable young woman, Izzy. I don't know if I'd have the courage and unselfishness you've got at your age." She rose and gathered the dirty dishes. "Call me after you talk to Ann. It doesn't matter how late it is." She moved toward the back door, then stopped and turned to Izzy. "One more thing. Paul said Faye will be on bedrest. I don't want you to worry about her while you're at work. I'll bring her lunches over and keep her company in the afternoons. Paul volunteered to come over anytime you need to leave."

Izzy opened her mouth to speak, but Mrs. Kimball put up her hand.

"It's no use arguing with me about this. We're happy to do it." She gave Izzy a warm smile and left.

A group of three nurses paused in their conversation and stared at Izzy when she passed them in the corridor. She heard one of them whisper, "She was with her..."

Faye was propped up in bed behind a tray of untouched food. A black and white television mounted from the ceiling droned just below hearing. The patient in the first bed acknowledged Izzy with a slight wave of a spoon before returning her attention to her pudding.

"Hey you," Izzy jiggled Faye's foot.

"Hi," Faye said.

Izzy dropped into the chair provided for visitors. "How are you doing?"

"I'm okay."

Izzy cocked her head and gave her a little smile. "Oh, yeah? Then what are you doing here?"

Faye gave her a look that said she wasn't in a mood for teasing.

"I brought you some stuff," Izzy said, and opened a paper bag. "Hairbrush and comb, bathrobe, slippers, some magazines, a crossword puzzle book, and a couple of candy bars."

"They gave me a comb," Faye said listlessly.

"Oh. Well I can take this one home. You don't want to be overrun with combs."

"No, I don't." Faye looked away.

Izzy glanced over the food tray. "How come you're not eating?"

"Not hungry."

"Looks good. Is that turkey with dressing and cranberry sauce? You've got fruit salad, some kind of pie." Izzy glanced at Faye. "Want me to open your milk carton for you?"

Faye didn't answer.

"Cut up your turkey maybe?"

Nothing.

"Butter your roll?"

"I'm not hungry."

"Want me to go away?"

"No."

Izzy sighed.

A nurse walked briskly into the room and picked up the empty tray from the patient who had finished her dessert. She looked over at Faye's dinner, shook her head and asked, "Was there something wrong with your food?"

Faye raised her chin, "I don't know, I didn't eat it."

"I can see that," the nurse said tartly. "You know if you don't eat, then your baby doesn't either." She tapped her foot impatiently, but the rubber sole made no sound on the linoleum.

Faye's face darkened. She picked up a fork and ate a bite of turkey.

"That's better," the nurse said, "I'll come back for your *empty* tray."

Faye continued to eat while Izzy watched.

"You want my pie?" Faye asked.

Izzy eyed the filling that had congealed between the crusts. "Thanks anyway." She told Faye about the meal Mrs. Kimball had delivered, but didn't mention her offer to take Ann into the Kimball household.

"I can imagine what she must be thinking about me." Faye stabbed at her plate.

Izzy considered her answer carefully before replying. "I think she's more concerned about what other people might be thinking. She didn't say anything mean."

"She wouldn't," Faye said "that doesn't mean she doesn't think it."

"It doesn't mean she does either."

Faye prodded her food with her fork. "Right. She's sitting at home right now saying, 'That Faye is such a sweet girl! You should marry her, Paul, and raise her little bas… bastard.'"

Beneath the quiet of the ward there was a collective gasp. Izzy, too, sucked in her breath. She tried to think of what to say, but the insurmountable truth blocked every thought that came into her mind.

Faye pressed a paper napkin to her mouth, smothering sobs.

Izzy pushed the food table out of the way and sat on the edge of the bed. She gathered Faye into her arms. Tears soaked Izzy's shoulder until Faye shuddered to a stop. Izzy continued to hold her, afraid to let go, afraid that only her embrace was keeping her friend together. She patted Faye's back, and the two of them rocked gently.

"Faye," Izzy whispered, "Why are you going through this alone? Shouldn't Stan help?"

Faye fell back, her face registering astonishment. "You think Stan's the father?" Tears welled again in her eyes. She shook her head. "There isn't a father, not the way you mean." She blew her nose into a tissue. "Izzy," she gulped and raised her swollen eyes, "I was raped."

Chapter Twenty-Seven

The words were spoken on a whispered breath, but they exploded in Izzy's ears. Shadows of Faye —sweet, gentle Faye— being assaulted clouded her mind, and she pressed her fingers over her eyes to dispel the vision. Instead, she sensed Sid's damp hand fumbling with her blouse, tasted the liquor on his lips as he tried to force his tongue into her mouth. Then her mind froze; she wouldn't imagine what else would have happened – the horror of what had happened to Faye.

Faye's face was buried in her pillow. Izzy reached out with trembling fingers. She pulled them back and wrung her hands. She longed to offer comfort, but where to begin? Her brain felt numb; she was ill-equipped to deal with this. *I'm just a kid! Someone is supposed to be taking care of me. How can I take care of anyone else?*

"Oh, Faye," she finally said and her voice sounded distant, "have you told anyone?"

Faye shook her head.

Izzy gulped. "I . . . I think you should. What about the social worker? Or the police?"

Faye shook her head again. "I tried to tell the police," she said and lifted bloodshot eyes to Izzy. "Promise me you won't tell anyone."

Izzy made herself nod and Faye buried her head again. A horrible silence filled the space between the two girls. As usual, whenever Izzy was upset, it went straight to her stomach, and she began to feel sick. She rose and opened the window. Leaning on the sill, she inhaled the cool air. Feeling slightly better she turned again to Faye.

"Kid, I'm so sorry. It's getting late, and I should try to get home before it gets any darker."

What am I talking about? Dark is dark and it's already here.

Faye nodded. "Be careful." Her voice was muffled.

"I'll see you tomorrow." Izzy hurried out of the room. The picture of Faye looking small and vulnerable under the covers pressed into her mind.

She entered the elevator when several people got on. She darted through the lobby and outside to fumble with the chain and lock on her bike. Throwing them into the basket, she mounted the bike and pushed away from the curb, into a night now filled with a new threat. Somewhere in the dark a predator lurked. Gone was Izzy's disguise. She didn't feel eighteen or fifteen. She was a child helpless and afraid. *Where should I go? Somewhere safe. Nowhere is safe!*

She aimed for the center of a peaceful street where she felt less vulnerable. Her knees pumped the pedals and her eyes cut back and forth at shadows on either side where every shrub or bush took on a human shape in the dark. She strained to hear over her thudding heart and gasping breath for rustling leaves, breaking twigs, running feet. Her senseless brain couldn't decide if it was safer to take busy streets or quiet ones. Only one thought made sense: home. She wanted to be home. But there was no one waiting there. No sister. No roommate. No mother.

Panicking, she twisted the handle bars right. A blaring horn told her she'd cut in front of a car. Standing on the pedals, she rode harder. Her lungs burned. Her thighs strained so hard that her muscles quivered. She was on Main Street and heading the opposite direction from her house. She passed block after block of closed businesses before she saw what she was looking for.

The lights were off inside the café. She glimpsed someone moving inside and sped her bike around the corner to the alley behind.

Ida was turning the key in the lock when the bike skidded to a stop. Startled, she whipped a small pouch from her bag, prepared to do battle. She stared open-mouthed.

"I'm . . . sorry . . . Ida," Izzy panted.

"Good Lord! What the heck is the matter?" Ida quickly unlocked the door. "Get in here! Bring the bike and get in here!"

With the last of her strength, Izzy pushed the bicycle over the threshold and collapsed onto the floor. Her shoulders and chest heaved with every breath. She leaned her forehead on the hand that still clutched the handle bar. A light flicked on. She heard Ida's footsteps and the sound of scooping ice and running water.

Ida placed a cold, damp towel on the back of Izzy's neck and held a glass of water to her lips.

Izzy concentrated all her might to force her fingers to let go of the bike. She took the glass and drank. Ida dropped down next to her and maneuvered herself so that she could pull Izzy in to lean on her. She took the damp towel and patted it over the girl's face. Her arm encircled her, and she made soothing sounds, "Hush now, and just relax. That's it. You're all right now. Take another sip. There, there. There, there."

They sat on the floor for what felt like a long time. The motor on the freezer ticked on and began to whir. Ida was both solid and soft under Izzy's cheek. She smelled like onions, French fries, and the Ben Hur perfume they sold at Woolworths and Sprouse Reitz. The freezer motor finished its cycle before Izzy could pull herself upright.

Ida groaned and reached for a rung on a nearby ladder to heave herself first to her knees, then to her feet. "Well," she said as she brushed the back of her uniform, "that took a few years off my life." She tugged at her girdle and adjusted a bra strap. Reaching for her purse she said, "And I don't mind telling you, cutie pie, you came damn near gettin' a goose egg from my sock full of nickels."

Izzy, still shaking, got to her feet.

"You still look limp as Saturday's dishrag." Ida put her arm around Izzy's waist and guided her to a booth in the dark cafe. "I think we could both use a Coca-Cola. What do you say?"

"Yes, please."

Ida chuckled, "That'll do. You like ice? I can never have too much ice, myself."

"Yeah, that sounds good." Perspiration still poured over Izzy's body. The trembling had subsided.

Ida set the drinks on the table and tossed Izzy a dry towel. "Just take it easy, honey. Drink slowly." She scooted herself onto the opposite bench, and unwrapped straws for both of them. "Put your legs up, and rest your back against the wall." She showed what she meant by turning on the bench and propping up her own legs. "If your legs are half as tired as mine, and I don't know how they couldn't be, they should be elevated."

Izzy followed her advice. They finished their drinks in silence. Ida refilled their glasses.

"Now, what happened? You rode up like every hound in hell was at your heels."

"It felt like it," Izzy paused. "Honestly, Ida, I'm not even sure how I got here. I meant to go home . . . but I couldn't."

"Why not?" Ida looked up sharply, "Is that pawnbroker still after you?"

Izzy shook her head, though the thought of Sid made her stomach lurch, and she shuddered. "I don't know. That's not it. He's leaving me alone." She remembered the bowling alley and added, "Mostly."

"Something's going on," Ida insisted, "out with it, girl. I should be home in my PJs eating rice pudding and watching TV reruns."

Izzy felt her face grow hotter. Ida patted her arm. "I'm just teasing. I got all the time in the world. Now, what's up?"

Slowly, Izzy told her about Faye, the pregnancy, how Faye needed a place to live so she rented her a room, then the trip to the emergency room, and finally the conversations, first with Mrs. Kimball about Ann moving out, then she told her about visiting Faye and – despite her promise – the rape.

Ida nodded at intervals while she gingerly worked a toothpick around her gums and between her teeth. "Anything else?"

"No."

"Did she say where or how it happened?"

Izzy frowned. "No. She didn't have a chance to tell me." Her head drooped in shame. "I left before she could."

Ida dropped the toothpick into her empty glass. "Well, of course you did, honey. I wouldn't hang around for the details myself. There are some people who just live for that sort of news. I'm not one of 'em. I can tell you're not either. Thing is, you hear of one person going through something like that and naturally you start thinking it could happen to you."

"But, it could," Izzy said. "Couldn't it?"

"Maybe. But just because it could, doesn't mean it will. Hell sakes, we'd all stay home under the covers if we thought that way."

Izzy tried to fix these thoughts in her mind, but they slithered away before she could get a grip on them. The thoughts that were firmly planted were the empty house and Ann leaving. All the things that she'd thought might be permanent for now in her life were slipping farther and farther from her fingers.

Ida cleared her throat. "Now, Ann – that's your sister, right? – She'll be there tonight won't she? I mean, she doesn't have to move before Faye gets out of the hospital does she?"

"That's right. She doesn't have to move out right away. She doesn't even know about it yet." Izzy felt a small spot of comfort begin to bloom.

Ida checked the neon-lit clock on the wall. "It's after nine-thirty. How about I drive you home and stay with you 'til she comes in?"

Tears sprang into Izzy's eyes, "Oh, Ida! Could you?"

Pulling herself out of the booth, Ida adjusted her girdle again. "Course I could. You got a TV, right? We'll check all the windows and closets and under the beds. I'm a devil with my sock of nickels! We'll batten down all the hatches and you'll sleep like a baby."

Izzy laughed over a sob. Ida pulled her into a hug, and for a full minute Izzy felt just like a protected child.

Chapter Twenty-Eight

They placed the bike in the trunk of Ida's car. Izzy gave her directions to the house.

When they turned onto the street, Ida commented, "This is a nice stable neighborhood with solid middle-class people. Safe, I'd call it. And all your streetlights work."

"It's the little house on the right," Izzy said. The fear that still gripped her chest loosened its grasp just a bit.

Izzy unloaded her bike while Ida walked through the house, flipping on lights as she went.

"All clear," she called from the back door.

Izzy secured her bike and went inside, turning the lock behind her.

"Tight as a drum," Ida declared when she returned to the kitchen. "Clean, too. You're quite a housewife."

"Not really," Izzy admitted, "it's mostly Ann and Faye who do the cleaning and cooking."

"Well, whoever does it does a nice job."

"Thanks."

Ida looked around, "You rent here?"

"Yeah."

"This looks like one of Beverly Call's places."

"I don't know her first name, but a Mrs. Call is our landlady."

"She have her mother living with her? A gal about a hundred years old, calls herself 'Puddin'?"

"That's her."

Ida rested her hands on her ample hips. "How many times has she raised your rent?"

"Twice. How did you know?"

"I know Beverly. Probably surprise you to know that we went to school together."

Izzy was surprised, Ida looked quite a bit older than Mrs. Call.

"Bev's worked hard to look younger than she is. Dyes her hair every color of the rainbow, hardly eats a bite, false eyelashes, fancy clothes. Even had a face lift. That's where she got that big toothy grin. Hell, her skin's so tight, every time she winks her knee jerks."

Izzy laughed, and Ida joined in.

"It's coming on ten o'clock. Should we watch TV while we wait? Perry Mason is on channel two." Ida moved toward the living room.

"If you want."

"Normally I skip the news. Don't read the paper either. Ignorance really is bliss." Ida turned on the TV, and they settled on the couch.

They were getting into the mystery on Perry Mason when a pair of headlights lit up the drive and stopped behind Ida's car. A door slammed and Izzy recognized Ann's voice. She got up to unlock the front door that Ann was already knocking on.

"Why'd you lock me out?" Ann began. Then she saw the visitor.

"This is Ida," Izzy said. "Remember I told you about her? She works at the coffee shop."

"Oh, yeah. You're the one who told Izzy about the job at the sewing factory."

"That's right. Your sister's told me a lot about you." Ida looked her up and down. "She didn't mention how pretty you are, though."

Ann blushed. "Not really; Izzy's the beauty."

Ida stood and reached for her handbag. "Well, I wouldn't be able to pick between the two of you. You're both very attractive girls. Don't look much alike for sisters though."

"Nope, we've never looked alike," Ann said with a smile.

"Well, I best be going. Oh, Izzy, I noticed you have a phone in the kitchen." Ida opened her bag and pulled out a notepad and pen. "Here's my phone number, just in case." She tore out the paper she had written on and tucked it into Izzy's hand. "Real nice meeting you, Ann. Good night."

When the door closed behind Ida, Ann turned a puzzled face to her sister. "In case of what?"

"You hungry?" Izzy asked, avoiding Ann's eyes. She bolted the front door.

"We went for burgers after the dance. In case of what?" Ann dropped her books on the

coffee table and shrugged out of her sweater.

"Who won the game?" Izzy asked.

"We did," Ann said. "In case of what?"

"What?" Izzy feigned ignorance. "What are you talking about?"

"That lady, Ida whatshername. She said just in case. What did she mean?"

"Oh, that. You know, just in case I wanted to talk or something."

"Well, I like that! Like you couldn't talk to me? What is she, your new best friend or something? What was she doing here anyway?"

Izzy walked to the bathroom, Ann followed on her heels. "I went to the coffee shop after I saw Faye, that's all. She gave me a ride home." Izzy pinned her hair back from her face and soaped her hands.

Ann watched her carefully. "What's going on? You know you can't lie to me."

Izzy scrubbed her face, rinsed, and picked up a towel. "Come in the bedroom and I'll tell you."

Once they were seated on the bed Izzy began. "Mrs. Kimball came over earlier tonight. She brought me some dinner and wanted to talk."

"What about?"

Izzy paused, looking around, "Rats!" she exclaimed, "I forgot to bring in the sheets. We'll have to sleep with just a blanket and the bedspread."

"Can't you go out and get the sheets?"

"I'm, un . . . too tired,"

Ann sighed, "Fine, so what did Mrs. Kimball want to talk about?"

"About you and the situation with Faye."

"What situation?" Ann stiffened a little. "What does she know about Faye?"

Izzy's fingers plucked at the old chenille bedspread. "Only what Paul told her. She knows that Faye's pregnant and not married," she said.

"Well, what does that have to do with her?"

Izzy cleared her throat. "Nothing. She's concerned about you."

"Me? I'm not pregnant!"

"No one thinks you are, Ann. The thing is, she's afraid of what will happen when word gets out about Faye. She said the school board might not think I'm a fit guardian when they find out I invited an unwed mother to live with us."

Ann was flabbergasted. "It's none of their business!"

"Yes, it is. They can make trouble, force you into a foster home or something."

Ann jumped up and began to pace. "I'd like to see them try! You're my sister. There isn't anyone more fit for me to live with!"

"I'm your twin, remember? They'll say we're abandoned and they'll be right." Izzy held up a hand to stop the protests from Ann. "Sit down, Sis," Izzy touched her shoulder, and Ann sat. "Mrs. Kimball suggested that you come live with them."

A look of excitement flickered over Ann's face and vanished in an instant. "I can't do that, Izzy. I can't do that to you."

Izzy took her sister's hand. "Yes, you can. You'll share a room with Jill. We'll see each other all the time."

Ann jerked her hand away and crossed her arms. "I'm not leaving you." She set her jaw.

"Then I'm kicking you out," Izzy said, just as stubbornly.

"The heck you are!"

"Listen Ann, you're doing great. You're popular, you have friends, and you're a class officer. Where would you rather invite people over for meetings or whatever other things you'd invite them to? Jill's house with parents and a normal family, or here with your uneducated sister and her pregnant friend?"

"They're not *my* parents!" Ann unbuttoned her blouse, pulled a nightgown over her head, and finished undressing beneath it. Izzy followed her around the room, impatiently waiting until she could have her full attention.

Ann pushed past her into the bathroom and started washing her face.

"Listen to me, Ann," Izzy began, but her sister turned the water on harder. "I can't hear you," she yelled.

Izzy waited until the soap was out of her sister's eyes, then she twisted the water off.

"Okay, now you can hear me. You see the difference, right? Between living here with me and moving in with Jill?"

Ann rolled her eyes and squeezed paste onto her toothbrush.

Izzy situated herself between her sister and the sink. "You're doing so great, Ann. There are bound to be people who are jealous. If they find out about your situation at home, there could be trouble. Not just for you, for me, too. I'll lose my job. We'll have nowhere to go, and we'll end up in homes with strangers, or maybe juvenile detention or wherever they stick kids when their mother takes off." Izzy drove her point home. "You see that, right?"

Ann sank to the edge of the bathtub. She dropped her toothbrush onto the sink and held a towel to her face. She sat like that for a while before she nodded. "When am I supposed to go?"

Izzy knelt in front of her and leaned her head on her sister's shoulder. "When Faye comes home from the hospital. Mrs. Kimball is so sweet, she's going to help take care of Faye while I'm at work."

Nodding, Ann added, "She really is nice. Their whole family is nice. Their house is nice, too. They have color TV."

"Well, damn it, Ann!" Izzy said in mock outrage, "Like this isn't tough enough, you didn't have to tell me that!"

Chapter Twenty-Nine

Izzy yawned over her sewing machine. Twice she'd caught herself putting wrong sides together and had to unpick seams. When break time came, she cradled her head on her folded arms at the table.

"Late date?" Betty asked, nudging her shoulder. Izzy moaned in response.

"Oh leave her alone; can't you see the kid's knocked out?" Marti said. She snickered and added, "Better out than up, I always say."

No one laughed. Izzy opened one eye to give her a dirty look.

"Shame on you, Marti," Betty muttered, "talking about poor Faye like that."

Marti protested, "I never meant Faye." She looked around the table, "Honest, I was only kidding."

"Relax Marti," Izzy said over another yawn. "You just have bad timing."

"Speaking of who, how was Faye last night? Did you visit her?" Betty asked.

Izzy sat up. "Yeah, she'll be coming home in a day or two. She has to stay in bed the rest of the pregnancy."

"Poor kid," Betty lit a cigarette. "We should pass around a get well card."

"Why?" Marti asked. "It's not like she's sick."

Betty blew smoke in Marti's direction. "Nobody's asking you to sign if you don't want to. But she's gonna be down for a long time, and I think we ought to do something."

Stan walked up and laid his clipboard on the table. He bought two cups of Coke at the vending machine and placed one in front of Izzy. She gave him a weak smile and took a sip.

He pulled out a chair and sat. "Faye still in the hospital?"

Izzy nodded.

"I need to take her some paperwork. Would you go with me?" He looked at Izzy. All of the other eyes at the table shifted back and forth between them.

"I guess. I'm going to see her anyway." Izzy finished the Coke.

"Okay, wait for me after work. Did you ride your bike this morning?"

"Yeah."

"I'll put it in my trunk."

Izzy smiled a little at that. "My bike's been getting almost as many rides as I have lately."

Stan returned the smile with a tilt of his head. "What do you mean?"

She brushed away his question and shrugged. "Nothing."

Izzy drank two more Cokes for lunch and ate a packet of cupcakes. Riding the sugar rush got her through the rest of the work day. By three-thirty she felt starved and shaky. Worse than that, she felt mean. She snapped at Marti when the older woman questioned some of her work. When Betty tried to ease the situation, Izzy told her to butt-out.

Stan loaded her bike and opened the car door for her. He drove out of the parking lot but didn't turn toward the hospital.

"Where you going?" Izzy asked.

"Ding Ho. You like Chinese food?"

"I thought we were going to see Faye. Visiting hours end in fifteen minutes."

"We are," Stan answered. "But I'm not taking you there until you've got something besides Coke and cupcakes in your system. The way you lit into Marti and Betty, poor Faye wouldn't stand a chance if she crossed you.'"

Izzy folded her arms and directed her pouting face out the window. "I wouldn't light into Faye," she muttered.

Stan patted the top of her head as if she were six years old. "I don't want to take the chance."

Ding Ho's parking lot was nearly empty. Few people under the age of sixty-five wanted dinner at four in the afternoon. It was dark inside the café.

The walls were draped in red tapestries and colorful, tasseled lanterns hung over the tables. It smelled like hot fat, ginger, and garlic. A hostess greeted them and showed them to a booth.

"You been here before?" Stan asked as he opened the menu.

"No."

"Let me order for you?"

"Why not?" Izzy replied, "I'm so hungry I'd eat fried lizard without salt at this point."

Stan smiled and scanned the menu, "Dang, they're fresh out of lizard. Maybe they can scrounge up a rat for you."

A waitress set water glasses on the table. "Keep your voices down please. The boys in the kitchen don't appreciate the humor." This was said with a wide smile and a wink.

"No offense," Stan said.

"None taken," the waitress said. "They don't speak much English, so you're okay. What can I get for you?"

"We'd like egg drop soup, sweet and sour pork, chicken chow mien, and fried rice, please."

"And something to drink?" asked the waitress.

"Two Seven-Ups, lots of ice."

The waitress walked away. Stan leaned closer to Izzy, "Hope that's okay. I think Seven-Up tastes better with Chinese food. Besides, any more Cokes and you might climb the walls instead of sleeping tonight."

Suddenly Izzy felt inexplicable tears fill her eyes. Stan frowned, "Hey! I'll get you all the Coke you want." He raised his arm for the waitress. Izzy grabbed his sleeve and pulled.

"It's not that," she said. "I'm just tired." She pulled a napkin out of the container on the table and blew her nose. "Soddy," she mumbled and sniffed.

Stan patted her hand. "I know you're worn out, but I get the feeling there's more going on. What's up?"

"It's so kind of you to buy dinner for me and I just," her voice broke, "I just . . . I mean I haven't exactly been nice to you lately, and I just . . . I just . . ." She couldn't find the words.

Stan cleared his throat and his hand closed over hers. "Listen, Izzy," he began, "I'm not nearly as stupid as I act. I know you thought I might be the father of Faye's baby."

Her head snapped up. She snatched another napkin and blew her nose a second time.

"I'm not," Stan said quietly. "Faye is a very sweet girl, but I've never felt that way about her. And . . ." his face darkened, "I could never, ever abandon someone that I–"

Izzy touched his arm and he stopped talking. She felt like she'd die of embarrassment if he went on. "I know. It's okay, I know."

Stan seemed to deflate in relief. "Thank heaven," he said.

Izzy wiped her eyes and blew her nose one more time.

"You're not going to keep doing that when the food comes are you?" Stan teased.

Izzy laughed the first true laugh she'd had in days. "I hope not. Spicy food does this to me, too."

"I didn't order anything too spicy. You should be okay."

The waitress brought their drinks and two steaming bowls. With the warm soup in her stomach, Izzy soon felt better. "What sort of paperwork do you have for Faye?" she asked.

Stan wiped his lips. "It's for a medical leave. She's entitled to disability until her doctor says she can come back to work."

Izzy wrinkled her forehead, "She's not getting fired is she?"

"No, after two weeks she'll get a portion of her regular paycheck, sixty percent. That's company policy."

Stan used chopsticks to eat his chow mien; Izzy resorted to a fork.

"That will be good news for Faye. I think she's worried about the money. Will she get the $150, too?"

Stan frowned, "What $150 are you talking about?"

"You know, the company money you brought me when I hurt my hand."

He still looked puzzled, "You got $150? I don't . . . Oh, that $150!" His face reddened. "I'm not sure, I mean we're not talking about a work related accident."

"You're right. It definitely wasn't work related." Izzy felt her own face warming.

Stan shifted in his seat. "I'll talk to Cudgel. Maybe we can do something to help until her checks start coming again."

"Thanks, Stan." Izzy thought for few minutes. "Stan?"

"Hmm?" His mouth was full of sweet and sour pork.

Izzy cocked her head. "Why are you so kind?"

He took a sip of his drink and swallowed. "What do you mean?"

"You came to my house and brought food and magazines, you took care of my hand, you even cleaned up the mess in the kitchen. You've given Faye and me rides to work, you had her over to your house for dinner on her birthday, and made sure she had a place to stay. None of those things are your job. That's what I mean."

Stan kept his eyes on his plate during this recitation.

"So, how come you do so much?" Izzy pressed.

He lifted a shoulder in half a shrug. "Too much time on my hands?" he offered.

"Maybe you need a hobby. Marti and Betty have mentioned you want to be a doctor, like your brother. You should start golfing."

Stan smiled, sort of shyly, Izzy thought. "I do golf. I'm taking a couple of college courses, too."

Izzy mulled this over for a minute. "Wow," she said. "That's pretty amazing. Can I ask a personal question?"

Stan laughed, "What have you been asking?"

"How old are you? Why aren't you going to school fulltime?"

"That's two questions. You only asked for one," he pointed out.

"Okay, then just answer the first one."

"As of two days ago, I'm twenty. And, since you were so good about it, I'll answer the second question. I'm not in school fulltime because I didn't get a scholarship. I'm saving up for medical school and taking undergraduate courses whenever I can."

Izzy nodded. She thought they had some things in common. Both of them were at a time of their lives when they should be focused on classes, football games, parties, hanging out with friends. She saw faint lines of premature worry on Stan's forehead and wondered if she had them, too.

The waitress brought the check on a little tray with a couple of fortune cookies. Izzy picked up hers and slipped it into her purse.

It was too early for evening visiting hours at the hospital, so they walked up the street to a florist shop, selected a bouquet of carnations and daisies, and a card. Izzy held them on her lap as they drove to the hospital.

Faye was propped up on pillows in her bed. She had brushed her hair and was braiding it. A vase of pink roses dominated the table next to the bed, and Paul was watching her. He smiled when he saw Stan and Izzy and stood to give the only chair to Izzy. "It's starting to look like a hot house in here," he commented and moved the roses to make room for the new arrangement.

"You guys didn't need to do that," Faye said, but her cheeks flushed with pleasure.

"How're you feeling?" Stan asked.

"Better than yesterday," Faye admitted. "The doctor thinks I can go home by the end of the week."

Izzy gave her a quick hug. "That's great! Mrs. Kimball is going to check on you during the day while I'm at work. I can put the TV in your room, or maybe you can lie on the couch in the living room."

"Leave it in the living room. The prospect of looking at the same four walls for three months is so depressing. Moving from the bedroom to the living room sounds like a vacation."

Paul and Stan stood awkwardly, as if they weren't sure where they should be looking. The other women in the ward were walking with their husbands to the nursery windows to see their babies.

"Thanks for the magazines Izzy, but you forgot to bring me a pencil for the crosswords," Faye said. "I don't suppose you guys would go to the gift shop and find me a pencil with a big eraser, would you?"

"Paul can go," said Stan. "I just got here."

"Don't be so thick, Stan. Can't you see Faye wants to talk to Izzy alone?" Paul grasped Stan's arm when he said this and commandeered him out of the ward.

Alone at last, Faye reached for Izzy's hand. "You okay? I'm so sorry I blurted out . . . well, what I said yesterday. That wasn't fair to you."

"I admit it freaked me out. Heck, I'm still freaked out! But it happened to you, Faye, not to me. It makes me feel sick to think of it. I'm sorry I ran off; I didn't know what to say."

"I told the doctor, and he had someone, a counselor or something, come in to see me. It was really hard to talk about it, but at least I know I can get help."

Izzy clung to her friend's hand, her heart was thudding in her chest, and she prayed the fear she felt didn't show in her eyes.

Faye must have seen it because she said, "You don't need to be afraid. It was someone I know. Someone I thought I knew. It wasn't random."

Bad as it was, this news did make Izzy relax a little. So it wasn't some maniac hiding in the shadows. Then she felt guilty for her selfish relief.

"You haven't told anyone have you?" Faye asked as she withdrew her hand and reached for a tissue.

"No," then she remembered Ida. "That is I did tell one person. She's sort of a friend of mine. She doesn't know you, and even if she did, she'd never tell anyone. I'm sorry."

"Don't be," Faye said. "You've been a true friend through this entire thing." She squeezed Izzy's hand. "So, Mrs. Kimball is going to look in on me while you're at work? How did that happen?"

Izzy told her about Ann moving in with Jill.

Faye fell quiet, even quieter than she usually was. "I should go to a home for unwed mothers," she said after a minute. "It's selfish for me to mess up your life like this."

"Don't be silly, Faye. No one wants you to leave, especially me. Ann's so busy with school and meetings and parties, without you there I'd be alone all the time. And what would Paul do?" She added the last question with a smile.

Faye met her gaze. "I didn't mean to come between you two, Izzy. It just happened."

"I admit I was a little hurt at first, but then I realized I was forcing myself to feel hurt, like it was expected. I had a crush on him, but that's all it was. It died a natural death. You and he are both so good. It makes sense for you to be together."

Paul and Stan sidled in with their hands hidden behind their backs. Paul presented a package containing a packet of pencils, an eraser, and a sharpener. "I thought of the pencil sharpener," he boasted.

"You must be so proud!" Stan said. "Imagine a big college boy like you coming up with that on your own!" Paul gave him a little push, and Stan offered Faye a box of chocolates.

The four shared the candy and visited until Paul had to leave. "I'd rather stay," he said. "But I've got a research paper that won't wait. See you later." He took Faye's hand for a second, then he left.

Stan pulled out the paperwork he'd brought and went over the details with Faye, showing her where to sign and explaining the terms.

They were getting ready to leave when Izzy said, "You see, Faye, I'm the one whose being selfish. I need your money." She was joking, but it came out a little flat. Faye was sitting up, and Izzy put her arms around her. "Don't leave me, Faye," she whispered into her friend's ear. "I don't want to lose anyone else."

"Okay," Faye whispered back.

Izzy picked up her purse and remembered the fortune cookie. "I almost forgot, I saved this for you. Open it."

Faye cracked the cookie open, unfolded the strip of paper and read, "Prepare yourself for a big change." She looked worried for a second then burst into laughter.

Chapter Thirty

At the end of the week, Izzy coasted into her driveway with a feeling of relief bordering on elation. It was the feeling she associated with Friday afternoons and completing another week of work.

Ann and Jill had changed their school clothes for cut-offs and T-shirts. They sat on the porch eating Popsicles and gave Izzy a wave. "How's Faye?" Ann called.

Izzy dismounted and laid the bike against the railing. "She's coming home tomorrow."

"Great," Jill said, a wide smile on her face. She nudged Ann. "We should move your clothes to my house. I cleaned out some drawers and made plenty of room in my closet."

Izzy looked down. "Good idea," she said without enthusiasm.

"I've got a better idea," Ann said brightly. "Let's go dancing tonight."

"At the Union Hall? Cool!" Jill jumped up.

"What's the Union Hall?" Izzy asked.

"It belongs to the union workers at the steel plant, but they have dances on the weekends. Everybody goes there when there isn't a dance at the high school."

"So, it's just for kids?" Izzy dreaded a night alone in the house.

"You have to be 16 to get in, but college students go there, too." Jill's face lit up. "You can come with us!"

"But—" Izzy stopped herself from saying "we're only fifteen" and changed her response to, "You two aren't sixteen."

"No one ever checks IDs. Oh, Izzy! Please come with us," Ann cried. "You never have any fun. You'd love it!"

"Paul can drive us," Jill offered the services of her older brother. "He spends every evening at the hospital with Faye, but it wouldn't be out of his way."

Izzy didn't even try to quell the yearning she felt for a night of music and dancing. "What should I wear?"

"Same stuff you wear to work," Jill answered. "Most girls wear skirts or dresses, but slacks are okay, too."

Two hours later, Izzy and Ann jostled for position in front of the bathroom mirror, mascara wands at the ready. The radio was booming "These Boots Are Made for Walking" from the kitchen. Clothes were laid out on the bed: a skirt and blouse for Ann, corduroy slacks and a sweater for Izzy.

"Just let me finish and you can have the mirror to yourself," Ann complained.

Izzy took a seat on the clothes hamper. "So, you've been to this place before?"

"Just once." Ann held her mouth open while she swept a light coat of mascara over her lower lashes. "Jill and I went with a bunch of kids after a football game." She put away the mascara, applied lip gloss, and studied her reflection for a second. "Okay. All yours."

Izzy's make-up was usually darker and more dramatic than Ann's, but tonight she wasn't worried about looking older, and she toned it down considerably. She brushed a soft gray shadow in the crease of her eyelids and lined them with a thin streak of black. Her lashes were thick and dark, and she kept the mascara light enough to just give them definition. She added blush to her cheeks and a hint of rose lipstick that matched the natural color of her lips to complete her make-up. She wondered if her co-workers would recognize this version of herself. She doubted it. The hair that she usually teased and wore up was brushed into a soft bob and held back with gold barrettes.

"I wish I had pierced ears," she sighed.

In the bedroom Ann paused while buttoning her blouse. "You what?"

"They make the cutest earrings for pierced ears. I think it would be fun," Ann laughed. "You know what Mom would say, don't you?"

"That I was trying to look like a beatnik," Izzy answered. 'I don't care; it's better than looking like a floozy." She turned off the bathroom light and walked into the bedroom to dress.

Ann zipped her skirt. "You don't look like a floozy!"

"I do when I want to look older." Izzy remembered the girls at the junior high calling her a "slut on a bicycle." Was that only weeks ago? It seemed like a year. Well, tonight she looked nice. She pulled the sweater over her head, it was an old one that fit taut over her chest. She checked for damage to her hair and make-up in the vanity mirror. In spite of the tight sweater – she felt a touch of pleasure – she actually looked pretty. Ann did too. Ever since she'd cut her hair, she had gained a confidence that showed in everything she did.

Izzy watched her sister put on knee-high socks and slip on a pair of loafers. She dabbed Chantilly perfume behind her ears and offered the bottle to Izzy, who turned it down. "It smells like soap on me."

"We should go shopping tomorrow and find a scent that works for you," Ann lifted her skirt to tug at her shirttails.

"You look cute, Ann," Izzy said.

Ann beamed. "You look good, yourself. That sweater is a little va-va-voom."

"I know but I don't have anything else that goes with these slacks." Izzy tried to stretch out the knit. It helped very little.

They heard a car horn and hurried to the kitchen door.

"Go ahead; I'll lock up," Izzy said. She moved through the house checking windows and flipping on lights before she turned the key in the back door and joined Ann, Jill, and Paul in the car.

"What's with all the lights? It looks like there's a party going on," Ann said.

Izzy slapped her forehead, "Damn, I forgot to leave the radio playing!"

"I don't think we can afford to leave on the lights and the radio," Ann pointed out.

Izzy shrugged. "I don't like coming home to a dark house."

"I had the radio on earlier, and they said there won't be a band tonight at the Union Hall, just a disc jockey," Jill said.

"I don't mind a DJ, they don't take as many breaks. I hope there'll be a good crowd. I heard that there was a fight in the parking lot last week," Ann said.

"You stay inside," Paul warned. "When I used to go to these dances, kids smoked and drank in the parking lot. Cops patrol there now, but you'll be okay if you stay inside."

"You're such a prude, Paul." Jill punched his shoulder.

"I'll pick you up at eleven."

"Maybe we can get rides for ourselves," Ann teased.

Paul stopped the car at a light. "I'm not joking. I'll be out front at eleven and you better be waiting inside for me. All of you!"

"Okay, okay. Don't burst a blood vessel. We'll be there." Jill turned up the radio.

Tires crunched on the gravel parking lot at the union hall. Paul parked near the entrance and turned around to talk to Izzy. "I'll tell Faye 'hi' for you. She'll be glad to come home tomorrow."

"Her room will be ready. Give her a hug for me." She stepped out of the car. A breath of autumn air met her with the scent of burning leaves and fermenting apples from a nearby orchard. Placed on the edge of town, the union hall was surrounded by small fruit farms. The building's exterior was dimly lit by one street lamp near the entrance and another on the other side of the parking lot.

The girls each paid fifty cents at the door and had their hands stamped. They moved through a small crowded lobby to the hall. Teenagers milled around the edge of the linoleum dance floor. Loud speakers hung from the walls. On a stage at the end of the room a disc jockey sorted through records and ran a "testing, one, two, three, testing" check on the sound system.

Some of Ann and Jill's friends joined them. "This is my sister, Izzy," Ann said. Some of the kids Izzy recognized from the student council meeting at the house. A tall, dark-haired boy waved a hand and moved in her direction.

"You look different," he said when he reached her side.

Izzy smiled. "Different from what?"

He shrugged. "The last time I saw you. You look good, though. Not that you didn't look good before." He seemed to be tripping over his tongue.

"Thanks, I think," Izzy said. "What's your name?"

"Nick Anderson," he raised his voice to be heard over the music that had started. "You want to dance?"

"Okay."

He took her lightly by the elbow and led her onto the dance floor. Mick Jagger was getting no satisfaction at ear-splitting decibels. They shuffled their feet in time with the song. The lighting was dim. Nick's hair was parted on the side and just long enough to brush the tips of his ears. It curled around the nape of his neck. His eyes were dark, but Izzy couldn't see if they were brown or blue. He had rolled the long sleeves of a Madras shirt halfway between his elbows and wrists. The song ended, and before Izzy could retreat he took her hand. "Where you going?" he asked with a smile.

Izzy returned the smile. "I don't know."

Peter and Gordon's "True Love Ways" began to play. Nick slid a hand around her back. "I'm better at the slow songs. Do you mind?"

Izzy shook her head.

"Ann said you work in a sewing factory."

"That's right."

His smile flashed. "You don't remember me, do you?"

Izzy frowned, "I'm sorry. Are you a class officer with Ann?"

"No, my kid brother is. I came by your house to pick him up one day."

"Did we meet then?" Izzy asked, still puzzled.

"Not really. But I've seen you around town. You're usually on your bike. A couple of times I saw you with Paul Kimball and once with that guy from the pawnshop."

Izzy stiffened, her skin prickled, and she suppressed a shudder. "Are you a senior?" she asked.

He laughed, "I graduated a while ago. I work at the steel mill. I'm probably the only guy here tonight who actually belongs to the union."

"What do you do at the mill?"

"I work on the furnaces. What do you do at the sewing factory?"

"Sew."

"I thought maybe you were in management," he said, straight-faced.

"No, they wanted me for management, but I told them I'd rather just sew. At least until my trust fund kicks in,"

Nick nodded. "Trust fund, huh?"

"I guess Ann never mentioned our trust funds."

He shook his head. "I would've remembered."

The music ended, and they wandered off the floor. "I don't believe in trust funds," Nick said. "I'm going to be a self-made man."

"Good for you!" Izzy said. "What are you going to self-make yourself into?"

"Professional skier. My dad says I have to graduate from college first. Here," he gestured to a vending machine, "let me buy you a drink."

They sipped Cokes and watched the dancers. Two hundred or so kids moved with the beat of the music. The air was thick with Elsha and Brut cologne with an underlying scent of Right Guard deodorant.

Nick took Izzy's hand and led her to a couple of chairs beneath a casement window. He cranked the window open and crisp air flowed in.

"How old are you, Izzy?" he asked.

Izzy took another swallow of her drink and considered how to answer. "How old do you think I am?"

He looked her up and down, and she was thankful it was dark. "I'd say eighteen," he finally said. "But you could be a little older."

She smiled, "Very good. You're exactly right. I could."

He reached up to adjust the window and let his arm rest on the back of her chair. Izzy inched away from him. He slid a little closer. They both pretended to watch the dance. After a few minutes, Nick leaned in to speak in her ear. "Would you like to go for a ride?" His breath warmed her neck. She was glad he had chosen Brut over Elsha. Elsha was so sweet it triggered her gag reflex. Then she noticed his finger tracing the line of her bra strap through her sweater.

"I'd rather dance," she answered. "After all I paid four bits to get in here. You know how many baby dresses I have to sew to make four bits?"

Nick withdrew his arm. "Okay, you have a good time. Maybe I'll see you later." He rose and ambled away.

Izzy stared after him. That's all he wanted? To find a girl willing to leave with him? She shook her head. She crossed the room to place her empty Coke bottle in the rack next to the machine.

Jill and Ann walked out of the Ladies Room. They were laughing.

"Having fun?" Izzy asked, lamely.

"The best," Jill replied. "Saw you dancing with Nick. What did you think of him?"

"I thought he was nice but he proved me wrong. What about you two? Any luck?"

"The boys line up to dance with Ann," Jill said. "I'm still waiting to be discovered."

"You are not! Plenty of boys would ask you to dance if you'd give them a chance," Ann said. She turned to Izzy. "Every fifteen minutes I have to drag her out of the Ladies Room. She hides in there."

"I'd rather stay hidden and wonder if the guys will like me than stand against the wall and find out they don't." Jill grimaced.

"Come sit with me," Izzy offered. "You might as well give them a good look at you." She threw an arm around Jill's shoulders and pulled her away just as Ann was asked to dance.

They found seats and made themselves comfortable, or as comfortable as one can be on a wooden folding chair. After a few minutes a lanky young man approached. He paused and cleared his throat before he asked Jill to dance.

Izzy got up and moved casually through the clusters of girls that rimmed the room. She saw Ann swaying in the arms of the Sophomore Class President, Nick's younger brother, Frank. Her eyes were closed, her head nestled against his neck. Jill was dancing with another boy now. He held her at a proper distance and seemed to be telling her something funny because she laughed, and Izzy saw his arms relax.

That is how my life should be, thought Izzy resentfully, *I should be having fun, not worrying about taking care of a pregnant friend and trying to keep food on the table and pay the bills.* Her throat tightened. She tasted the salt of tears and blinked hard. She turned toward the Ladies Room.

Safe in a toilet stall, she unraveled tissue, blew her nose and dabbed at her eyes. *Stupid, stinking self-pity! I'm doing what I have to. What else can I do? Damn Willa! Wherever you are, I hope you're as miserable as I am.* She heard the outer door open and some girls entered.

"If he asks you to go for a ride, don't even think about it," a girl stated.

"Why not?" asked a second girl.

"It's a one-way ticket to Passion Flats, that's why."

"Like you've never been there!" scoffed girl two.

"Yeah, but I didn't have to walk home that time," answered girl one.

"You're kidding! He made you walk home?"

"It was either that or you know what."

Izzy wondered if she should make some noise so the girls would realize they weren't alone. Before she could, they continued.

"What a jerk!" girl two said.

"Yeah, that's what I thought. I walked about half a mile before he found me and said he'd take me home."

"What'd you do?"

"Are you joking? I wouldn't get in a car with him for anything. I went to a pay phone and called my dad."

Izzy felt a stab of jealousy. *What would that be like, having a father to come and rescue you from trouble?*

The Ladies Room door opened again, the music blared followed by a muffled silence. Izzy left the stall and checked her face in the mirror. She repaired the damage to her mascara with a paper towel and ran a comb over her hair.

Back in the auditorium, she looked for Ann and Jill. The clock over the entrance said it was only 9:30, an hour and a half before Paul would pick them up. The room was oppressively hot and humid. Music thrummed in her ears. Her skin felt sticky. The dancers reminded her of a large mass of amoebas writhing together. Izzy's head spun under the colored lights.

A boy in a T-shirt and very tight jeans strode up to her and took her hand. "Come on," he said, "let's dance." His grip was like a vice, and he dragged her into the crowd. The strains of "Unchained Melody" by the Righteous Brothers played. The boy pinned Izzy's hand behind her back. He towered over her and clamped her to him. She squirmed and used her free hand to push at his chest. He snorted. "Relax, honey. It'll be over in a minute. Enjoy yourself," he suggested in a voice like a growl. She smelled smoke and the sour tang of beer.

"Let me go!" Izzy said through gritted teeth.

He laughed again and moved a hand to the back of her head. Grabbing a handful of hair, he forced her face up. His mouth pressed on hers, chapped lips scraping, a hot tongue tried to explore her mouth, and she gagged. His hips ground against her. Izzy brought the heel of her shoe down on his instep. He didn't flinch.

He whispered in a course voice, "Try that again, and I'll follow you home."

Izzy panicked. Where was everyone? Didn't anyone notice what was going on? Weren't there any adults around?

Furious, she pulled a hand free, grabbed one of his ears and twisted it. "Listen jerk, you come anywhere near me and you won't walk away in one piece!" She looked him straight in the eye when she spoke. Whatever he saw there made him let her go. She pulled back her arm and slapped him with all her might. Four dark streaks marked the path of her fingernails against his cheek. People stopped to stare. He staggered into the darkness.

Izzy stood shaking. She saw traces of blood under her nails. Pushing through the crowd, she made her way once more to the rest room. She washed her hands over and over. Too angry for tears, she rinsed her mouth then drank cool water from the faucet.

After several minutes, her breathing and heartbeat returned to normal. Now she only felt sick. Sick and sad. She checked a pocket in her corduroys for a dime. She wanted to go home. She could call . . . who? Ida? She didn't have her number, and didn't know her last name to ask Information. Paul? No, he was already coming to pick them up at 11:00; she couldn't ask him to make two trips. She knew Stan's number.

※

Ann and Jill were drinking sodas and talking with their friends when she found them.

"I feel sick, Ann" she said. "I called Stan. He's coming to pick me up."

Ann looked at her. "You want me to come with you? You don't look so hot."

Izzy shook her head. "I'll see you at home."

She waited by a window near the entrance and watched for Stan's car. She hadn't lied to Ann. She felt awful. Why, she wondered, in a room full of potentially good guys, had she been targeted by two creeps? Sid, she could understand because she'd played a part to deliberately deceive him. But tonight she thought she would blend in. She shook her head and rested a cheek against the cold glass next to the door.

Some guys in the parking lot horsed around, pushing and shoving each other. She spotted a patrol car driving slowly down the street. It stopped. A cop got out and walked over to talk to the boys. That was why she didn't see his car, didn't see him until he was standing next to her. Stan, with his kind face, his straight hair, his ears that stood out a little from his head, his eyes that smiled so easily.

"Hey, do you want to dance?" he asked mildly.

And, suddenly, she did. Just one, uncomplicated, slow one.

With Stan.

Chapter Thirty-one

Izzy followed Stan to the one corner of the dance floor that didn't feel like a sauna. He held her lightly, one hand resting on her back, the other holding hers. He stood near enough to show he was interested, yet he didn't crowd her. "What the World Needs Now is Love" played over the loudspeakers, and Izzy felt every note. She felt the safety of Stan's arms. He was easy to follow. She closed her eyes.

"Do you want to tell me what happened?" His voice came from just above her ear.

"Not really." Her head swayed to the music.

"Okay."

Stan smelled refreshingly clean, like soap. His shirt felt freshly ironed, it was smooth beneath her hand. The space between them bristled lightly with a kind of static and, blushing, she opened her eyes and backed away.

The song ended. Stan held onto her hand. "You want to go? We can stay if you want."

Izzy hesitated. The thought of spending the next hour dancing with Stan had a definite appeal, but in the recesses of her mind, a little voice reminded her that she was not who Stan thought she was. She shook her head. "I want to go, please."

He guided her through the crowd. "Did you wear a jacket?" he asked when they reached the coat rack.

"No."

He tried to look stern. "You should have, it's getting cold."

She tilted her head up. "You'd be a great big brother, you know that?"

The parking lot was quiet now with no sign of troublemakers.

"You hungry?" Stan asked when he held the car door for her.

"Kind of."

Stan drove to the A&W and parked. The carhop skated over and took an order for burgers and root beer.

Izzy remembered the day Paul had brought her here. Her cheeks reddened when she recalled the way she'd flirted and how he had kissed her.

"Penny for your thoughts," Stan said.

Izzy laughed, "Not for a million dollars!"

"You look a little warm. Should I roll down the windows?"

She shook her head. "I'm fine. I was thinking of something embarrassing."

"Really? Anything you want to confess?" Stan reached over and ruffled her hair. "You look different tonight."

"Quit that!" She took the comb from her pocket and repaired her damaged hairdo. "What do you mean?"

"I don't know. Softer, I think. Less, I don't know, less tough."

Izzy turned the comb over in her hands. "I look tough?"

"I think you make a big effort to look tough."

The neon sign flickered colored lights over his face. Something about him felt so secure. Dangerously secure. She cranked a window down a little. He had been right. The night was turning cold.

"So, am I right? Do you try to look tough?" he asked.

"Maybe."

"Why?" His voice was soft. "You can tell me, Izzy."

Could she really? She twisted on the car seat to face him, though she couldn't quite bring herself to look him in the eye. "It's not easy taking care of myself and Ann. I didn't think my life would be like this. Working, I mean. I planned on going to school. Learning, doing homework, going to parties, being a kid for a little longer." She stopped herself, afraid he might catch on to more than she was saying.

The carhop rolled up with their food. Stan paid her and handed Izzy a burger and mug of root beer. They ate in silence for a few minutes.

"It's got to be hard making your own way. I don't know about partying; I was never that guy, but there's no reason you have to stop learning. I take night courses at the university. Maybe you can too."

Izzy swallowed and reached for her root beer. "I can't afford it."

"You might qualify for a scholarship. You should talk to an academic advisor."

"I'll think about it. What kind of classes are you taking?"

Izzy listened, watching the way Stan's face lit up when he described his courses and talked about the things he was learning. His eyes glowed with enthusiasm. She had to remind him that his sandwich was getting cold.

When they'd finished eating, Stan flashed his headlights and the carhop came for the tray.

They rode across town to Izzy's place. The movie theaters had turned off their marquees, and the streets downtown were dark, except for the traffic lights and occasional street lamps. Gauzy clouds stretched overhead obscuring the stars and the moon.

"Do you think it will rain tonight?" Izzy spoke to break the silence.

Stan looked up at the night sky. "I dunno, maybe."

They turned onto her street, and Izzy wished she lived farther away.

Ann was sitting on the porch with Frank when they drove up. She hadn't worn a coat and was sharing Frank's jacket.

"Thanks for everything, Stan." Izzy reached across the seat and squeezed his hand.

"You're welcome." Stan held onto her hand for a second. "Would it be okay if I came over tomorrow?"

"Of course."

"I'll see you then. Hey, is that Frank Anderson there with Ann?"

"Yeah. You know Frank?"

"I went to school with his brother, Nick. Tell him I'll give him a ride home, would you?"

Ann and Frank stood when Izzy walked up to the porch. "I forgot to take my key," Ann said, pulling off the jacket.

"Stan says he'll give you a ride home if you want, Frank."

"Great! I wasn't looking forward to that long walk." Frank and Ann both looked a little awkward, so Izzy busied herself unlocking the door and went inside.

Ann followed after a few minutes.

"You look better," Ann said while she changed into a nightgown.

"I definitely feel better." Izzy ran a soapy washcloth over her face.

"What happened?"

Izzy told her about Nick and the boy she had slapped. Ann lay on her stomach, her chin resting on her bunched up pillow. "I don't get it, Izzy," she said. "I've been to half a dozen dances since school started, and all I do is dance. You go to just one and get hit on twice."

"I don't get it either. The tight sweater didn't help." Izzy pulled the blanket and bedspread up to her chin in the chilly room. "Honestly, Ann, I could have puked. I hated it."

After a minute Ann spoke again. "I saw you dancing with Stan."

Izzy ducked her head and smiled to herself. She wanted to close her eyes and relive the sweetness of his touch. She switched off the lamp on the nightstand. They were shadows sharing secrets in the dark. Well, some secrets.

"You like him, Izzy." Ann yawned. "I can tell."

"I like his type."

"What's the difference between him and his type?"

"I don't know." It was Izzy's turn to yawn. "I just think that maybe someday, a long time from now, I'd like to meet someone like him. Fall in love. Get married."

"Now tell me about Frank."

Ann giggled. "He's sweet. It's nice having someone to talk to and eat lunch with. It's not just him though. There's always a group of us—Jill and some of the other kids."

Izzy felt a twinge like a toothache in her heart. "Yeah, that would be fun."

She thought of Stan's comment about her looking tough. It was intentional, but more and more the persona she played was taking over her life. She had wandered so far down her solitary road that when she looked back she could no longer see the beginning.

Ann made a soft snoring sound next to her. Izzy snuggled close and tried hard not to think that in the morning Ann was moving out. This was the last night they'd talk together in bed. The looming separation was temporary but it felt so permanent.

※

Izzy put clean sheets on the bed in Faye's room while Ann ironed the pillowcases. Together they added a blanket under the spread because nights were definitely colder. Then they dusted the furniture and ran a damp mop over the wood floor. Everything looked fresh and comfortable.

"Wish we had flowers for her," Ann said.

"She'll probably bring the ones from the hospital." Izzy straightened the shade on the bedside lamp.

Back in their room, Ann returned to packing her things. Izzy sat on the bed to watch.

"Well, one good thing, you'll have plenty of closet room." Ann folded a skirt and placed it in the grocery bag she was using as a suitcase.

"I don't need more room."

Ann took her nightgown from the nail in the closet door and stuffed it into the bag.

"Maybe you can get more clothes now that you don't have to worry about me." Her voice sounded small.

"Maybe. I could use more shirts for work. I'll get a bigger sweater, too. You want my old one?"

"Okay, I can't fill it out like you, though." Ann folded it and added it to the rest of her things.

"Good, you'll be safer."

Jill called hello from the back door.

"We're in here," yelled Izzy. She went into the bathroom and blew her nose.

"Mom said don't worry about toothpaste or shampoo 'cause we have plenty." Jill bounced into the bedroom. "This is going to be so fun!"

Ann glanced toward Izzy leaning against the doorframe. "I'll only be through the back hedge, since Mr. Kimball cut that hole in it. We'll come over every Friday night to watch the horror movie with you and Faye."

Izzy studied the floorboards. "We haven't watched the horror movie for weeks. You always have school stuff on Fridays."

Jill looked back and forth between the sisters. "This bag looks full. Why don't I carry it over to the house?"

"Thanks," Ann said.

After the backdoor closed, Ann turned to Izzy. "You're not making this easy."

"I know."

"Well?"

"Well maybe it shouldn't be easy." Izzy sniffed.

"It isn't. But it doesn't have to be the end of the world either." Ann emptied a drawer of socks and underwear into another bag.

"Not for you." Izzy was being deliberately mean, and she hated herself for it.

"Then I won't go." Ann began tossing her things back into the dresser drawer. "The heck with what people say. We'll take our chances with the family courts or anyone else who interferes."

For a split second Izzy felt relief, then she grabbed Ann's hand. "No! I'm being a jerk." She swallowed hard. "It'll be fine. We'll see each other all the time. I'm. . . I'm sorry."

Ann paused. "I hate leaving you, Izzy. I really do." She unrolled and re-rolled a pair of knee socks. "Remember that night you showed up at Mrs. McKinley's and asked me not to leave you?"

Izzy nodded and didn't try to hide the tears spilling down her face.

"I feel like I'm running out on you," Ann said through tears of her own.

Izzy put her arms around her. "Don't Annie. We couldn't have known what we were facing. I'll be okay. I'll be here with Faye and working. It'll be lonely without you, but like you said, you're not going that far."

"I'll come over every day," Ann promised.

They heard someone at the door and quickly wiped their cheeks.

"Anybody home?" Paul called.

They hurried to the front room. Paul carried Faye in his arms. "Quick," he said, "where do you want her? She weighs a ton."

Faye kicked her legs, "I told you I can walk,"

"Put her on the couch." Izzie smoothed the throw pillows.

Stan followed them, carrying a small bag from the hospital and a vase of flowers. He handed Izzy a typed list of what Faye could and could not do while on bedrest.

Paul, faking exhaustion, dropped onto the sofa. "Man, you sure you're not having triplets?"

Faye laughed, but Izzy thought she looked pale.

Izzy took the flowers and bag from Stan and put them in Faye's room. When she returned the boys were gone. "Where'd everybody go?"

"They're coming back later." Ann turned her attention to Faye. "How do you feel?"

"Okay, just a bit tired." Faye pushed herself up a little higher on the couch.

"Do you want to go to bed?" Izzy asked.

"No, I'd kind of like to stay here and watch TV."

Izzy laughed. "Well, it is Saturday morning. Which cartoons do you want to see?"

"Bugs Bunny, if he's on. You may laugh, but after sharing a TV that I couldn't see and could barely hear, I'm excited to watch anything."

Ann turned on the set while Izzy made some punch and poured a glass for Faye. She set both the glass and the pitcher on the coffee table within easy reach. "You hungry?"

"Always," Faye replied.

"I can make bologna or grilled cheese sandwiches."

"Anything as long as it's not Jell-O or custard." Faye looked around the room. "It's so good to be home," she said and sighed contentedly.

Izzy glanced at the worn furniture, the fuzzy picture on the TV, the faded rug and said, "Such as it is."

When she opened the cupboard she saw that the bread was blooming blue and green with mold. "Oh yuck! The bread's no good. We're down to soup and crackers. You want tomato or chicken noodle?"

"Tomato sounds good," Faye called.

"I'll have to make it with water, we're out of milk."

"Chicken Noodle then."

Izzy used a cookie sheet for a tray when the soup was ready. She folded a dishtowel to fit and placed a steaming bowl of soup, a spoon, and a sleeve of saltines on it. She carried it into the living room. Returning to the stove, she divided the remainder of the soup between herself and Ann. Still hungry, she buttered some saltines and ate them while she drank punch.

"I've got to go to the store, Ann. Can you stay with Faye until I get back?"

Ann, who was buttering some crackers for herself, said she could.

Izzy wrote up a short list, no more than she could fit in her bicycle basket. She combed her hair and changed into a clean shirt.

"I'll be right back. Anything you want, Faye?"

"I'd love a Coke and a Mars bar," she said.

Izzy scribbled the addition to the list. "Okay." She grabbed a jacket, jammed her wallet into a hip pocket of her jeans, and went out to her bike.

Saturday traffic was heavy due to a football game at the college, and Izzy focused on getting to the market without accident. The sky was gray, and she was glad she'd remembered a jacket. When a car with pennants flying from its antenna swerved and nearly clipped her, she turned her bike onto the deserted sidewalk. At last she coasted into the grocery parking lot and chained her bike to the rack.

Inside the store she filled a cart with milk, bread, and other necessities. She added the Coke and Mars bar and chose a Heath bar for herself. Heath bars came in two pieces. Candy twins, she thought. She could share it with Ann, or she could save it for later and eat it all herself. So far that was the only bonus she could think of from having Ann move out. It wasn't enough, but it was something.

"Hello, Izzy," called a familiar voice.

Izzy turned and saw Ida waving at her. She looked different out of her uniform and cap. She wore a floral printed dress and low heels. Her hair was combed into its usual bun. A wide smile creased her kind face.

"How you doing?" The older woman stopped her shopping cart next to Izzy and put an arm around her shoulders.

Izzy smiled, "Okay, I guess. Faye came home from the hospital today. Ann is moving to the neighbors."

"That's today huh?" Ida offered a stick of gum and took one for herself.

Izzy accepted the gum. "Yep, even as we speak. Ann's all packed. She's just waiting for me to get back."

"Think she'd mind waiting a little longer?"

"I guess not, why?"

"Thought you might join me for some lunch. Blue Plate Special at the diner is Chicken ala King today. It's not bad. I always get so dang hungry when I shop. Why don't you check out and we'll walk across the street. My treat."

Izzy was tempted. She'd already worked off the scant bowl of soup with her bike ride. "I don't know. I'd have to bring my groceries with me. I'm on my bike."

"Put 'em in the trunk of my car for safe keeping." Ida wasn't going to take no for an answer.

"You've got a deal." Izzy hurried through check-out right behind Ida.

The café was quieter on the weekend. Ida prepared two plates and led the way to a booth.

"Smells good." Izzy took a bite. "Umm, oh, wow."

Ida grinned. "Told you. It's my mother's recipe."

Izzy watched her friend buttering a roll and realized how little she knew about her. "Ida, who do you live with?"

"Me, myself, and I. Why do you ask?"

"I just wondered. Where's your family?"

Ida sopped some sauce with a bit of the dinner roll. "I have a sister who lives out in California. Some nieces and nephews scattered around. Some ne'er-do-well kids I gave birth to. That's about it."

"What about your husband?"

"He worked for the railroad, but he died in an accident."

"I'm sorry," Izzy said awkwardly. "I shouldn't have asked."

Ida patted her hand. "It's okay, sweetie." She sighed. "I still miss him, but I can hardly remember what it was like being married. We had three daughters. I hear from them sometimes. Mother's Day, Christmas."

Izzy changed the subject, "So, do you make the Chicken ala King for the café?"

"Couldn't trust anybody else to do it right. It's the only thing I cook for 'em. I shared some recipes, but I'd rather be serving the customers than slaving over the stove. Glad you like it! Can I get you some more?"

Izzy had cleaned her plate. She shook her head. "I gotta get home. They'll be wondering where I am."

Ida stacked the dishes. "Hold on just a minute while I clear the table, then I can walk back to the car with you." She went to the kitchen and came back with three take-out containers. "I know how crazy it gets when folks are moving in and out, so I put up some Chicken ala King, vegetable soup, and a couple of lemon tarts for your dinner."

Izzy threw her arms around Ida's neck. "That day I came in here was the luckiest day of my life."

"Pshaw." Ida patted her back. "I just hope you'll have room on your bike."

"If I don't I'll throw away the groceries."

They crossed the street and Izzy managed to fit everything into the basket.

"Thanks for the lunch, Ida, and the dinner." Izzy balanced her bike.

Ida gave her a little squeeze. "Let me know how things are going. You still got my number?"

Izzy nodded, "Right next to the phone."

"Okay then. You best hurry before that milk begins to turn, or the rain starts." Ida waved her away.

Izzy rode slowly through quiet back streets, careful not to spill anything. She thought of Ida's solitary life and felt a touch of melancholy. The autumn afternoon harmonized with the sadness of her mood. Change was happening all around and through her, and it brought an unspeakable sorrow. Leaves dropped sporadically as she glided beneath the trees arching over the road. A squirrel scampering onto a limb caught her eye, and she stopped to watch it. She wondered if it, too, was lonely. It came to her again that Ann was all she had by way of family, and she realized that, of everything she feared, being alone topped the list.

Chapter Thirty-Two

Ann wrapped her toothbrush in a square of waxed paper and placed it in the last bag. Izzy held out the pillow Ann always used.

"No," Ann said, "you keep it. I don't need it."

"Okay." Izzy wished she would leave. The entire experience had taken on the anguish of slowly removing a Band-Aid. It was time to rip it off and let the pain happen. She couldn't start healing until then. Though it stung like a paper cut, it was actually an amputation. No matter how much time passed, she knew she would never be the same. Ann moved toward her as if to hug her. "Don't." Izzy backed away. "It will only make it worse. Just go."

Ann picked up her bag. "I can't come over tonight. I have a date with Frank."

"Just as well, Ida only gave me enough food for two."

"Mrs. Kimball is planning on me eating there. They've even put my name on their Chore Chart. I'm supposed to dry dinner dishes today."

Izzy walked her sister to the back door. "Where're you and Frank going? Did he get his driver's license?"

"Next week. We'll walk downtown to a movie. I forget what it's called. I have to be in by eleven. Kimball's have a curfew."

"Good."

"Yeah. Well, bye."

"Bye."

Izzy closed the door. She stood by the window and watched Ann cross the backyard and disappear through the hedge. Izzy wrapped her arms around herself and stared, willing her sister to come back. Come back and say it had all been a joke. Ann would never really leave. They'd laugh, recalling Izzy's old threat that they would probably die in the same bed and have to share a coffin. The lump in Izzy's throat ached so much her molars hurt.

"Izzy?" Faye's voice sounded distant.

Izzy shook her head, took a deep breath, and walked to the living room. "You getting hungry?"

"A little. I need to go into the bathroom. The nurses said I should have someone help me when I first get up just in case I'm dizzy from sitting around so much."

"Oh, sure." Izzy held out her hand and helped her up. "What do you want to do tonight? After dinner, I mean. We could play cards."

"Whatever you want," Faye stepped into the bathroom. "You don't need to wait."

Izzy returned to the kitchen to heat up dinner. It turned out that Ida had packed more than enough for two. Izzy tore some lettuce and sliced a cucumber for a salad, then she set the table. She had the unnerving feeling that she was watching herself as she worked. Her body felt partly empty, a crucial piece of herself missing.

Faye came into the kitchen, her hair freshly combed, her face washed. "It smells good," she said as she took a seat at the table. Izzy dished up the food and deliberately took the chair that Ann had always used. Best to start acting like she'd never been there. A voice in the back of her mind said that she was over reacting, that Ann would certainly be back at some point. It wasn't like she had died. But Izzy ignored the voice. Right now hope hurt.

Faye cleaned her plate and had a second helping. Izzy ate little, pushing her food around her plate with her fork. They ate their lemon tarts in front of the television while they watched *Shindig*. Just like two normal girls, Izzy thought, except that one of them was pregnant and the other an imposter.

The show ended, and they turned on the radio to listen to the top forty.

"I know," Faye said, "let's do our nails. I can never get my right hand to look decent. We can give each other manicures. In my nightstand drawer there's a little case with nail tools. I have a couple of bottles of polish, too."

Izzy fetched the items and they spent an hour trimming, filing, and painting their nails. Her malaise lifted as they sang along with the radio and lost track of time. They decided to paint their toenails too. Faye had just finished Izzy's when there was a knock at the front door. Izzy walked on her heels, cotton balls between her splayed toes, to answer it. Paul and Stan stood under the porch light, their arms full of boxes.

"This some new kind of dance?" Stan asked, observing Izzy's feet.

"Very funny." Izzy backed up and held the door open.

The boys came in and placed the boxes next to Faye. "What's all this?" she asked.

"It's a bedrest boredom kit. See?" Paul held up a couple of paperback books. One was called *Christy*, the other was a murder mystery. "My mom just finished these and thought you might like them."

"We also have Clue, Monopoly, and Chinese Checkers." Stan sorted through the rest of the boxes. "One jigsaw puzzle that may, or may not, be complete, and a gift for Faye." He presented a sloppily wrapped package.

Faye ignored her newly finished nails and tore into the paper. "A clock radio! It's beautiful!"

It was pink with a gold face in a sleek very modern design.

Paul sat next to her. "See, it has an automatic sleep setting so you don't have to worry about shutting it off. You can set it and it turns off by itself."

Faye's eyes shone. "You guys shouldn't have. You've done so much already."

"It's nothing," Paul said.

Faye began to protest, but Stan interrupted her. "He's not being modest. It really is nothing. We bought it with green stamps we got from my mother. She saves 'em and forgets she has them. She was glad to see them go."

"Well, thank you anyway. No matter how you paid for it, I love it."

They plugged it in and made sure everything worked. Izzy turned off the old radio in the kitchen and they listened to the new one. She cleared the coffee table, and they all started on the puzzle.

At eight o'clock Izzy noticed Faye beginning to wilt. Her face paled, and she seemed to slump on the couch.

"I think she's had it for tonight," Izzy whispered into Stan's ear. "You two better go."

"Hey Paul, we should take off. Faye needs to rest. You can come back tomorrow." Stan stood and stretched his back.

Paul seemed reluctant but agreed after he looked at Faye. He slipped his arms under her and lifted her off the couch. Stan unplugged the new clock radio and followed.

"This way." Izzy went ahead and turned down the covers. Paul set Faye on the edge of the bed and kissed her lightly on the lips. "See you later."

"Thanks, Paul,"

"You two showed up just in time," Izzy said.

"Yeah, it looked like you'd run out of things to paint." Stan ducked the slipper Faye aimed at his head.

Izzy followed them to the front door and locked up before she returned to Faye's room.

Faye had changed into a fresh nightgown and was climbing under the covers. "Those two are crazy."

Izzy placed the radio on her nightstand and reset the time. "In the nicest way."

"Yes. The nicest way. Oh, this bed feels so good." Faye sighed. "Don't go Izzy; stay and talk."

Izzy sat near her feet.

"It's so strange. This is the hardest thing I've ever been through, but in some ways it's also the best." Faye extended her hand and Izzy took it. "I feel more cared for than I ever have, at least since my mother got sick."

Izzy watched her friend's face in the dim light. "When did she die, Faye?"

"Eight years ago; I was twelve. She'd been sick for a long time. It was some kind of cancer. Nobody ever said exactly."

"That must have been hard." Izzy felt how lame that sounded.

Faye's fingers squeezed Izzy's hand. "You ought to know. How old were you when your mom died?"

Izzy shifted her gaze. "It was a few years ago. Car accident."

"So you must have still been in high school. You poor kid. You've never mentioned your dad. Where's he?"

"We never had a father. He took off before we were born." This, at least, wasn't a lie.

Faye began to pick at the fabric of the chenille spread. "I wish I could forget mine. That sounds awful, but it's true."

Izzy studied her face. "Why? Was he mean or something?"

Faye's complexion darkened. "He was more than mean. He used to yell at my mother. Really scream. I can still hear him calling her lazy because she was too sick to fix his meals." She paused and Izzy could see how hard she swallowed before continuing. "I tried to keep the house nice. I did the laundry and ironed his clothes. That's how I learned to sew, repairing his clothes. I did everything before he got home from work so he'd think Mom had done it. I cooked, too. Mom would tell me what to do, and I just went in the kitchen and did exactly what she said." Faye reached for a tissue.

Izzy waited.

"Not long before she died, Mom got a cough. The doctor said it was because her heart was failing. It woke Dad in the middle of the night. Mom slept in the living room. He came stomping out of the bedroom and slapped her. Right across the face. He . . . he . . ." Faye swallowed. "He told her to die a little quieter; he needed his sleep." Her voice fell to a whisper. "It happened the next day while he was at work. I was so glad he wasn't there. I wanted it to be peaceful. I came home from school and our next door neighbor, Mrs. Montrose, was waiting for me. She used to bring over lunch and sit with Mom in the afternoons. She put her arms around me and said, 'Your mama went to heaven.'"

"What did you do?" Izzy asked.

Faye blinked back tears and plucked another tissue from the box. "I called the mortuary, then I washed Mom's face and combed her hair and waited. They came and picked her up in their hearse. I took the sheets off her bed. It was a roll away, so I folded it up and put it in the closet under the stairs." Faye's voice took on a wooden quality as she recited her activities from that day. "I made a meatloaf and put it in the oven with some potatoes. I hung up my school clothes and finished the ironing."

"Wow." Izzy stared. Just like that. The worst thing a kid could face and Faye had just kept going. She wondered what had happened when Faye's father came home, but had no desire to ask. What had Faye's life been like for the last eight years? She suspected she already knew the answer. It was more than enough for Faye to deal with what was in front of her now.

Faye's eyes drooped shut. Izzy rose carefully and switched off the lamp. She left the door ajar so she could hear if Faye called to her.

Back in the kitchen she rinsed the dirty dishes in the sink. She straightened the living room. Fatigue crept up her spine and spread through her shoulders. She picked up one of the books Paul had brought and went to her room.

The bed felt much too big. She propped both pillows in the center, changed into her nightgown, and slid between the covers. She thumbed the pages, but her mind refused to focus. Weariness weakened the barriers she had erected in her mind. Faye's voice recited the tragedy of her mother's death, and Izzy's thoughts turned to her own mother. Was Willa dead? Not likely. A person doesn't get a chance to pack their clothes if they're being abducted. No, that leaving was deliberate. Switching off the light, she pulled Ann's pillow to her chest and buried her face in it. The worn pillowcase was as smooth as satin against her cheek. It smelled like hair spray and Ann's Chantilly perfume. The lump from her throat had shifted during the evening and was now lodged somewhere near her heart where it grew with each breath.

Izzy thought of Ann lying in a strange bed tonight, probably talking with Jill just as she and Faye had done. Was it only weeks ago that Ann had said she'd never leave? Everything had been out of place since Willa disappeared. Izzy, Ann, and Faye were like the unfinished puzzle in the living room, and Izzy was powerless to see how the whole picture would come together. All she could do was to keep placing one piece after another and pray it would somehow make sense at the end.

Monday morning Izzy made breakfast and threatened Faye to not wash so much as a spoon. "I'll take care of it when I get home. Mrs. Kimball is going to check in on you, but if you need anything, call her. If she's not home, then call me at work. Stan said it would be fine."

Faye gave a mock salute from her place on the sofa. "Yes, ma'am."

Izzy put on the plum-colored sweater that Ann had bought for her, picked up her lunch bag and went out the back door. A thin layer of frost crusted the leaves on the ground, and Izzy's breath puffed in the cold. She was going to need a coat soon. Her old one had been too small last year.

Her fingers and nose were stinging cold when she reached work. She was glad of the heated factory and hurried to the breakroom for a hot chocolate before she clocked in.

Stan joined her at a table. "You surviving?"

She blew on the chocolate. "Just about."

"How's Faye?"

"Okay, I think. Paul came over Sunday and kept her entertained."

Stan nodded. "Yeah, I think he's pretty smitten. But then I thought he was smitten once before." He ducked his head to look into Izzy's eyes.

The corners of her mouth turned up. "He got over it."

"What about you? Did you get over it?"

She let out her breath. "I liked him. A lot. But it wasn't serious."

Stan raised an eyebrow.

Betty and Marti came in, bought coffee, and seated themselves at the table.

"Really, I'm fine," Izzy said.

"Why wouldn't you be fine?" Marti stirred her drink.

"Don't be so thick, Marti," Betty said. "She's had quite a week with Faye being in the hospital and all. How's she doing, by the way?"

Stan excused himself and left the women to talk.

Izzy watched him walk away. "She's doing okay. She came home on Saturday."

"Is she coming back to work?" Betty asked.

"The doctor has her on bedrest. She probably won't be back until the baby comes."

The older women exchanged a look.

"About that," Marti seemed to be making an effort to sound disinterested, "what's she going to do with the baby?"

"She hasn't said anything one way or the other." Izzy finished her hot chocolate.

"Still no word about the father?" Marti asked, and Betty reached over and pinched her.

"Ouch! What was that for?"

"For putting your pointy nose where it don't belong!" Betty scowled. "It's none of your business. If Faye wants to tell us, she will."

Izzy stood and put on her smock. "Well, I don't know any more than you do." She turned, walked to the time clock, punched in, and went into the production area.

A new girl was at Faye's place. Izzy grabbed a stack of collars and began stitching.

The music on the intercom annoyed her, like a rash she couldn't scratch. The thread on her machine broke every few minutes, and she had to get a new spool. She finished the collars and began sewing tiny tucks on romper pieces. These were a pain, as the fabric didn't want to crease, and she had to stop several times to unpick what she'd done and start over. By break time she was in a foul mood. She bought herself a packet of cookies and a milk. The cookies were little more than crumbs and the milk wasn't cold. She ate them anyway, listening to Betty and Marti snipe at each other until the buzzer called them back to work. The square of sunlight near her workstation disappeared before lunch, and rain spattered on the metal roof. The only good thing about this was that the deafening noise drowned out the music.

She felt the beginnings of a migraine, spent all of her change on a lunch she couldn't eat and then had to borrow a dime to buy a tampon when her period showed up unexpectedly in the afternoon.

Izzy biked home in the downpour. Her sweater got soaked. As soon as she was inside, she rolled it in a towel to squeeze out the water, then laid it flat to dry. In her bedroom she peeled off her damp jeans and wrapped herself in her bathrobe to get warm.

Faye was asleep on the couch. The dishes were drying in the drainer. Mrs. Kimball must have done them. Izzy found a note on the table:

Izzy,
I'm going to the market tomorrow. If you'll leave a list, I'll pick up whatever you need.

Hope you've had a good day,
Paulette Kimball

A good day? Izzy thought of the frustrating day at work followed by the ride home in the rain and had a perverse urge to laugh. It was going to be that or a blood-curdling primal scream that would certainly wake Faye. She pressed a dishtowel to her mouth and laughed until tears streamed from her eyes. The tightness in her shoulders eased, and the cold in her feet and hands gradually warmed. She got up, turned on the oven, removed two pot pies from the freezer, and put them in to bake.

"Izzy? That you?"

"Yeah, Faye, it's me. What do you need?"

"Bathroom, please."

Izzy wiped her cheeks on the towel and went smiling to help her friend. After all, things could only get better from here.

Couldn't they?

The End

Coming
Summer of 2022

Book 2

Izzy & Ann

Apart

Izzy & Ann

Apart

By
Sherri Peterson Curtis

Chapter One

"She doesn't wear it anymore," Ann said as she held out a coat that looked like it had never been worn. It was exactly the coat Izzy would have chosen for herself: heather gray wool with maroon piping and toggle buttons with leather loops.

"It looks new," Izzy said, one eyebrow raised in suspicion.

Ann shrugged. "Mr. Kimball gave it to her for Christmas last year, and it never fit her right."

"She should take it back to the store."

"It was on sale, no returns."

Izzy slipped it on. "You've got an answer for everything haven't you?"

Ann grinned. "Yup. If you stop arguing now. Fit, sale, and no returns are all I've got."

Izzy looked at her reflection in the dresser mirror. The coat could have been made for her. "I'll buy it from her."

"Izzy," Ann moaned, shaking her head.

"I can give her a couple of dollars from each paycheck. How much do you think it cost?"

Ann crossed her arms over her chest. "Two thousand dollars. American."

Izzy took off the coat and held it out to her sister. "Either I pay for it, or she can send it to the Salvation Army."

They locked eyes until Ann flinched. "Honestly! Would it kill you to let someone do something nice for you?"

Izzy looked longingly at the coat and tried it on once more. "It might. I can't start accepting gifts. It feels like a trap."

Ann put her arms around Izzy. "It looks beautiful on you. The color is perfect and it fits. Just this once please. . . "

Izzy melted a little in her sister's embrace. "Okay, Annie. But only once." She hung the coat in her closet.

This was Ann's first visit since she moved out, and an awkward tension crept through the room. "So how've you been?" Ann took a seat on the end of the bed.

"Since Saturday?" Izzy asked. "It's only been two days."

"I know." Ann twisted her fingers in her lap.

Izzy took a seat next to her. "Okay, I guess. I mean riding home in the rain today was a drag, but I'm okay. How 'bout you?"

Her sister shrugged. "Fine. The Kimball's are great, but it's not home."

Izzy looked around at the faded curtains, the paint peeling on the door, the battered hardwood floor. "Yeah, well you can't expect to find this kind of glamour everywhere you go."

Ann kept her head down. "You know what I mean, Izzy. It's not the same."

"Did you think it would be? Honestly, Ann! Sometimes I think they've got the wrong twin in school. I mean, open your eyes! This is a two bedroom, one-bath shack with cracking linoleum. And you're living with what? Four bedrooms, wall to wall carpet, and color TV? Poor you!"

"I never said I had it hard. I know I'm the lucky one. You don't have to remind me," Ann said.

"When have I ever reminded you?" Izzy shot back. "And keep your voice down, Faye's just in the other room."

The girls stood, faces flushed.

Ann spoke, "You don't say anything, but you walk around like a martyr. Every time you stand still, I feel like I should be lighting candles at your feet."

"Take that back!" Izzy hissed.

"No one asked you to be some big hero. I wanted to get a job, too, but you said I couldn't. I didn't want to go to school without you. You think it's been easy being on my own? Well, it hasn't!"

"On your own? Exactly how have you been on your own? You have friends at school. I'm here every night. You don't have to lie about your age, pretend to be someone you aren't. Someone you never—" her voice broke, she swallowed and started again, "Someone I never wanted to be."

Ann looked like she had been hit. She covered her face with her hands and began to cry. "I'm," she gulped on a sob, "I'm sorry. I'm so darn sorry."

Izzy slumped back onto the bed. "You don't need to be sorry." She picked up the roll of toilet paper she kept on the dresser to use for tissue and tossed it to her sister.

Ann blew her nose. "None of this is your fault, Izzy."

"Yeah, well it's not your fault either."

"It stinks," Ann said after a minute.

"Yeah."

"Remember that night I told you I'd never leave?" Ann dabbed at her eyes.

"Yeah." *How could I forget?*

"I meant it."

"Things changed."

Ann sighed. "I guess."

Twilight crept up the walls.

"We were never going to have a normal life, Annie, even if Willa hadn't run off." Izzy took the wad of tissue from her sister's hand and dropped it in the trash can.

"But we'd still be together."

"You think you'd be a student body officer and everything if we were together?"

"No. I think you'd be Homecoming Queen, and I'd still be your shadow."

"Neither one of us would be anything. We never made friends," Izzy said.

Ann flopped on the bed next to Izzy and studied the ceiling. "What was the point, we never knew when Willa would pull up stakes and move us."

Ann took more tissue and blew her nose again.

"So, in some ways we're doing better now than we were." Izzy sat up straighter.

"Maybe I am, but what about you, Izzy?" Ann's eyes searched Izzy's face.

"It's not so bad working at the sewing plant. I don't mind it. I met Faye and Stan. I like making money and knowing that the bills get paid."

"But what about school?"

Izzy stared at the darkening window, but she looked beyond it to the shadowed trees as if there were answers in the dusk. "I'll get to school, Ann. I really will. Somehow I'll make it happen." She rose and pulled Ann up. "Come on, it's getting dark. You need to get back to the Kimball's. Go wash your face or they'll think I've been torturing you."

Izzy followed Ann to the bathroom and watched as she splashed cool water over her eyes.

After her face was dry, Ann said, "I miss you, Izzy. I miss you so much it hurts."

"I miss you, too. We need to remember it's only for a while." Izzy's heart skipped a beat and her stomach clenched. A voice deep inside her mind began to whisper *It's forever, forever, forever.*

The rain continued through the week. Faye found a sturdier raincoat to lend her, but Izzy came home every day with her jeans soaked from the knees down. A stubborn part of her didn't want help from anyone. She suspected it was self-pity, but told herself it was independent pride.

She was relieved when Friday came. As she coasted into the driveway, the clouds parted and sunlight shone.

"Now you show up? Thanks a heap." She hopped off her bike and put it in the garage.

Ann and Faye sat at the kitchen table, heads together, looking at a dress pattern. They looked up when Izzy walked in.

"Hi!" Ann jumped up and gave her a brief hug.

Izzy hung the raincoat on a hook behind the door. "What's going on?"

"I'm going to make a dress for Ann." Faye held out the pattern for Izzy to see. It was a party dress.

Izzy poured herself a drink of water. "Cute," she said. "Kind of fancy for school."

"It's for the Homecoming Dance," Ann said.

"Frank ask you?" *Is this water bitter?*

"Yeah. He passed me a note in history class."

"Nice." Izzy tapped her fingers on the counter. "So, how much will you need for the dress?"

"I don't need anything. Faye's going to make it."

"Right. Out of newspaper?" She refilled the water pitcher and returned it to the fridge.

Faye and Ann laughed. Izzy did not.

"Mrs. Kimball is buying material for me. She's making one for Jill, but she doesn't have time to make two." Apparently nothing was going to shake Ann's happiness.

Izzy felt her jaw tighten. "That's really kind of her." She folded her arms over her chest. "You know, Faye gets paid to sew."

Faye waved this point aside. "Oh, Izzy, don't worry about that. I'm looking forward to having something to do. I have my portable machine, and I can sit at the table for a little while each day. It'll be fun." Faye smiled. "Tell her the other part."

"What other part?" Izzy frowned.

"You're coming to the dance, too!" Ann said grabbing Izzy's shoulders and squealing.

Izzy thought she was past being surprised by anything, but this surprised her. She couldn't have been more shocked if Ringo Starr had walked in and said, "That's right, luv. With me!"

"We're going to make a dress for you, too!" Faye added.

Izzy's mouth hung open. Her brain tried to make sense of what was going on but fell short of the task.

"I'm on the dance committee, and someone mentioned chaperones, and I volunteered you!" Ann said.

"So, I'll be a babysitter?"

"Izzy! Seriously, we're in high school. We don't need sitters. All you have to do is make sure no one spikes the punch or wanders off to neck in the hallways."

"Gee, sounds fun," Izzy said, sardonically.

"It will be. The other chaperones can take care of that stuff. They're all parents."

"I think you need to tell her the rest," Faye said.

"There's more?" Izzy began to feel a little faint.

"You have a date!" Ann was practically jumping up and down.

Izzy stared.

"We called Stan and asked if he'd chaperone, too." Ann *did* jump up and down.

"He was so sweet, Izzy. He said it's his civic duty and he'd be happy to do it," Faye said.

Izzy took a seat. "Wow, flattering."

Faye shook her arm. "Silly! He was teasing. He said he'd love to. He's going to wear a suit and buy you a corsage and everything."

"Mrs. Kimball will do our hair, well mine's too short, but she'll do yours." Ann threw her arms around her sister. "Oh, Izzy, aren't you excited?"

Izzy wished the room would stop shifting under her feet. Her first real dance. A high school dance with kids her own age. Her heart raced then dropped with a thud. She wouldn't be part of the crowd. She'd be playing her part. Still, a whole evening dancing with Stan. She closed her eyes briefly and recalled the Union Hall. Opening her eyes, she saw the happiness on Ann's face. "Yes," she admitted, "I think I am excited."

Acknowledgements

Over the years and the many revisions of this story I have been guided, influenced and inspired by many. Foremost among these are the members of the two critique groups with whom I meet on a regular basis. These wonderful people are: Betty Briggs, Linda Calhoon, Karen Pool, Phyllis Gunderson, Estel Murdock, Rene Murdock, Norma Mitchell, Linda Orvis, Erica Prechtel, Karla M Jay, Rich Casper, Andy Walker, Jeff Lowder, and David Tippetts. An extra measure of appreciation to Karla, Linda, Jeff, and Andy for mentoring me through the morass of preparing a manuscript for publication. You are angels, bless you all again and again! In addition I must also thank some who volunteered to be early readers who gave me valuable feedback, Isabella Curtis and Sharleen Thomas among them. And, as always, my built-in editor, style guide, computer expert, and amazing husband, Lawrence Curtis.

I'd also like to thank my English teachers through school and college. They led me to believe in possibilities. They opened my eyes to the beauty of the written word and what may be achieved. I have a long way to go but I'm making a start. Thank you.

Made in the USA
Coppell, TX
07 July 2023